Extraordinary Visions

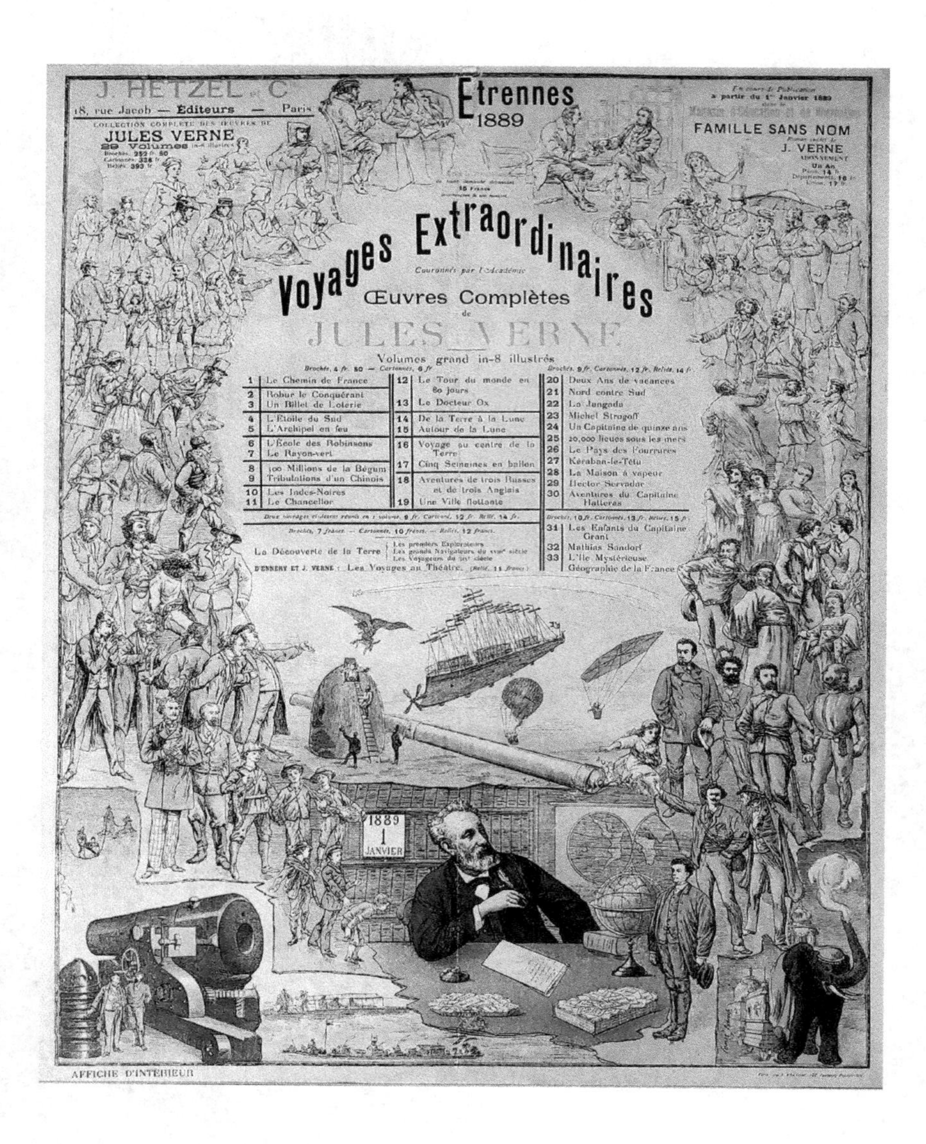
J. HETZEL et Cie
18, rue Jacob — Éditeurs — Paris
COLLECTION COMPLÈTE DES ŒUVRES DE
JULES VERNE
29 Volumes
Étrennes
1889
15 Francs
à partir du 1er Janvier 1889
FAMILLE SANS NOM
J. VERNE
Un An
Voyages Extraordinaires
Couronnés par l'Académie
Œuvres Complètes
de
JULES VERNE
Volumes grand in-8 illustrés
Brochés, 4 fr. 50 — Cartonnés, 6 fr.
Brochés, 9 fr. Cartonnés, 12 fr. Reliés, 14 fr.
1 Le Chemin de France
2 Robur le Conquérant
3 Un Billet de Loterie
4 L'Étoile du Sud
5 L'Archipel en feu
6 L'École des Robinsons
7 Le Rayon-vert
8 500 Millions de la Bégum
9 Tribulations d'un Chinois
10 Les Indes-Noires
11 Le Chancellor
12 Le Tour du monde en 80 jours
13 Le Docteur Ox
14 De la Terre à la Lune
15 Autour de la Lune
16 Voyage au centre de la Terre
17 Cinq Semaines en ballon
18 Aventures de trois Russes et de trois Anglais
19 Une Ville flottante
20 Deux Ans de vacances
21 Nord contre Sud
22 La Jangada
23 Michel Strogoff
24 Un Capitaine de quinze ans
25 20,000 lieues sous les mers
26 Le Pays des Fourrures
27 Kéraban-le-Têtu
28 La Maison à vapeur
29 Hector Servadac
30 Aventures du Capitaine Hatteras
Deux ouvrages ci-dessus réunis en 1 volume, 9 fr. Cartonné, 12 fr. Relié, 14 fr.
Brochés, 10 fr. Cartonnés, 13 fr. Reliés, 15 fr.
31 Les Enfants du Capitaine Grant
32 Mathias Sandorf
33 L'Île Mystérieuse
Géographie de la France
Brochés, 7 francs. — Cartonnés, 10 francs. — Reliés, 12 francs.
La Découverte de la Terre
Les premiers Explorateurs
Les grands Navigateurs du XVIIIe siècle
Les Voyageurs du XIXe siècle
D'ENNERY ET J. VERNE : Les Voyages au Théâtre. (Relié, 11 francs)
1889
1
JANVIER
AFFICHE D'INTÉRIEUR

Extraordinary Visions

Stories Inspired by Jules Verne

by the North American
Jules Verne Society

edited by
CDR Steven R. Southard, USNR (Ret.)
and
Rev. Matthew T. Hardesty

BearManor Media
2023

Extraordinary Visions: Stories Inspired by Jules Verne

Published in the United States of America by:

BearManor Media
1317 Edgewater Dr #110
Orlando FL 32804

bearmanormedia.com

Printed in the United States.

Typesetting and layout by John Teehan

All internal images, except Fronticepiece, are cropped from the

Project Jules Verne Illustrations, Collection B.Krauth, www.jules-verne-club.de

ISBN—978-1-62933-954-2

Story Copyright Information

Table of Contents

Dedication:

We dedicate this collection to the memory of these NAJVS members who've passed on. They made significant contributions to the Society during their lifetime and continue to inspire us:

Brian Taves, Edward Baxter, Tom McCormick,
Bert Grollman, Norman Wolcott, Walter James Miller,
Sidney Kravitz, Edward Palik, Betty Harless,
Dr. Zvi Har'El, Prof. Robert Pourvoyeur,
Prof. Stanford Luce, and Henry Sharton

"It is my intention," concluded M. Verne, "to complete, before my working days are done, a series which shall conclude in story form my whole survey of the world's surface and the heavens; there are still left corners of the world to which my thoughts have not yet penetrated."

– "Jules Verne at Home" by Marie A. Belloc,
Strand Magazine, February, 1895

Foreword

HOW MANY AUTHORS, however popular in their own time and country, have a fan club still going strong over a century after their death, on a different continent?

Jules Verne has one. At least one.

In particular, the North American Jules Verne Society has over 70 members in 9 countries. It's been in existence since 1993 and is dedicated to promoting interest in Jules Verne and his writings, providing a forum for discussions of his works, and stimulating research on this fascinating French author. Over its history, the Society accomplished many things, but never compiled an anthology of short stories inspired by Verne.

Until now.

This book features the stories of authors who felt the wonder and passion for science, exploration, and adventure of Verne's novels and sought to recapture that experience in their own way. Each tale sparkles with the boundless imagination, wit, and wanderlust of Verne himself.

Among the baker's dozen stories in this volume, you'll enjoy many based on Verne's major classics—*A Journey to the Center of the Earth*, *Twenty Thousand Leagues Under the Seas*, *From the Earth to the Moon*, and *Around the World in Eighty Days*. Other tales drew their inspiration from Jules Verne's lesser-known works, and might motivate you to read those more obscure novels as well.

Of those stories based on *Twenty Thousand Leagues Under the Seas*, Eric Choi's "Raise the Nautilus" speculates about a British attempt to salvage the famous submarine. Mike Adamson's "The Highest Loyalty" has Captain Nemo and his crew undertaking a rare land mission to rescue a slave sympathizer from North Carolina in the aftermath of the U.S. Civil War. Demetri Capetanopoulos' "Rust and Smoke" takes us to the Lofoten islands to discover the fate of the Nautilus' dinghy and a missing artifact. Janice Rider's "Want of Air" is a charming tale about how even a single chapter of Verne's novel can stimulate the imagination of young and old alike. Christopher M. Geeson's "Tyranny Under the Sea" provides a rollicking adventure with several submarines, divers, and an underwater city.

Around the World in Eighty Days gets a fanciful twist in David A. Natale's "Nellie and Jules Go Boating" when journalist and world-traveler Nellie Bly meets Jules Verne. Readers will recall *From the Earth to the Moon* and be amused when ballistic obsessions go too far in Michael Schulkins' "To Hold Back Time: A Baltimore Gun Club Adventure." In Joseph S. Walker's ominous story, "The Dominion of All the Earth," you'll learn more about the mysterious beings from *Journey to the Center of the Earth.*

It's not necessary to have read all (or any) of Verne's novels to enjoy this anthology, but some stories may prompt you to delve deeper in his oeuvre. "Old Soldiers," by Gustavo Bondoni shows what really happened to the mechanical steam-powered elephant of Verne's *The Steam House.* Kelly A. Harmon's "Trumpets of Freedom" echoes characters and settings from both *The Lighthouse at the End of the World* and *Robur the Conqueror.* "A Drama in Durango" by Alison L. Randall gives a Wild West slant on *A Drama in Livonia.*

Most of Verne's novels form a collection called the *Extraordinary Voyages,* and the title of this anthology is a nod to that. Two stories capture the entirety of his collection in different and fascinating ways. In Joel Allegretti's "Gabriel at the Jules Verne Traveling Adventure Show," you'll experience Verne's works through the eyes of a young boy at a mid-Twentieth Century carnival, reminiscent of the setting in Verne's *Cesar Cascabel.* "Embrace of the Planets" by Brenda Carre transports you to a book and antiquities shop with rather unusual connections to Verne's works and history in a manner similar to Verne's play *Journey Through the Impossible.*

The North American Jules Verne Society is pleased to bring you this anthology of short stories. In addition to its two co-editors, this book wouldn't exist without the hard work of several other Society members, namely Dana Eales, Alex Kirstukas, Andrew Nash, Reggie Van Stockum, and the Society's current president, Dennis Kytasaari.

We hope you enjoy these stories and will be motivated to read the novels that inspired them. Join us at NAJVS.org and Facebook.com/groups/NAJVS for conversation, annual gatherings, and scholarship on a wide spectrum of Vernian and steampunk-related interests. Through Verne's books, he lives forever, and in many ways, we now live in the extraordinary world he envisioned over a century ago.

CDR Steven R. Southard, USNR (Ret.)
and
Rev. Matthew T. Hardesty

2023

The Dominion of All the Earth

Joseph S. Walker

DISTINGUISHED SCIENTIST, EXPLORER TO SPEAK

The famed geologist, Dr. Axel Lidenbrock, will deliver a public lecture, entitled "On a Passage from Iceland to the Mediterranean Under the Earth," at the Majestic Theatre at 7 o'clock this evening. Tickets may be purchased for fifty cents at the box office.

Dr. Lidenbrock is presently touring North America to commemorate the fiftieth anniversary of his celebrated 1863 expedition into the subterranean realms, undertaken alongside his late uncle, the much-honored Professor Otto Lidenbrock of Hamburg. Copies of the classic account of that voyage, A Journey to the Center of the Earth, *will be available for purchase at the theater.*

Dr. Lidenbrock will recount the origins of the great adventure and some of its most memorable episodes, and will share his theories as to why every subsequent attempt to explore the mysterious regions beneath the ground has ended in either disaster or disappearance.

Questions from the audience will not be entertained.

– CHICAGO TRIBUNE, *July 8, 1913*

The talk went well, Axel thought. Every seat was taken, the applause was genuine, and only twice was his presentation disrupted by audience members leaping to their feet to scream he was lying. These accursed skeptics would bedevil him until his dying day. So far, the only stop where they had not made a nuisance of themselves was Pittsburgh, where a packed crowd of coal miners proved entirely willing to believe that there was more under their feet than rock. Poor Uncle Otto had spent the last years of his life refuting charges of fraud, even after a panel of scientific experts from two dozen nations, following an exhaustive examination of every scrap of evidence, concluded that his story was true.

In private moments, Axel understood the doubters. There were times even now when his own memories seemed too fantastic to be believed. Every night, however, brought fresh evidence of their reality, for no fabrication could account for the vividness of his dreams. Dreams of enormous creatures emerging from the waves, water streaming from their reptilian hides. Dreams of riding an untamable column of flame and steam upwards, the stifling heat and rushing stone walls vying to see which would kill them. Worst of all, dreams of crushing, endless, hopeless isolation, and the most complete darkness ever experienced by any man. Those were the nightmares he dreaded, the ones he woke from with cries of despair as Gräuben rocked him and made her soft sounds of comfort.

Ah, his poor Gräuben. Gone now to join Uncle Otto. Axel supposed he would see them again soon enough.

To avoid falling into melancholy, he began thumbing through the stack of new scientific journals on the table, the fruits of a morning spent at an excellent bookstore near his hotel. Finding the still heat in his room unpleasant, he had taken his acquisitions to the hotel's rooftop club, where, cooled by the breezes of the upper air and shielded from the sun by an enormous parasol, he enjoyed a commanding outlook of the waters of Lake Michigan, lapping at a narrow beach twelve stories below. He was looking forward to spending much time here in the two days before his train to St. Louis.

Absorbed in a series of letters debating the new model of the atom proposed by Niels Bohr, Axel was unaware someone had approached his table until a melodious voice spoke at his elbow. "Do I have the pleasure of addressing *Herr Doktor* Axel Lidenbrock?"

Axel rose, as quickly and smoothly as his sixty-nine years would allow. The woman standing there was, he saw with pleasure, charming. She was perhaps twenty-five years old, with dark hair and a frank, direct gaze. She carried a large bag but had no hat, and his attention was distracted for a moment by a strand that had come loose from her coiffure and stirred softly in the light wind. "I am he, madam," he said. "My pardon, I was somewhat startled just now."

"You were absorbed in your studies, sir, as befits a man of science. My name is Lenora. I have come a great distance to speak with you."

Axel bowed slightly. "I am honored to be the object of such attention. If we are to converse, however, may I first be assured that you are not of the faction that believes me a charlatan?"

Lenora smiled. "I promise you, sir, that I know you to have truthfully reported your underground experiences." He could not place her accent, but she did not sound like any American he had encountered.

"Then by all means." Axel pulled a chair back from the table and held it for her. "Please, join me. I welcome the company of such a lovely young woman in my old age."

"You are too kind." She sat. As Axel returned to his own chair, she examined the stack of his books. A much wider smile touched her lips as she picked one up. "I am not surprised to see scientific books and journals in three languages here, Doctor. I must confess, however, that I had not expected to find, as well, *The Patchwork Girl of Oz*."

"Ah, Mr. Baum's latest fantasia," Axel said. "Just published this week, I believe."

"Yes," she said, paging through the volume and stopping at illustrations. "The American Grimm. Fairy tales without the awful, violent, bloody parts. Without the terror."

Axel folded his hands. "I read his books to my grandchildren. It helps them with their English."

Lenora snapped the book shut and restored it to the stack. "And yet terror has its place," she said, seemingly to herself. She looked Axel in the face. "You have, I believe, recently prevailed upon your children and their families to move to New York, and you intend to live there yourself when you have completed this tour."

Axel narrowed his eyes. "Where did you acquire such a detailed account of my plans, madam?"

She ignored the question. "May I ask, Doctor, if your relocation reflects your concern over the growing likelihood of open warfare in Europe?"

"Are you suggesting I am abandoning my homeland in her time of need? That I am a coward?"

"I wouldn't put it that way, no," Lenora said. She sat forward and propped her chin on her fist. "I would say that you might find it convenient to put on the identity of an American, as you put on the identity of your uncle all those years ago. Even taking his name."

Axel gripped the arms of his chair. "I was honored to assume the patronym of the great man who was my only real parent," he said stiffly. "Though I know of no reason to account for my name to you. Are you a reporter?"

"Of a sort," Lenora said. "I am primarily an emissary."

"An emissary on whose behalf?"

"You saw one of them once," she said. "He was in a forest, herding mastodons."

"Herding—" he stared at her. She returned his gaze calmly.

"You're mad," he said, when he was able to speak. He started to turn in his chair. "I'm going to have you removed."

"Wait." She put her hand on his, surprising him so much that he fell still. "I have two things to show you, Axel Lidenbrock, and a message to convey. I'm going to show you the first thing now. After you see it, if you still wish me to leave, I will."

Lenora reached into her handbag and set a small object, wrapped in a handkerchief, on the table. When she pulled aside the cloth, the blood drained from Axel's face. He reached out a trembling hand.

"It cannot be," he breathed.

"It is," Lenora said.

The glass had been shattered and the wooden casing was crisscrossed with scars and blemishes, but when he touched it, he knew immediately she was telling the truth. He turned the ancient barometer over and found, as he knew he would, his uncle's name neatly engraved on the underside. He traced a finger wonderingly across the familiar letters. How many times had he held it, just so, in the glare of the lanterns, his back to a slab of solid stone?

"This was one of the instruments we carried," he said. "It was lost in the chaos after the explosion at the Lidenbrock Sea."

"Lost and then found," Lenora said. "Brought here as testimony to the truth of the message I carry."

"It is a message itself," Axel said. "Holding this I hear the voice of my dear uncle. I see the brave, calm features of Hans. You bring me shades of the dead and a fragment of the past."

"I have come to speak of the past. And the future."

Axel put the barometer down, though he longed to continue holding it. "You have certainly captured my attention, madam. Pray, deliver your message."

"You accept, then, that I represent those below? The inhabitants of the world you so briefly visited?"

Axel pursed his lips. "Let us say that I accept it conditionally. I can imagine other possibilities. Perhaps the instrument was brought to the surface in the same eruption that delivered us. I am a scientist, Miss Lenora. I shall require more evidence than this."

"May I inquire of you the time, Doctor?"

He glanced at his pocket watch. "It wants fourteen minutes of three o'clock."

"You shall have your additional evidence soon, Doctor, very soon." Lenora leaned forward. "I have read your book, and its account of the being you saw, near the coast of what you call the Lidenbrock Sea, after your exploration of the boneyards. Would you add anything to that account?"

"I would not," Axel said. "I described the creature as accurately as possible, based on a few minutes of observation. He was some twelve feet tall, roughly clad in furs, his hair wild and disheveled. My uncle and I debated his nature many times in the years between the voyage and his death. I remain convinced that the being was a primate, akin to the great apes of Africa, or perhaps the sasquatch said to occupy the wilds of this continent. My uncle insisted that he was human, though of some lost, primitive branch of our species. In essence, a caveman."

To his surprise, Lenora laughed.

"A caveman," she said. "I suppose, in a strict technical sense, that is true. Whatever your quibbling over terminology, in other words, you agreed he was bestial. More animal than man."

"Of course."

She shook her head. "Imagine seeing a shepherd boy in the fields," she said, "and never knowing that Rome was just on the other side of the hill."

"An astonishing comparison, madam," Axel said. "If you can claim to know more of the creature, pray enlighten me."

"We have but limited time, Doctor. I fear I can give you only a glimpse of the truth." She looked out over the lake. "But I will try to tell you something of the people in the world below this one. Their name for themselves in their own language would sound harsh and absurd to you. Let us honor Mr. Baum and, for the moment, call them Nomes."

"Very fitting," Axel agreed. "The wicked little jewelers in their caves. I have often wondered if Mr. Baum had my book in mind when he created them."

"Perhaps he did," Lenora said. "But the real Nomes I speak of have nothing in common with his absurd villains. They are not little, they are not jewelers, and they are most assuredly not wicked, though many may soon have cause to think them so."

"How very ominous," said Axel.

"Do not mock that which you cannot hope to understand, Doctor. The Nomes are beyond you in every way. When your ancestors and mine were just beginning to craft crude clay huts and scratch in the dirt to plant seeds, their race was already ancient. You have seen with your own eyes that they are larger and stronger than us. Indeed, the Nome you saw must have been an adolescent, for the adults are nearer twenty feet tall than twelve, and gifted with enormous strength. Yet I assure you that this is but the most trivial measure of their superiority. They live ten times longer than us. They are much more intelligent, and much more honorable. War is repellent to them, as are all the other vicious stratagems we humans employ to elevate ourselves by causing harm to others."

"Paragons indeed," Axel murmured. He would humor this madwoman, if only as recompense for the nostalgic thrill that had seized him at the sight of the barometer. Plainly some disturbance in the lower world had brought it back to the surface, and this young woman had found it. The name on the casing had led her to his book, and the disorders of her mind had woven about it a dreamworld. He would indulge her, but cautiously, for the other possibility was that Lenora's enchanting exterior concealed what the Americans called a "confidence artist." On no account would he open his purse in her presence.

Lenora sighed. "I did not expect to be believed immediately. Naturally you are skeptical, for the Nomes are unknown to the history you have learned. Examine, however, myth and legend, Doctor. Consider Prometheus, Cyclops, and Goliath. The Nomes have always been a subterranean people, but some few of them used to wander the surface of our world, striking wonder and fear in humanity."

"And why did they cease the practice?"

"I believe I would call it disinterest. They found the quarrelsome, violent, selfish behavior of our race increasingly troublesome. And they have no love for the things that bring us pleasure." She gestured. "The sunlight, the open air. They are creatures of rock and water, of long, slow, careful thought."

Axel lit a cigarette. "This would seem to argue against your own hypothesis," he said. "How superior could your Nomes be if they ceded the world to us?"

"Ceded the world? I said no such thing. Tell me, Doctor, who is the true master of a home? The man who lives within, or the insects crawling on the walls without?"

"Come, child." Axel found himself wearying of this fairy tale. "Do not seek to enlighten those older and wiser. Your story contains the elements of its own undoing. If your magnificent Nomes withdrew themselves to the world below, then how do you know of them?"

"I have spoken of their wisdom," she said. "With wisdom comes foresight, and caution. They do not fear us, but neither do they think it prudent to simply ignore us. You have traveled much of the world, Doctor. Tell me, have you never encountered a small town which seemed odd, disquieting in a way you could not name? A place which seemed, in some undefinable way, cut off from its country, its region, its neighbors? An insular place, full of secrets?"

Axel blew out a stream of smoke, shaking his head. "You speak in riddles, madam. It is a large world, and there are many strange places."

"Indeed there are," she said. "There are perhaps a hundred of these communities I speak of, scattered around the globe. Small towns, with families that stretch back for generations beyond counting. They do not easily welcome strangers or travelers, though they are eager for news of the world, news which they can pass on to their hidden masters."

"Meaning your Nomes." He stubbed out the cigarette and immediately lit another.

"I come from such a town myself," Lenora said. "I was eight when my parents took me into the hidden cave in the hills, and showed me what the world really is. Last week I was summoned there, for the first time, and the Nomes sent me here. They sent me to you."

"And why should they do such a thing? What am I to them?"

"Can you not imagine?" She rose from her seat. For a moment she stood, her hands on the railing, looking out over the lake. She turned and put her back to the view and addressed him, her arms crossed. "The world below is vaster than you can imagine, Doctor. What you insist on calling the Lidenbrock Sea is one of fourteen such subterranean oceans. The Nomes built them."

Axel laughed. "One cannot build an ocean, young lady."

"We cannot," Lenora said calmly. "They can, and they have had untold millennia to shape the underworld to their designs. They built it, Doctor. They gathered the waters, and they filled the space with light, and they brought to it creatures they wished to preserve who could no longer occupy the surface." Her mouth tightened. "And then you came." Axel was startled to realize she was sneering. "You, and your uncle, and his bomb."

"Surely you do not dispute the value of scientific exploration," Axel said.

"Scientific?" she asked. "Does science destroy what it discovers, Doctor? Perhaps yours does. Perhaps ours does. Can you have any conception of the devastation you wrought with your little bomb?" She rubbed her forehead and sat back down, seeming suddenly weary. "I cannot pretend to understand the electrical means by which they light those vast chambers. Whatever it is, your explosion disrupted it. An area larger than Europe was abruptly plunged into darkness as the sea poured into the chasm. Winds stronger than any hurricane ever known to mankind swept the shores, flinging every living thing against the rocks. A storm to shake the pillars of heaven that lasted for days."

Axel shifted. "I cannot accept that," he said. "We had only a little powder."

"Sometimes the weight of a fly is enough to start an avalanche," Lenora said. "Tens of thousands of Nomes died, Doctor. Even now, they are still recovering, still attempting to restore some vestige of what was destroyed. For years, they had no idea what happened. Until one of their agents, in one of those odd little towns, told them about your book."

"So you have come in pursuit of revenge."

"Revenge? No, Doctor. It is unknown to them. I have told you they do not have humanity's capacity for hostile action. They would have accepted what happened as an aberration, an accident with results far beyond your knowledge or comprehension. One does not kill a child for spilling milk."

Axel spread his hands. "Then I am at a loss, child, to understand why you have tasked me with listening to this outrageous tale. Perhaps you should seek out Mr. Baum. He may be in need of such phantoms for his next volume."

"But neither does one allow the child to continue willfully making such messes," Lenora said, as though Axel had not spoken. "War is coming to Europe, Doctor, and perhaps to the entire world. Everyone knows it, though we conspire to act as though we do not. The great nations of the world—of the surface world, that is—know of your voyage. Can you not imagine their plans? The strategies they construct for destroying London or Berlin or, indeed, Washington, from below?"

"Now I believe you are simply being paranoid, or else your gargantuan masters are," Axel said. "There has been no successful expedition beneath the surface since the one led by Otto Lidenbrock."

Lenora cocked her head. "And why do you imagine that is, Doctor?"

Axel opened his mouth, prepared to share his intricate theories concerning atmospheric pressure and the inherent instability of subterranean landscapes, but she went on without giving him a moment to speak.

"Two months ago, Great Britain dispatched a secret expeditionary force to follow your route," Lenora said. "They were stopped, but they were armed with sufficient explosives to more than duplicate the damage that you three men inflicted unwittingly. Humanity's weapons will only grow more powerful in the years to come. The Nomes were willing to suffer an accident. They are not willing to suffer more, or to see our bent for greed and destruction extended into their realm. A decision has been reached, Doctor, and I was sent here because it was felt fitting that you should be the first to know of it."

Axel felt cold, despite the heat of the midwestern summer day. "What decision?"

"The Nomes are coming. They will be benevolent overlords, Doctor Lidenbrock, but overlords they will be. Your grandchildren will grow up in a world where mankind is a subject race, no longer free to bring ruin wherever it goes." Lenora stood, and picked up her bag. "And that is my message, Doctor. That is what I came all this way to tell you."

Axel's mouth was dry. He shook himself, willing the sense of dread that had settled over him to depart. "This is absurd," he said. "Even if I believed your ridiculous fable, mankind would never accept such dominion. We would not bow to the yoke. We would fight."

"Would we?" Lenora said. "Indulge me, Doctor. What if the Nomes announced themselves with such a demonstration of their power that the futility of resistance was immediately obvious? What if they made it plain how easy it would be for them to deprive us of the very materials we need for life?" She stepped closer and put a hand to his cheek. "I might have spared you this, Doctor," she said. "I believe you innocent of any malign motives. But this day has come, for you and for us all, and it is time for the second thing I came to show you. Do you not feel the wind rising?"

Yes, Axel realized. The wind was rising and had been growing stronger for some minutes. And he could hear something. Screams, coming from below. He stood and looked over the railing, hardly registering Lenora's final sad look before she walked away.

The wind was accelerating more, beginning to howl. Axel's hat was snatched from his head and spun away, but he barely noticed, entirely consumed as he was by the view before him. Beyond the narrow strip of the beach, where mighty Lake Michigan had been, now stretched a vast muddy plain, obscenely animated by the death throes of untold thousands of fish. The receding water was a roaring white line, a mile away, two, then vanishing, faster than seemed possible, out of sight.

Axel Lidenbrock heard the cries of confusion and despair rising all around him. He fell back into his chair. His hand groped out blindly and grasped the barometer, its familiar shape providing no comfort. He didn't need to read the instrument to know the storm had arrived. He had the wild thought that it would have been better had he died, alone in the darkness, all those decades ago. Better that individual oblivion than to bear witness to this.

The hour of mankind's dominion was over.

To Hold Back Time: A Baltimore Gun Club Adventure

Michael Schulkins

J. T. Maston sat in the smoking room of the Baltimore Gun Club discussing matters of natural philosophy with his colleagues. President Impey Barbicane had just treated the club to a lecture on the feasibility of sending items of cargo (such as bales of cotton) across the Atlantic by means of projectiles fired from stationary cannon, and returning manufactured goods (such as textiles) to America in the same way. All present agreed that Barbicane's scheme had merit and that they would arrange a test when their busy schedules permitted.

Maston scratched at his ceramic cranium with the hook that served him in place of a right hand, took up a tumbler of bourbon whiskey with the other, mostly whole, appendage, and said philosophically, "There are any number of scientific and commercial ventures we all would like to pursue, such as President Barbicane's estimable idea, but alas, there is never enough time. Certainly not time enough for a fraction of what I'd like to do." Several members expressed agreement with this sentiment, and Maston continued, "I often find myself wishing there were simply more hours in the day."

"Yes," said Mr. Bilsby, fixing his one good eye on Maston. "Think of it! What might I accomplish given a steady, reliable twenty-six-hour day?"

"Why content yourself with a paltry twenty-six hours?" said Maston. "Consider the efficacy of a thirty-hour day, or forty!"

"I must confess," said a member who still sported two intact limbs, "at my age, I believe I would require a nap before little more than twenty of the thirty had elapsed."

"Ha. I'd thought you were made of sterner stuff," opined a member graced with but a single remaining limb.

"It is indeed a splendid notion," said President Barbicane, "but imagine how long one would have to wait for suppertime to arrive." This elicited mild mirth from the members, as supper was imminent, but perhaps not so imminent as some thought it ought to be.

"Simply an additional hour a day, for extended gunnery practice and such, would be a godsend," said Captain Nicholl. "But such a notion is the sheerest fantasy. The length of the day is twenty-four hours, and that's the end of it."

"Not necessarily," said Barbicane. "A solar day is indeed 24 hours long, but the sidereal day varies by as much as 16 minutes, depending somewhat upon the location of the observer, and averages only 23 hours, 56 minutes, and 4 seconds."

"Then to the devil with the sidereal day," proclaimed Captain Nicholl. "With that as our measure, we would have to make up four minutes just to get to where we started." His colleagues received the proclamation with laughter, and he continued, "Nevertheless, the day has always been twenty-four hours, and so it will always be, until the final trump sounds and we are all recalled to our Creator."

J. T. Maston smiled and said, "Ah, but it depends upon the date of Armageddon, my dear sir. If it is quite distant, and I sincerely hope that it is—say some millions of years hence—the day will by then have lengthened without any intervention."

"Yes, I suppose that is so," said President Barbicane.

"Indeed? Why?" asked Mr. Bilsby.

Barbicane said, "It is a matter of a gradual, inevitable, imperceptible loss of angular momentum."

Mr. Bilsby looked at the club's president with anticipation, rather than admit to ignorance.

"The property that all rotating objects possess," added Barbicane. "Among its other accomplishments, it is what causes a shell fired from a rifled barrel to fly true."

"Then bless it," intoned Captain Nicholl, and the members briefly bowed their heads.

Barbicane continued, "The Earth, of course, has a tremendous amount of this wondrous property due to its mass and its swift rotation."

"And what does that have to do with Armageddon?" asked Tom Hunter, knocking ash from his cigar.

"Nothing, sir. But over millions of years the Earth will, of necessity, lose a portion of its angular momentum due to friction with the aether, if for no other reason, and thus the rotation of the planet will be slowed and the length of the day increased."

"So we must wait for Armageddon to squeeze in another hour of work?" said Captain Nicholl, sounding dour.

"I'm afraid so," said Maston.

The Club's president was uncharacteristically silent for nearly a minute, occupying himself with the rekindling of his cigar. But, as every member of long standing knew, his remarkable mental faculties were running at a breakneck pace.

"Not so fast," said Barbicane at last. "I believe it could be done. I should require a raft of calculations, my dear Maston, in order to verify it, but if my notions are sound, such a thing could actually be accomplished."

"And what is that?" said Hunter.

"Why, the lengthening of the day, of course. Is that not what we have been discussing? All that would be required would be to slow the rotation of the Earth."

"All, you say?" exclaimed Captain Nicholl. "It seems quite a tall order."

Barbicane waved this away. "Slow it just a bit, sir, or two bits perhaps. Barely enough to notice."

Nicholl replied, "We have attempted to alter the conditions of the Earth's orbit before, if you'll recall, and with embarrassing results."

Captain Nicholl referred to the Gun Club's attempt to alter the position of the axis of rotation of the Earth by 23 degrees, to permit exploitation of suspected coal deposits at the North Pole—an enterprise that had earned them the enmity of most of the world's governments and struck fear in the heart of nearly everyone on Earth. Fortunately, the project had failed due to a crucial miscalculation, undoing much of the favorable reputation the club had earned from their trip around the Moon in 1867.

"It is one thing to alter the position of the Earth's axis of rotation, but quite another, and far easier thing, to slow that rotation."

"And why is that?" asked Nicholl.

"As I've been saying, it is a matter of angular momentum. To alter the axial tilt of the planet, by even a tiny fraction of the amount we attempted, would require—we now know—a nearly inconceivable amount of force. Whereas, altering the rate of rotation, which is what would be required in this instance, is relatively paltry, quite trivial in comparison. Would you not agree, Maston?"

"I expect you are correct. I would need to perform some calculations," was his answer.

Few of those present wished, or dared, to mention the twelve orders of magnitude error in calculation that had preceded their attempt to displace the Earth's axis. Fewer still wished to draw attention to the fact that the wealthy widow, Mrs. Evangelina Scorbitt, now sitting beside her beloved J. T. Maston, had contrived to distract the great mathematician at a crucial point in his work, and thus had precipitated the fatal error.

"Allow me a crude demonstration," said Impey Barbicane. He rose and called to a servant, ordering him to locate one of the Gun Club's several velocipedes and bring it to the smoking room. The vehicles were useful, for any members still owning two lower limbs in working order, for traveling efficiently to the armory or firing range and back.

In less than a minute the servant returned with the requested bicycle. It sported a primary drive wheel, with pedals, having a diameter of one hundred and fifty centimeters, handlebars and a small leather seat atop it, a small thirty-centimeter wheel behind for stability, and a curving green-and-white-striped canopy overhead in case of rain. Barbicane took the velocipede and placed it in the center of the room, swept his gaze over the company, then released his hold on the device. It teetered a moment, then fell sideways onto the carpet with a crash.

"That," said Barbicane, "is how the machine operates without angular momentum."

He righted the velocipede, held it off the floor by the frame, with one hand, then spun the great wheel by cranking the pedal until it was rotating too fast for the spokes to be seen.

"Now the vehicle will stay upright, and most persistently so, because the considerable angular momentum of the wheel requires a considerable torque to dislodge it."

He withdrew a small snuff box from his coat pocket and tossed it onto the carpet.

"This, gentlemen, represents the jolt we must give the Earth." He hoisted the velocipede suggestively. "See how she slows once she hits it!"

He lowered the velocipede to the carpet. The machine flew from his hands in great haste, running over the snuffbox and losing a bit of its angular momentum and most of its stability in the process. Veering wildly, it sped across the room and raced down the adjoining hall. A loud, rattling crash followed, along with the tinkle of broken glass and a servant's shriek. President Barbicane resumed his seat without expression.

For several moments there was only the ticking of the grandfather clock to be heard in the smoking room, then Mrs. Scorbitt spoke.

"I wonder if the day isn't more than long enough already," she said, gazing after the lost velocipede.

Another few moments of silence passed before J. T. Maston, sitting beside her, said, "Nonsense, my dear woman. Whatever makes you say that?"

She laughed discreetly. "If you were a woman, my dear Maston, you would not need to ask. Or a servant, for that matter, but perhaps that is redundant. When one does the work other men refuse to do, the day can be quite long enough, I assure you."

This only led to more silence.

At last Barbicane said, "Nevertheless, gentlemen, and lady, I believe it can be done. Once again, there is much calculation still to be performed." He looked benevolently upon Maston the mathematician. "But I believe the scheme is viable, and should be far easier to execute than our voyage around the Moon."

"But how, sir?" asked Mr. Bilsby. "However is it to be done?"

"Need you even ask, my friend? By the means through which most of the great things in the modern world are accomplished, namely, gunnery." He rose again to his feet. "Cannon, sir. Long, large-bore cannon, securely anchored in bedrock, or perhaps carved into the bedrock so all the recoil will be absorbed by the Earth. Cannon firing the most massive balls we can create." Barbicane began to pace. "I should think that four such cannon will suffice. There should be one placed in each quadrant of the planet, located on the equator for maximum lever arm, and directed along its line, firing simultaneously for maximum effect, and oriented so as to fire against the rotation of the Earth."

"And what result would these four great guns produce?" asked Captain Nicholl.

"Why, a longer day, sir."

"Yes, conceivably. Only how much longer? A second? A minute? An hour?"

Barbicane began, "That would depend once again upon the calc—"

But J. T. Maston interrupted him. "By Jove! Don't you see? That is the great advantage to the scheme Impey has contrived. If the change is not enough for our liking, we must only fire the cannon again, as many times as we please, until the desired amount of slowing has been achieved."

"Exactly," affirmed Barbicane. "If we would like a twenty-five-hour day, we need only fire our cannon the requisite number of times."

"And if we're lucky," said Tom Hunter, "it will take scores of simultaneous firings, perhaps even hundreds. Think of it, gentlemen. While the project continues, we shall be up to our ears in gunnery! Why, I dare say, it's nearly as fine a thing as a war."

This was too much for the assembled members and they jumped to their feet—what feet they had between them—and cried, "Hip hip! Three cheers for President Barbicane! Three cheers for the longer day!"

Mrs. Evangelina Scorbitt was the only one present who did not rise nor take up the cheer.

The world's reaction to the Baltimore Gun Club's latest enterprise, once its details had been released to the press, was almost immediate, and furious in its tone, both from those who approved of the notion of a longer day, and those who opposed it. The latter fell into two camps, one of which wished to do nothing and keep the length of the day the same, and another that wished to see the length of the day reduced. Fortunately for Impey Barbicane and the Baltimore Gun Club, press coverage showed that a substantial number of prominent men were in favor of the proposition, so a subscription fund was created and the capital accumulated for the construction of the necessary guns.

The general placement of the guns was decided upon considerations of geography and the likelihood of the presence of accessible bedrock. The first site identified was in South America, at Ambato, in the newly formed nation of Ecuador; the second was in Malaysia near Singapore; a third was in West Africa, near Monrovia in Liberia; and the last was on a remote volcanic island in the Pacific called Ocean Island, in the Gilbert Islands chain. All four locations were on the equator, or as nearly so as could be managed. As these places were all rather remote and quite some distance from Baltimore, the construction and alignment of each of the four cannon was assigned to a Club member in good standing and was to be completed on site on his own recognizance. Thus Captain Nicholl set off for Liberia, J.T. Maston for Singapore, Tom Hunter, who had a high tolerance for sea voyages, to remote Ocean Island, and Impey Barbicane, who still had two good legs for climbing, chose Ambato. The task took more than a year, with the four men and their aides working in isolation, but at last all four had relayed messages to Baltimore announcing that their guns were finished. The massive cannonballs they were to fire had already been cast, and the enormously powerful gunpowder Captain Nicholl had invented was sent to propel them.

They chose a date for the commencement of the operation, and since this time there was no astronomical or geographical reason to choose one date over another, the first day of December was selected, in honor of the date upon which their successful trip around the Moon had commenced. Since they wished to fire all the guns at once for maximum effect, they agreed upon a time for firing the first volley, and chose an interval of ten minutes for reloading the cannon so the next could be sent. They would continue to fire at ten-minute intervals until a total of one hundred rounds had been fired from each gun.

As the four gun emplacements were spaced at roughly equal distances around the globe, the moment of firing would be approximately at dawn for one, at noon for another, at sunset for the third, and at midnight for the fourth. However, nothing had been left to chance, and each man carried an excellent timepiece synchronized with the grandfather clock in the Gun Club's smoking room, so they might be as precise in their timing as possible. Only Barbicane did not have to convert the time, because Baltimore, contrary to expectations, is along the same longitude as Ecuador.

Thus on the first day of December, 1873, Captain Nicholl stood a healthy distance from the cannon he had anchored into the rock, gazing out into the Atlantic, idly fingering the switch that would cause a spark to ignite the powder and launch the first ball.

"Mr. Bilsby," he called, for Bilsby had accompanied him and assisted in the work, "how much time have we? It will be dark soon."

"Only another minute, Captain," he said. "I'll count it down for you if you like." And he did.

At the mark of zero, Nicholl closed the switch and an instant later the air exploded with a tremendous roar and a gigantic ball shot with inconceivable speed from the mouth of the immense gun. Nearly a minute later, far, far out to sea, a towering fountain of water rose up against the setting sun. More shots followed at regular intervals, and continued on through the night and into the morning.

A month later to the day, the participating members of the Baltimore Gun Club reassembled to assess the results of their effort to alter the rotational speed of the Earth. So distant were their various points of departure, one being literally halfway around the world, that they had had little or no time to do anything but travel, primarily by steamship, and had heard no news of any kind, not even about the new length of the day. The reunion took place in Baltimore, near Fort McHenry on the Patapsco River, and was scheduled for the otherwise unpleasant hour of sunrise, and even a bit before, so that they might be in place and ready with their instruments when the blazing orb appeared over the horizon. Fortunately, the weather was clear, although in early January, even temperate Baltimore was windy and cold.

Of course they knew the ostensible moment of sunrise, or Barbicane and Maston did, and comparing the incontrovertible event with their timepieces should tell the tale. Would the day indeed be longer, and if so, how much longer would it be? They had allowed a month for the small change in time to accumulate, although they had only a rough idea of just how much it ought to be. J. T. Maston had done his best, but as he reminded his colleagues, without precise data, there is only so much that mathematics can do. Thus they stood close together on the windswept shore, staring east and awaiting the rising of the sun.

JV

"Let us hope that we are still in the dark an hour from now," said Bilsby.

"What's that you say?" shouted Tom Hunter.

"I said, let us hope it is still dark an hour from now," Bilsby shouted in reply.

"Yes. Or a dozen," hollered Hunter.

Soon thereafter, however, one of the company noted that the sky was lightening to the east.

"I wonder if we haven't—" began Impey Barbicane.

"For heaven's sake, Impey, please speak up!" hollered Captain Nicholl. "Even after a month, I'm still as deaf as a post."

All of the men who had witnessed the firing of the great balls were so afflicted, and thus the conversation, although not particularly elevated in tone, was necessarily elevated in volume.

"I wonder if we haven't outsmarted ourselves and gained exactly twenty-four hours," shouted Impey Barbicane. "How much of a change would that amount to, compounded over a month, Maston?"

The mathematician bowed his head in thought for a moment, then said, "Approximately forty-eight minutes. That would be quite a significant dilation for the first attempt."

The sky continued to lighten, the stars faded, and soon it was clear that sunrise was imminent.

"Have your timepieces at the ready," called Barbicane loudly, and a moment later, the sun appeared.

— JV —

How do you explain it, then, Mr. Maston?" shouted Mr. Bilsby, as the adventurers walked into the Club's smoking room. "Is it possible that we have added exactly twenty-four hours in thirty-one days? That we have, in effect, added one day to every month of the year?"

"Certainly it is possible, sir, as that is essentially what we intended to do. Nevertheless, we shall have to check to be sure."

He raised his voice even higher to call for the butler, from whom he requested that morning's Baltimore Sun.

"Ah, but we have just seen the Baltimore sun," japed Tom Hunter, "and it has failed us."

The servant soon returned with the newspaper. Maston took it with hook and hand and looked immediately to the top of the front page for the date.

"I was afraid of that. It's January first, by Jove. So we have not gained forty-eight minutes a day after all."

"Can it be yesterday's paper?" shouted Bilsby.

"I very much doubt it," hollered Maston. "See? the ink smears when rubbed."

"So, what have we accomplished, then?" called Tom Hunter, who like the others had traveled to the ends of the Earth to conduct the project.

"Apparently nothing," said Impey Barbicane, "or very little in any case. All of our timepieces agree to within a few seconds, and what's more, they agree with the almanac." He waved the book for emphasis. "And the sun, may the devil take it, was right on time. I can only conclude that we have failed."

"What a shame," said Captain Nicholl.

"Yes," mused Tom Hunter, albeit loudly. "Still I must admit, even if the experiment was a failure, and turned me deaf in the bargain, it did my gunner's heart good to send so many balls so far into the sea."

"And yet you had it the worst of all of us," called Maston, "facing as you were directly into that fierce tropical sun."

"What's that, Maston?" barked Tom. "I must have heard you wrongly."

Maston repeated what he had just said, this time more distinctly.

"But no," Tom said. "Surely you're mistaken. That's not how it was at all. I was facing—"

"I'm glad to know that the conditions did not discommode you," said Barbicane casually, but with added volume, "as the result was apparently nil."

"But, sir," Tom said, "I must tell you—"

"What's that?" said Maston.

"Sir, I must insist that when I fired the cannon, I was not facing into the sun, but away from it, as indicated by President Barbicane's instructions."

"Why ever would you do that?" exclaimed J. T. Maston.

"Because Mr. Barbicane's instructions, as relayed in the letter composed by Mrs. Scorbitt, clearly stated that—"

"What's all this?" rumbled President Barbicane, having detected the presence of his name above the ceaseless ringing in his ears.

"I fear I have made a most dreadful mistake," said Tom, just loud enough for the others to hear. "I can hardly bear to say it, but I believe I fired all one hundred of my shots in the wrong direction."

"Nonsense," insisted Barbicane. "You fired east of course, into the rising sun. The thing is simplicity itself, sir, a child could understand it."

Tom Hunter said nothing, but felt utterly shocked and dejected, as only a master gunner who has fired a hundred balls and missed the target with every one can feel.

"Wait now," called Captain Nicholl, "what is that you're saying?"

Barbicane, raising his voice, said, "If I correctly understand what he is saying, Tom here contrived to fire all of his shots, all of them mind you, in precisely the wrong direction."

"Impossible," said Nicholl. "Surely he fired his cannon to the west, as we all did." He looked around at his colleagues. "Did we not?"

Overcome, President Barbicane collapsed into a chair and put his head in his hands.

"How can this be?" he said at last. "I thought the instructions were perfectly clear, and in any case, a child should be able to see it. To slow the rotation of the earth, one must point one's gun to the east. Nothing could be simpler. Maston!" He glanced up at the mathematician. "Surely you fired your gun in the right direction."

"Well, yes. To the east, certainly. As you say, it is elementary."

"But hold on now," said Tom Hunter, "your instructions clearly indicated the contrary."

"Yes," agreed Captain Nicholl. "So it appeared to me as well."

"See here," said J. T. Maston, "let us simply consult the message Mrs. Scorbitt was kind enough to transcribe. That is, the instructions given by President Barbicane at our initial meeting." He looked at the woman once more sitting beside him. "Mrs. Scorbitt, Evangelina my dear," he said in the tenderest tone of which he was capable, "is it possible that you made an error in recording what Impey said?"

Mrs. Scorbitt took a paper from her bag and offered it to Maston. "Here is a copy, my darling. See for yourself."

Maston took the paper, inspected it for a moment, then said, "I must say, it seems in order to me. Precisely as I remember it."

"Read the relevant passage aloud," called Captain Nicholl. "And loudly as well, if you don't mind."

Maston looked down at the paper and said, rather loudly, "Here is the salient part." And he intoned, "There should be one placed in each quadrant of the planet, and located on the equator for maximum lever arm, and directed along its line, firing simultaneously for maximum effect, and oriented so as to fire against the rotation of the Earth."

President Barbicane said, "If I am hearing it properly, that is entirely correct. 'Oriented so as to fire against the rotation of the Earth.'"

"But gentlemen," shouted Captain Nicholl, "that is exactly what I did."

"And I as well," insisted Tom Hunter.

"Surely, as everyone knows, the Earth rotates towards the east, thus causing the Sun to be overcome by the horizon to the west. So as per your instructions, I fired my gun against the direction of the Earth's rotation, and that direction is west. Is that not so, sirs? How have I erred, if indeed I have?"

There was silence for a long moment, except for the ringing of ears, then President Barbicane said, "Hmm. Perhaps I should have said 'fire in such a direction as to reduce the rotational motion of the Earth.'"

"Yes," agreed Maston, "I suppose that would have been clearer, if not as concise."

"But it amounts to the same thing," shouted Tom. "The Earth is rotating toward the east, as we all agree. Therefore, to counter that rotation we must fire our cannon to the west. It seems simple."

"No," said J. T. Maston.

"Certainly not," agreed Barbicane.

Maston continued, "You must understand, gentlemen, that the direction of the ball means nothing. It is the direction of the recoil that concerns us. The force exerted on the Earth by the gun, as produced by the firing of the ball, is what must slow the Earth's rate of rotation. Thus, for the gun to act against the direction of rotation, the gun must actually face in the direction of that rotation." He looked at the men. "Do you see?"

"Yes. Indeed I do," said Captain Nicholl, "but my interpretation of the instructions made it seem the opposite."

"So two of us fired to the east and two of us to the west, and the result was to cancel each other out completely," said Tom Hunter.

"I'm afraid so," said Barbicane.

"If only the sodding instructions had been a bit clearer," added Tom, but as he did not shout, it was unlikely to be heard.

Yet J. T. Maston did hear it, if just barely. He turned to Mrs. Scorbitt, who, it shall be remembered, recorded them, and asked, "Did you find the instructions to be clear, Mrs. Scorbitt?"

"Certainly, my dear Maston," said Mrs. Scorbitt with a wry smile. "As far as I am concerned, they served their purpose perfectly."

A Drama in Durango

Alison L. Randall

Ila Nichols stepped up to the post office window. "I'd like a stamp please." She plunked her two cents on the counter and pushed them toward the postmaster, Walter Johnson.

He grinned, like she'd just made his morning, and passed over a tiny square.

"Thank you kindly," Ila said. She licked the stamp and pressed it to her envelope, which contained an order for another of Jules Verne's *Extraordinary Voyages*. She made certain not to let their fingers touch as she placed the envelope into the postmaster's care. That lopsided grin of his seemed especially fixed on her the past while, although she couldn't imagine why. According to a suitor best forgotten, she was too tall and as sturdy as a workhorse, which still stung when she thought about it. So, she tried not to, and it was best that the postmaster not think about her, either.

She turned to go, but a "Miss Ila?" made her swing back. Postmaster Walt hooked his thumb to the left. "Did you see that new wanted poster?"

Ila shifted her gaze and spotted the new one right away. *Rob in the Hood*, the bandit was called—a clever name, that—but Ila's eyes were drawn to the bolded letters underneath.

$1,000 reward for capture.

Heavens, but she could do a lot with money like that. This town was squeezing her tight as a corset, and she itched to go on a voyage of her own, not just read about them in Mr. Verne's novels. A low, unladylike whistle escaped Ila's teeth.

"You saw it too, then?" Walt said.

Ila looked at him, and his grin was gone. He'd turned serious, deadly so.

"Those banks he's robbed so far." The postmaster pointed at the bottom half of the poster. "He's heading this way."

Ila peered at the list of robbed banks. Being a lover of maps, she knew exactly how far away those towns were—ninety miles, fifty-eight, thirty-two.... The postmaster was right. Their town was next in line.

If that wasn't enough to startle her stays off, the description of the outlaw struck out at her like a snake: *Rob in the Hood walks stiff legged, like his knees have been shot up and won't bend no more.*

Why, Ila had seen someone walking just like that, only the night before. She'd gone outside around midnight for a whiff of cool air, and a dark figure had passed by on the other side of the road. She hadn't seen his face, but maybe no one ever had. There was no photograph on the poster, just a sketch of a man in a black hood.

"Miss Ila?" A voice cut through the bee-swarm in her head. "Are you all right?"

Postmaster Walt was leaning over the counter, his hand stretched toward her arm.

Ila stepped back. "I... I'm fine."

"Well, if that no-good comes into the bank while you're manning the till," he said, "you step out the door and holler." He lifted the closest thing at hand, a rubber stamp, and let it fall with a thud.

Ila turned away before the laugh in her throat could bubble out. "I'll do that," she said over her shoulder. But if a masked man did break in, calling for the postmaster to stamp him into surrender wouldn't be her first thought.

But as she descended the post office steps, she pondered the possibility. What if that outlaw—Rob in the Hood—really was the person she'd seen in the night? That teeter-tottering gait had seemed comical at the time, like that of the wind-up tin soldiers that were all the rage in town. But now, the thought wasn't comical at all.

It meant that the bandit with shot-up knees was in town for a robbery, and she was willing to wager—ladylike or not—that he would make his attempt that day.

Well, Ila would see about that. She could take care of Rob in the Hood and snag that $1,000 reward for capture while she was at it. She might not be able to go around the world in eighty days with it, but even a quarter of the way would be far enough from this dreary place. And she had an idea for how to do it, too, thanks to that thought of tin soldiers. Once those little men tumbled, they couldn't get back up again. She counted on that for shot-up knees as well.

— JV —

Come opening time, Ila had put her plan into place. She'd strung a trip wire just inside the vault and stashed a pair of ropes behind a cash box for tying the scoundrel up. She hadn't told the bank manager, though. Gerald Croft would hightail it to Sheriff Farr and then she'd turn out to be wrong. She'd be the girl who cried bandit and the laughingstock of the town.

The clock ticked off the minutes. Ila fidgeted behind her counter, nearly jumping out of her skirts every time the door opened. Gerald sat at his desk in the corner, fiddling with his tin soldiers, which he, along with half the town, collected.

Around noontime, it happened—a black-hooded figure slid through the door, turned the Open sign to Closed, and slid the deadbolt, all while pointing a revolver Ila's way.

Ila discovered a curious thing about being on the receiving end of a barrel—her knees were shaking. She'd read that they could, but never really believed it. And then, a clatter and a screech from the corner told her Gerald was feeling it, too. He'd probably just spilled his toys.

"Here now!" He came bounding in between Ila and the bandit. "No need to turn violent." He spread his arms wide in a shield. "Tell us what you want."

"Give me all your money," the bandit said in a halting way that made Ila wonder if he was foreign. He threw a cinch-top sack to Gerald. "Vault." Tossed a second sack to Ila. "Till."

But no, that wasn't the plan. "I'll. Take. The. Vault," Ila said, stressing each word, hoping Gerald would catch on.

But he only spread his arms wider. "I'm not letting this son-of-a-gun anywhere near you."

Ila could have clobbered him. Why did he have to turn all gentlemanly now? But the plan might still work if Gerald let the bandit go in first. Once the wire tripped him up, Ila could rush in and tie him tight.

She waited until they'd passed into the back room and then tiptoed after them.

Peering around the door frame, Ila caught sight of a bulge under the back of the bandit's leather vest. He was hiding something under there, and in the smaller room, the *tick, tick, tick* of it was plain to hear.

The bandit had a time bomb.

Ila froze, just as Gerald pulled open the vault, and stepped inside. His foot caught the wire and he toppled like a tree in a storm, face first onto the concrete floor.

A horrified glee surged through Ila—her plan had worked. Too bad she'd downed the wrong man.

The bandit raised his stiff-kneed legs, stepped over the wire, and into the vault. With a groan, Gerald sat up and spied Ila peering in.

"This your doing?" He pointed to the wire, and Ila had to nod. "Smart," he said. "But next time, let me in on it first."

Well, she'd tried, but Ila didn't bother pointing that out to Gerald because the bandit had swung her way. "Till," he said, and that ticking echoed ominously off the steel walls of the vault.

Ila stalked back to the till and practically threw the stacks of money and rolls of coins into the sack, but the more she threw, the slower she went, and the more sick-at-heart she became. There went Mabel Green's savings and Ethel Moore's. There went Clive Cornaby's and Olive Thompson's.

She couldn't let this greedy rascal get away, but if she did any of the rash thoughts she had, like jumping on his back or knocking the revolver away, he had the bomb in reserve. Something else then, something sly. Ila spied a piece of paper on the counter, and an idea flared. She took up a pencil and began to write.

I have information about an upcoming bank shipment that will interest you.

Yes, that would capture his attention. Now, a place to meet. When she'd seen the bandit sneaking down the street, he'd headed west, toward the fields. She'd thought it strange at the time, since no one lived out there, but it would do.

Meet me at midnight, at the first field to the west, under the tallest tree.

That was clear enough, and the place would be private that late at night. She had to have a reason to be offering information, though. Otherwise, he'd never trust her intentions.

All I ask is a cut of the goods. 20%.

There. That sounded sufficiently traitorous.

Ila folded the note and placed it at the top of the sack, where the bandit would find it when he checked his loot. She cinched the sack shut just as boot-falls and that horrible ticking sounded behind her. It seemed even louder now, and it sent Ila's knees jiggling again.

Maybe the thief would blow them up now that he had the money.

Ila turned to see the bandit, waving his gun at Gerald.

"Fetch two chairs," the bandit said. "Put them back to back."

Gerald scurried around the room, doing the bandit's bidding, until he, too, was forced to sit and submit. Soon, Ila found herself trussed to a chair, her hands behind her back and tied to Gerald's by the very ropes she'd stashed in the vault.

For a moment, she thought the bandit would leave his bomb with them, too, but he lifted a hand to his hood in a sort of salute. He dropped his loot out the side window, tipped himself after it, and slid out as stiffly as a log passing through a sawmill. Ila breathed a sigh at the clunk of his boots hitting the ground.

They were alive—stuck, with the door locked, the sign turned to Closed—but still in one piece, or, rather, two.

When the rescue came, it wasn't at all dignified. Two old widows who'd spotted the captives through the window wailed about their lost savings, and Sheriff Farr scolded Ila for being too proud to come to him right away. She told him she'd had no proof—a suspicion only—and didn't want him chasing after what might turn out to be just a thought in her head. What she didn't admit out loud was that she'd wanted that $1,000 reward for capture all to herself.

Gerald, on the other hand, was making a fine showing of himself. He told the widows he wouldn't let them starve, even if he had to drain his own savings. Ila had never seen this side of him before. She liked it but doubted the depths of his savings, especially considering the amount of money he must spend on his collections.

The bank customers would be fine, though. Ila would make sure of it. She would catch that thief and get back what belonged to them.

That night, Ila was early to the tree. It stood under a fat moon, as round and golden as an overripe squash. She arrived there, pushing a wheelbarrow that contained a bag of wheat with a rope around its middle and more ropes for binding the bandit after she'd knocked him down. It took all the extra time she had, and every bit of strength, to hoist the bag of wheat into the tree. Then she drew the rope around the back of the tree, so that it wouldn't dangle down, and tied it to her ankle where it was covered by her skirts. One swift kick should tighten the rope and tip the bag off the limb, right onto the bandit.

That was the plan, anyway, one she'd plotted out as she'd stood fuming behind her teller's counter. She could picture it all, especially the result, which would leave the bandit on his back, his arms and legs waving about like an upturned beetle's. Satisfied, she smiled to herself and leaned back against the trunk to rest.

She'd only just caught her breath, when sounds from an off-kilter walk joined the nightly rustlings of the fields around her. By the light of the moon, Ila glimpsed the dark shape of the bandit lurching toward her, a gun glinting in his hand, which surprised her and set her knees quivering again. Surely, she'd made it clear to the bandit that she was on his despicable side.

Ila wrested control of her coward knees. "I'm here," she said.

The bandit stopped. "What have you come to say?"

He was still too far away for her plan to work, but close enough for a ticking sound to reach her ears. He'd brought the gun and the bomb then.

She forced her thoughts away from the bomb. "Lower your gun and come closer. I'm not going to shout out my news for the whole town to hear."

He holstered the revolver with a jerky motion and then took a step toward her—*teeter*—another step—*totter*—*teeter, totter, teeter, totter*, until he was under the limb, exactly where she needed him.

"Well. . . ." he said.

"Well," she said, "you asked for it." And she kicked out hard.

The rope stretched taut, and the wheat rustled as the bag shifted on its limb. But it didn't fall.

Drat! She should have known there would be complications. Mr. Verne's books were full of them.

She looked to the bandit, sure that he would have pulled the bomb from under his vest and thrust it in her face. But he just stood there, and the ticking slowed, slower and slower, counting down the last moments of her life.

Ila reached back, seized the rope, and pulled hard.

The bag tumbled. It hit the bandit in the back, and he fell forward—right into Ila. She felt herself going down with the bandit on top of her and the fifty-pound bag of wheat on top of him.

And then—silence. No moan or curse from the bandit, and no ticking, either.

Ila closed her eyes, waiting for the *flash* and the *boom* and the *whoosh* that meant she'd met her end. But nothing happened.

The bandit was still. Not kicking or thrashing. Not speaking. Or breathing.

Not breathing?

No. She hadn't meant to kill him. She'd only meant to topple him, capture him, and turn him over to Sheriff Farr for a reward.

She was a murderer.

It couldn't be. Ila whipped the hood off the bandit's head, hoping that fresh air would revive him.

She screamed, long and loud, a scream those fields had never heard before, because the man on top of her was not a man.

The face was painted white, with circles of black for eyes, tiny lines for a nose, and a thicker one for the mouth that might have been red in the light. She raised a hand and rapped on his forehead, and it rang out, hollow and echoey, like an empty water can.

He didn't just walk like a tin man. He was one.

Again, a horrified glee rose up in her—the same sort Professor Aronnax might have felt when he realized the sea monster he'd been seeking was actually a mechanical wonder. Then and now, the impossible had come to life. But now that the breath was being squished out of her by an impossible thing, she wanted it to be over.

Ila pushed and pulled until the wheat slid off and she was able to shimmy out from underneath the tin bandit. Gasping for breath, she clambered to her feet and then leaned close to study the downed bandit, who lay still and unmoving, face down in the dirt.

Perhaps this tin man was like the small ones she'd seen on Gerald's desk. Even if this bandit was savvy enough to step over a tripwire, he might still need a wind-up key like Gerald's toys did. Ila stooped and made a move that would have brought on a blush only minutes before—she slid her hand underneath the bandit's vest. Gingerly, in case the lump on his back was indeed a bomb, she inched her fingers closer until they hit up against a square metal post about as big around as her thumb. The pole passed through a hole in the bandit's shirt and down into his back. Connected to the post were two flat, round paddles.

It was a key then, not a bomb, that had been the source of the ticking sound. Now that she knew it, Ila felt silly that she hadn't thought of it before.

Ila raised up, undecided about what to do. She could run for Sheriff Farr, but that would mean leaving the bandit alone, unattended, and there were things she had to know before she could do that. She had to find out if this thing was a thinking being, one who had planned and executed the robberies on his own, or if someone had invented him, sent him to the tree that night, and was expecting him back. If the latter, then the maker might come looking when the bandit didn't turn up. Ila would come back with help only to find an empty space where the bandit had lain.

Without proof, Sheriff Farr would never believe that a tin man had robbed their bank. She wasn't sure she believed it herself, even though the evidence lay at her feet. No. She couldn't leave the bandit. She had to see what he would do next.

Ila pulled in a strengthening breath, rubbed her hands together, and then leaned over to crank the bandit up. The key turned easily at first, then slower and harder, until it would turn no more.

She released it, and the bandit's legs gave a jerk. His arms flapped against the ground, and he rolled from side to side. It was clear he wouldn't be able to get up without help.

"What...." he said. "What... have... you... come... to... say?"

That was the same question he'd asked earlier. He was repeating the same tune, like a pianola does when it plays the patterned roll of paper inside it. He wasn't a thinking being, then, only saying what had been placed in his innards.

Ila took hold of his gloved hands and pulled him to his feet. She brushed him off so that whoever sent him wouldn't know he'd fallen and suspect she was seeking his inventor.

"Thank… you," the bandit said. "You are…." He hesitated. "Kind."

Startled, Ila stepped back. She couldn't imagine his maker placing that word in his inner works, but the bandit couldn't have come up with it on his own. That truly would have been extraordinary. Well, there was no time for wondering. She had to get the bandit going before his maker came looking, and she ought to play her part, too, just in case there were real thoughts in that tin head of his.

She stepped forward again and straightened his clothes. "You're not so bad yourself," she said, and then she pulled the hood back over his head. "Now, here's the information I promised. Wells Fargo is bringing a shipment of ten thousand dollars in gold through next Tuesday. The coach should arrive around ten. Like I said, I want twenty percent. You bring the money to me here, by midnight of that day, or I'm going to the sheriff with everything I know. And I mean everything."

"Fine, fine, fine," the tin bandit said, and he made to turn away, but Ila stopped him, worried now that the bag of wheat had jarred something loose.

"Are you all right?"

"Fine," he answered.

He tottered away, lurching down the lane and deeper into the fields. Ila, of course, had to follow. She had to see if someone was waiting for him. And then she could go to Sheriff Farr and he could arrest the robbers. He couldn't call her proud after that.

Freshly wound, Rob in the Hood walked quickly ahead of her. She held back, keeping his dark shape in her sights, until she saw he was headed for a small shed at the corner of one of the fields. The bandit went to it, opened the door, and walked in.

Ila crouched and crept toward the shed. There were no windows, but the boards had gaps between them, and lantern light trickled through. She found a big enough crack to peer through and saw the bandit facing the door, a man working at its back. After a moment, the man stepped to the side, and Ila dropped to her knees.

Gerald was in there, tinkering with the tin bandit.

It all made sense now. Gerald had built it! So, that was why he'd seemed brave enough to jump between her and an armed man—he was in on the plan. He knew his own bandit wouldn't harm them and wanted to be sure his tin bandit succeeded in the robbery. Ila rose a little, peered through the crack, and saw other parts on shelves in the shed. Rolls of tin, steel barrels with pins jutting out of them, stacks of paper cards. Piles of discarded arms, and legs, and heads made Ila think that Gerald had tried multiple times to get the bandit right.

She understood now why he'd offered his savings to the widows. He would only be giving them ten cents back on the dollar he'd stolen, and he'd be a hero for it.

Ila shifted—her knees paining her as much as the thought of Gerald being hailed a hero—and spotted a pair of boots at the edge of her view, one of them tapping the floor. Someone else was there. Ila leaned toward the next crack over, hoping for a better look, and nearly went tumbling.

Sheriff Farr was in there, too.

Ila plopped to the ground again, her mind a tumbleweed, rolling down the road.

He'd called her proud, that sheriff, and all the while, he knew who the bank robber was. She wanted to break down that door and give those two a telling-off. But she had to be clever if she was to stop them. She rose to kneeling and pressed her ear to the crack.

"This opens up new possibilities," Gerald was saying, "Her telling Rob about the bank shipment, planning a place to get her loot."

"What do you mean?" Sheriff Farr said. "Surely, you already knew about the shipment."

"Of course, I did," Gerald said. "But I wouldn't have touched it. Robbing banks is one thing—anyone with guts can do that—but hitting a bank shipment requires inside information. Usually only the manager knows when one's coming through so suspicion would fall on me."

"What's changed now?" Sheriff Farr said.

"Well, Ila's in the picture. That's why I risked sending Rob to her. I let word of the shipment slip to her and I had to see what she would say. Now, I know she'll take that money and skedaddle. Suspicion will fall on her, not me. Especially not after what I did today, offering them old widows my savings."

"*Hee, hee, hee,*" Sheriff Farr slapped the table. "You sure played it smooth. So, you don't think she'd try to pin it on you?"

"Nah," Gerald said. "She's not even trying to hide who she is. Only the teller could have put that note in the sack with the money. That makes me think she won't even look back. Not that I'm surprised. That girl's always reading, always going on about traveling, like she's too good for this town."

Ila pulled back in surprise at the picture Gerald painted of her. Was everyone in town whispering the same thing—that Ila Nichols thought she was too good for them?

"It's not right for a woman to be that smart," Gerald went on. "But we're smart too, and we can't let this chance get away from us. I've got an idea for what we can do."

He went on talking, laying out how they would stop the stagecoach at the north pass with an obstacle on the road. Ila listened to the details in disbelief, wondering when Gerald had become so, well, manager-like. She'd never seen it in all the months she'd watched him laze about at his desk. It seemed that all he'd needed to kindle a fire beneath him was the possibility of doing bad deeds.

She eased away from the crack, sick in the middle, raging in the head, and tiptoed toward home so they wouldn't catch her listening between the boards.

She had to do something—and not just to make sure she didn't get blamed. If she didn't stop them, the robberies would never end. People would get hurt. More would go hungry. Gerald—curse him—was wrong about her. She did care, and she was sorry if the townsfolk thought she didn't.

But Gerald was right about one thing—she was smart. Smart enough to stop him. And smart enough to have learned by now that she couldn't do it alone.

Only problem was, she didn't know who else to go to since both the sheriff and her bank manager were corrupt. Who else in town could she trust?

It would have to be someone who wanted to see those bad men caught as badly as she did, someone who cared about justice and old widows and....

The answer was obvious, but, oh, it was hard to think of running to him when she hadn't wanted him getting ideas about her. Still, as long as she was swallowing pride, she might as well eat the whole hog, hoofs and all.

It was time to enlist Postmaster Walt.

The next morning, she came early to the post office, long before anyone was expecting their mail. While she told him the whole story, she watched his face, waiting for a skeptical raise of his brows. She was talking about a tin bandit after all. But he only listened.

"Stranger things have come to pass," he said in a deep-throated way that made her think he was quoting something.

"Where...." She hesitated, pondering the words, and then the answer came to her. "That's from—"

"*Around the World in Eighty Days.*" He grinned and pointed to something at his left side. Ila had to lean across the counter and peer around to see a shelf fixed to the wall, topped by a row of books. There sat the same *Extraordinary Voyages* she had read.

She looked back at him with what felt like new eyes. "So, you'll help?"

He rubbed his hands together. "It would be my pleasure."

Under the guise of courting, they spent the next few evenings preparing the scene of the future crime. Sheriff Farr had seemed well acquainted with the terrain around town. He'd suggested a place for the ambush, and Ila recognized it on sight. Brush-covered hills rose to the west of the road, but there was one spot where hill and road almost met. The rocky outcropping was steep, with a jutting point that looked to Ila like the bow of a great sailing ship attempting to thrust itself through the ocean of sagebrush that lay on the other side of the road. On that side, the sagebrush intermingled with stunted trees, which would make it hard for a moving coach to careen around an obstacle if the driver suspected a trap. The coach would meet rock on one side, brush and trees on the other.

Sheriff Farr had also mentioned a nook next to the outcropping where he and Gerald could hide. Ila and Postmaster Walt found two such places situated on either side of the ship-like outcropping. Small boulders had tumbled from above and piled into a semi-circular rock wall, perfect for concealing two crouching people. The twin crannies were so alike Ila half-expected to find a rusty old anchor in each hollow, half-buried in earth, halting the huge vessel in its forward progress. Instead, she found brush and a scattering of smaller rocks.

The hollow on the southern side was less overgrown with brush and not quite as cramped. Ila figured that it would be the lair Gerald and the sheriff would choose. She and Postmaster Walt would take the north.

That decided, Ila presented her plan.

"Once the coach stops, I'll run out in front of it so they can't gun down the stagecoach guards. While I'm doing that, you send down a fall of rocks from above." She pointed to a spot on the hill, above the southern hollow, where they could gather a large pile of rocks. It would be easy enough for Walt to push it down and it would fell Gerald and the sheriff at once. Ila went on: "The guards and driver will help us tie them up and take them to the sheriff in the next town over."

Ila looked for a lopsided grin of approval but found a consternated look instead.

"What if they shoot you?" he said.

"Shoot a woman?" she said. "They wouldn't dare."

He didn't seem convinced. "How about I just come around behind them with my gun?" He moved his coat aside to show her a revolver in a holster on his hip.

The sight of the postmaster with a gun made her queasy. He should be stamping letters and grinning at customers, not shooting people, and she was the one who had brought him to this. Like it or not, though, they might need a revolver on their side, but only if things got desperate. "All right," she said. "Bring it. But let's try the rockslide first."

They climbed the hill and built their rock pile, and then the plan was in place.

This one would work—she was sure of it—so long as Gerald and the sheriff really were averse to putting a bullet in a woman's back. Or front.

Tuesday morning found Ila in her own little hollow at the north side of the point. Gerald had told her he'd be out of town for the day, and she'd played along, offering to watch the bank and pretending not to notice the smirk he gave when she said she'd sign for the shipment. She felt a little guilty about leaving the bank closed that morning, but not as guilty as she would have felt if she'd gone to work knowing what was about to happen.

She glanced up, but Postmaster Walt wasn't visible from where she hunched. He must be uncomfortable up there, lying flat under the sagebrush.

She didn't have to wait long before Sheriff Farr, Gerald, and Rob in the Hood showed up in a big wagon. They swung it around and backed it up into the tightest squeeze between rock and brush. Then they shifted six big canvas bundles from the back of the wagon to the ground, arranging them to make it look like the whole mess had slid off the back of a supply wagon by mistake. Ila heard the clinking of what sounded like tent poles from beneath the canvas and wondered where they'd rustled up big old army tents.

She had to hand it to them, though. It was cunning. And so was having the tin bandit stoop over and pretend to be lifting the bundles back onto the wagon, although they were big enough that he would have been hard pressed to do it alone. Gerald then placed a hat on the bandit's head, so that his hood wasn't visible from the back.

Not long after, the stagecoach came, lickety-split, down the road. Ila crept out of her hollow, ready to launch the plan, just as the driver hollered, "Whoa!" The coach creaked to a stop. "I'll come help," he called.

The tin bandit swung around and aimed his gun at the driver. "Give me all your money."

That was Ila's cue.

She rushed out from hiding and stood between the stagecoach and the tin bandit. "Stop," she yelled, arms wide and waving at Rob in the Hood. "Don't shoot them. Please."

Rob in the Hood jerked as though his innards were sifting through punched cards, trying to find the right one for the situation. But he didn't shoot. And that was what she'd wanted.

Ila swung around, daring to put her back to the bandit. "And don't shoot him, either!" she called to the coach. "He's not the real robber. The real ones are back there." As she pointed in the direction of Gerald and Sheriff Farr's hideout, the edges of the coach's oiled-leather curtains twitched aside, and two rifles were thrust into view. She watched the tips of both rifles waver, as though the men wielding them didn't know where to aim.

Ila looked at the tin bandit, and he, too, seemed unsure what to do. The tip of his revolver swung up and down, from the driver to her and back again.

"You don't want to do this," she said, hoping to confuse him even more.

And then she heard a sound she'd been hoping for—the clatter of tumbling rocks. But she didn't expect the cry of "Whoa!" that came along with it. Ila turned to see Postmaster Walt sliding down the hill on his backside along with the fall of rock.

"Hey!" came another shout, and Gerald and Sheriff Farr strode out from their hidey-hole.

No!

Ila thought they would have stayed back there as the rocks rained down on them. But not a rock had touched them. They didn't even look dusty.

Sheriff Farr drew his revolver. "Drop your weapon," he said to Rob in the Hood. "Can't you see you're surrounded?"

The bandit's revolver clunked to the ground, and the sheriff stooped to pick it up. Then he looked at the coach. "Hey, fellas," he called to the guards. "It's uh, it's all right." He leaned toward Gerald who had grabbed his arm and was muttering something in his ear. As he listened, Sheriff Farr sprouted a grin. "We, uh, we heard that this gal," the sheriff jabbed a finger toward Ila, "was in league with this outlaw and we followed her here. Looks like she sweet-talked the postmaster into it, too. You got ropes in there for tying them up?"

"No!" Ila wailed. "They're the ones, not me."

"She works at the bank," Gerald said. "She told the outlaw you'd be passing through, right about now. She's demanding twenty percent of the take." Gerald pulled a note from his pocket and dangled it in evidence. He sneered at Ila. "Isn't that right?"

"I… no." Ila looked from Gerald to the guard who was approaching her, a big burly man with his hat pulled low over his eyes. She glanced at the coil of rope he carried. "Well, I did write that, but only….

"There," Sheriff Farr said. "You've heard it from her own mouth. Go ahead and tie her up. The outlaw, too. We'll shift this stuff off the road for you."

Ila felt her hands pulled behind her and ropes tighten around her wrists, but she couldn't fathom what Gerald and Sheriff Farr were up to as they started moving the canvas bundles and propping them upright against the back of the supply wagon. They wouldn't just let the coach go, their tin bandit captured. As soon as that hood came off, people would know something strange was going on. They might wonder, like she had, if someone was behind his actions. They would look for someone to blame.

And they would blame her. Gerald had just seen to that.

A high-pitched roar echoed off the rock of the outcropping. Ila turned to see the canvas-wrapped bundles burst open. The wraps were flung aside to reveal six tin men, not tents. These bandits had no hoods. Their faces shone bone-white in the sun, and their red mouths were painted into a snarl.

Gerald had built himself an army.

The bandits launched themselves into a full teeter, heading toward Ila, her guard, and the coach. Ila heard a yelp behind her that must have come from the other guard and the driver.

"What in the...." the guard at her hands hollered. "Ahh!" He toppled as two tin bandits bowled him to the ground.

Ila's feet wanted to run, but she didn't know where. Gerald and the sheriff had moved to crouch behind some rocks, pretending they'd had nothing to do with the onslaught of tin bandits. And Walt—where was Walt? He might be bleeding to death under the fall of rocks, and it was all her fault.

Ila searched the scene—there had to be one good thing she could do. The guards were fighting tin bandits, but her hands were tied. Rob in the Hood was nearby, still hooded, his hands tied, too, but maybe, together, they could get free.

Even as she stumbled toward him, she wondered if this was another bad plan. He was a bandit, after all.

But only because they'd made him to be.

She came up behind him. "It's me. Ila," she whispered into the hood. "I'm going to untie you. Can you please untie me?"

He didn't answer, but she turned anyway, and her fingers grasped the rope that bound his hands. She'd trusted him earlier, and he hadn't shot her. Hadn't shot the guards, either. He'd been awfully quiet since then, which made her wonder what was going on in those inner works of his.

For once Ila was grateful for the hours she'd spent unraveling knots in the knitting that was supposedly the ladylike thing to do. It wasn't long before the ropes around the bandit's hands fell to the ground. And then she felt his fingers set to work on her bonds. The ropes loosened, dropped, and Ila spun and wrapped the bandit in her arms. "Thank you."

"You... saved me," he said, and she thought she heard wonder in his halting voice.

"You saved me, too." She showed him her freed wrists. "It feels nice, doesn't it?" She tapped his chest. "In here."

The bandit cocked his head, as though listening to that place inside him.

"You don't have to be what they want you to be," she said. "You don't have to be Rob in the Hood. You can choose another name. Another way of life. Anything you'd like."

"I... I don't know," he said.

Ila realized there was no way he could. He only knew two other men. He only knew this life. "I once read about someone like you," she said. "His name was Pittonaccio, from Mr. Verne's story, *Master Zacharius.* Would you like that name? We could call you Pete, for short."

He was still for a moment. "Pete," he said at last. "I... like it."

He looked around at the fight still raging and suddenly yanked off his hood. "Company," he cried. "Halt!" And just like that, the tin bandits stopped. "At ease!" he called, and they reached down to help up the battered guards and driver, as though they'd only been engaged in a training exercise.

"There's them, too." Ila jerked a nod toward Gerald and Sheriff Farr. They'd raised from their crouch and looked ready to run.

"Company!" Pete called, and he pointed at the two men. "Capture!"

Another roar echoed off the outcropping as they sprinted toward their maker. Ila watched long enough to see the guard who'd tied her up sprint after the tin army.

"Pete," she said. "Come with me. Please."

They hurried to the southern hollow and found Walt, covered by rocks. This time, Ila felt no horrified glee that her plan had worked, only horror.

Pete bent and began shifting the rocks. Ila helped, though she hardly breathed. After a few minutes, Walt sat up, somehow wearing a lopsided grin on his scraped-up face.

"Did you get them?" he said.

"*We* got them." She pulled him to his feet, and somehow found her arms around him, something that would have made her blush days before. It was surprisingly comfortable.

After a moment, she pulled back, hooked one elbow through the crook of Walt's arm and the other through Pete's.

"Well," she said, looking at the crooked smile and the red-painted one, too. "That was extraordinary." And, now that the villains were caught and the townspeople were saved from starving, she felt free to add something more: "Would you two be interested in a voyage?"

Old Soldiers

Gustavo Bondoni

Goûmi watched Sergeant Major Peter Watters trudge through the October mud, a constant in India's rainy season, and knew, from the shuffling, almost unmilitary way the man walked, that they were nearing the end of a long relationship. The once-black whiskers, still bushy and intimidating, were white now, and the once-imposing chest had receded to merely human proportions. But the man still walked straight as the proverbial ramrod, ignoring the drizzle.

The Indian man allowed himself a sad smile, knowing that, while Watters would never retreat from a hard task, or even refuse to advance, the man could slow his walk to a snail's pace. He even paused to play half-heartedly with the village children, in whom he inspired a mixture of awe and mirth that was difficult to explain.

His evident reluctance to advance hid the same sadness that Goûmi himself felt stirring within. Since Watters would never allow himself to show open emotion, Goûmi had learned to read his companion. Over the decades that they'd spent together, the old Sergeant and the loyal retainer and friend, had come to read each other's signs. The slow gait was an obvious indicator.

But eventually, he arrived where Goûmi waited. "Hello, sir," Goûmi said.

"I already told you not to call me sir," Watters replied. "Sir is what you call an officer. I am not an officer, and you, therefore, are impertinent."

"You are the master of my household," the aged servant replied. "That means I must address you in the correct way. Sir."

Watters grinned at him.

Goûmi knew that Watters might pretend to find him impertinent, but he was also aware that his service had always been impeccable and he had, despite the differences in status and nationality, become the closest thing the old soldier had to a brother. Neither would admit that, but the life they'd lived, so far from the world's power centers had cemented the bond.

They'd worked side by side to save the old colonial mansion from falling into tropical ruin, and each had a large room at a different corner of the house. But the division of labor was still defined by how it had started, when Goûmi was a minor servant, only tolerated because his father had been a front-line servant in the traditional style.

"You old pirate. The day you acknowledge a master is the day I'll stop getting up at dawn."

"But of course I need a master. I have not the wisdom to make the larger decisions in life, sir."

"You mean that you want someone else to take the blame when something goes wrong. That's also what officers are for, you rogue."

"Ah, sadly, we have no officers here. But it is good to have a master, sir." He paused. "Were you able to procure the item you were seeking?" He already knew the answer, but he also knew his old friend would want to break the bad news himself.

Watters pulled a package out from under his arm with a dramatic flourish. "Here it is!"

Goûmi swallowed back the emotion. His fears were confirmed: the final piece of the mechanical puzzle had been located, and Watters would soon be leaving him.

They set the oilcloth package on a table and unwrapped it with near-religious reverence. Inside was a large valve, nearly as long as Watters' forearm. It was a steel or iron casting, with the words Disnault Frères, Paris molded into it. Watters held up a letter, dampened and with ink-runs. "They say it's the last one anywhere in France, and that we were lucky that the new owners of the factory didn't throw away the old stock. They never knew what this was meant for, and were delighted to receive the photograph we sent them. They told us they would not accept payment for the valve. We may consider it a gift, as long as we use it to restore the Elephant."

"Let's go see if it fits."

Watters sensed the power of the beast. Even in its dormant state, he could feel its desire to be free of the shed that had served as its prison for so long.

Goûmi stood beside him, holding his thin, dark frame nearly reverently in the mechanical monster's presence. Sweat glistened on his bald pate, framed by white hair.

The plaque on the front of the machine, just beneath the trunk, proclaimed its name: Behemoth. It was all of that and more, a symbol of the days when the Empire was still synonymous with monumental undertakings.

A cool-minded person – an engineer, perhaps – would just have seen a traction engine, and one with a ridiculous design, at that. But within the lines, one could see both the ingenuity and the humor which had once characterized the Empire in India.

The steam engine was there, of course, but it had been clothed in a much more suitable skin than that of a typical traction engine. For this one had its power plant buried within a sheet metal elephant. The roads in India forty years before had been less than ideal—how Watters remembered marching in the mud during the monsoon—so the designers had sensibly decreed that their tractor would not employ virtually useless wheels, but would walk along on broad feet.

Just like a true elephant.

But within this elephant beat a modern heart, one that would serve it as well in the mud of Flanders as in that of India. A steam engine nestled in its belly, created to power an Anglo-French expedition and left to rust in the Indian humidity after the death of its last owner. With the rise of nationalism in Europe, Watters had predicted it would need to serve the Empire once again, and after building a waterproof barn around it, had spent ten years painstakingly wiping it clean, commissioning new parts, and finally locating the last piece still needed: the safety valve for the pressure control system.

Just in time, too. An incident in Sarajevo of all places had ignited the tinderbox of Europe. Though not a religious man, Watters gave a silent prayer to both the Christian God of his parents and the Hindu gods of his adopted home, and inserted the final part.

The valve slid into place. They spent about two hours adjusting the springs and covers for the pressure release system, finally finishing the dirty, fiddly task at the stroke of midnight.

"Do you want to try to turn it on?" Goûmi asked.

"If I were still a young man, I would do it in an instant. But I'm seventy-three, Goûmi, and I need to sleep. Do you think your father's spirit would mind terribly if we left it 'til morning?"

Goûmi's father, also known as Goûmi, had been bequeathed the mechanical beast and the two wagons it had been designed to pull from the Englishman who'd headed the original expedition as a reward for decades of loyal service. One of the wagons had long been sold off while the second, a fully-mechanical travel trailer, was in the barn behind the elephant. Goûmi had gifted the remaining trailer and the elephant to Watters as soon as he'd heard about the plan to restore them.

"I don't think so. He always seemed more interested in showing off the inside of the trailer than actually making the traction engine run again. I think he felt that a working steam engine was a privilege only Europeans should have."

"You never seem to think those things."

Goûmi smiled at him. "India has come a long way since my father's time, sir."

Watters thought about the war-torn European continent and sighed. Perhaps Europe has come backwards a certain amount, as well. But he didn't say anything.

— JV —

The following morning, it took some time to get the boiler going. Goûmi assisted Watters when he could, and watched when he couldn't as Watters worked slowly, and they sat under cover a safe distance away as pressure built up. Watters explained to him that boilers frequently failed catastrophically.

But it didn't explode. When the pressure was sufficient, the elephant moved, one leg lifting as another pushed the whole ensemble forward. The beast walked with a close, if slightly jerky, reproduction of the gait of the noble animal it was based on. Nothing seized or broke in half as Watters moved the levers up in the howdah, and the vehicle, lovingly restored, found its stride as it walked into a light drizzle, undisturbed by the soft earth.

Goûmi watched the old man drive it into the unkempt garden. Tears rolled down his cheeks, but he didn't even bother to wipe them away. Despite what he'd said the night before, he wished that his father could have been there to see this. As a child, he'd been told innumerable stories of the Behemoth in motion. None lived up to the reality, and only now, twenty years too late, did he understand what his father had been going on about with his interminable tales. Goûmi wished he could tell him that yes, it was as marvelous as he'd always claimed.

The elephant stopped with a final clank and Watters descended stiffly.

"Will you change your mind and come with me?"

Goûmi shook his head. "I'm much too old to leave India, sir."

"Hah!" the sergeant barked. "Just like you to claim that you are too old. Why, I'd be surprised if you're a day older than fifty-five. Look at me."

"You know exactly how old I am," Goûmi responded with a sad smile. "And you know my answer isn't going to change. You aren't planning on leaving your home, you are returning to your home."

"I'm doing no such thing," Watters growled. "This is my home, and once I've done my duty, then I shall return here to live out my remaining days. I only wish you'd come with me. We could sail straight back once we kick the Kaiser back to Berlin."

"No, my friend. You go on. I'll keep the manor in running order for your return."

"Then I'm off."

"Right away?"

Watters gave him a hard look. "A soldier in His Majesty's service is always ready to travel at a moment's notice. I loaded my valise into the travel trailer before you woke this morning."

"I wish you'd called me to help with that. It is my station, after all."

"I managed all right. It was just some clothes and my old rifle. I don't have much else that I want to take with me."

Goûmi suspected that leaving his single friend and confidant behind after all these years was what would hurt him most. Watters would never be able to put it into words, and he would rather die than show the tears that his dear friend would have had no trouble shedding. They both knew the truth, though.

What Goûmi felt was equally weighty. Though he'd buried his wife, and his children had moved to neighboring villages, this mansion he and Watters had resided in all those years was his home. It was much different to be a day's walk from his eldest son than to be a world away in a cold and muddy battlefield. The former, Goûmi could live with, the latter was not something he could even contemplate.

"Do you still think it's wise to take the overland route?" Goûmi asked. "Is it even possible to do?"

"Up through Persia into Russia? Of course. It's child's play. And the Russians will help me get to France. They're happy for any help in this war."

"It is not child's play," Goûmi retorted. "This is a long journey. Even if the local rulers are friendly, there is no guarantee that they are even in control of their territory. Bandits, usurpers, and minor rulers might not be so well-disposed. A ship out of Bombay. . . ."

"Is more than I can afford. Besides, I've always wanted to see Russia. I was too young for Crimea."

"Hard to believe that you were ever too young for anything."

They stood in silence for a moment, each knowing that separation was near, neither knowing what to say.

Finally, Peter Watters held out his hand, solemnly.

"It's not proper for a servant to shake his master's hand, sir," Goûmi said.

"I see no servants here. Only the best friend a man could ever have asked for."

Goûmi took the proffered hand and wiped away the tears that flowed. Watters made no comment and kept Goûmi from embarrassment by turning away and climbing the ladder to the controls. As the elephant lumbered off, dragging the travel trailer behind it, Goûmi saluted and reflected that his father would have been delighted to hear its roar again and see the elephant plod its way through the gardens and onto the road. He was happy to have gifted the contraption back to an English soldier. That was where it belonged.

Children immediately swarmed the beast, seeming to appear out of the undergrowth, just like in his father's stories, and they laughed as they followed it, creating an impromptu procession. The legend of how the old British Sergeant Major had ridden into the distance on a grinding, smoke-belching monster would be born that day. It was the way legends should begin.

But Goûmi didn't follow. He waited until the last child disappeared around a bend and then let his tears flow more openly, while standing at attention rendering the old British salute.

"Good luck, sir."

— JV —

At first the letters reached Goûmi frequently, every two days. They told of irritation with the state of Indian roads and of impatience to get to lands the Sergeant didn't know.

Then, as the Sergeant crossed into Persia, they came less often, and related how some brigands followed him for miles, but learned to respect the power of a long-range British rifle. They told of unsettled lands and suspicion. More than once, it appeared, Watters had needed to walk a diplomatic line to be allowed passage.

He received only two letters from Russia, four weeks apart. The first, a long note, was about how the Azerbaijani troops at the border had arrested him in the belief that he was an Ottoman spy until a Czarist delegate inspecting the border had happened along and freed him just hours before he was scheduled to be shot. The other, much shorter, confirmed that a diplomat he'd known in the army had secured passage north through the Baltic to France.

The final letter arrived in August of 1915. It told Goûmi that Watters arrived in France safely and that he was speaking to some British engineers about armoring the trailer for action along the front. The elephant's armor had been deemed adequate. "It seems," the Sergeant wrote, "that a major offensive is in the works for September. Since it would take too long to train another soldier to operate the elephant, they've allowed me to stay around for now. I think they aren't quite sure what else to do with me."

After that, there was nothing.

Goûmi read all the news that arrived in India, and even used some friends in the army to peruse a copy of the official lists of all British dead and missing after the war was over. Watters name was not among them.

And, remarkably, nowhere was there any mention of a mechanical elephant nor an old sergeant-major from India.

It seemed impossible that in this day of news that traveled the world on wires, no one would know the fate of his friend. In desperation, after asking all the local officers—some of whom were familiar with the particulars of Watters' journey—he wrote to the War Minister, with a detailed explanation of the situation. He even included one of the precious photographs of the elephant, taken before restoration.

He received a curt answer saying that there was no record of such a person, or the machine described. The man who answered then wrote a postscript wondering whether, perhaps, Goûmi read a little too much adventure fiction.

Goûmi laughed and folded the letter. He placed it carefully with all the other correspondence he'd received since Watters set out.

On the eve of another world war, a generation later, an old man nearing his eighty-fifth year lay on white sheets. He propped himself up and looked around, eyes alert, even though his body had little of the energy he once called his own.

"Grandfather Goûmi, Grandfather Goûmi," Himmat said. "Are you awake?"

"I am now," Goûmi replied.

"There's a man. A man to see you."

"From the government?"

"I don't think so. He says he's a friend."

"My friends are all dead," Goûmi replied. "Long ago."

"Father told him he has to wait until you come down. So I came to see if you were ready."

"You mean you came to wake me up."

"No, no," Himmat said, holding up his hands. "Just to see."

"All right. You can tell him I'll be down in a moment."

The rascal disappeared and Goûmi shook his head in wonder. Was he really old enough to have great grandchildren? Truly, his had been a blessed life.

The stairs, on the other hand, were the bane of his existence. He stubbornly refused to move to a room downstairs. For one thing, going up and down the stairs gave him some exercise. But mostly, he imagined what Watters would have said: "A man must take care of his body if that body is going to take care of the Empire." Even two decades after he'd disappeared, the old Sergeant Major helped define Goûmi's view of the world.

The visitor was a man in his forties, blond hair turning grey, wearing the uniform of an English soldier—not the glorious red, but a greenish light tan. Though he'd never seen the man before, Goûmi held out his hand.

"I am Goûmi," he said.

The British man's expression conveyed something Goûmi seldom saw in the eyes of the English, and never when faced with an Indian: a reverent look approaching awe.

"My name is Reginald Cooper, and I'm honored to shake your hand, sir," The man said. "I owe you my life."

"I am not an officer."

The awe was replaced by confusion.

Goûmi smiled. "I'm sorry if I'm cryptic. What I meant to say was that, in this house, the word sir is reserved for officers."

"Ah. I understand."

"Please, sit. Tell me your story."

The man sat and Goûmi's granddaughter, the woman who'd taken over the house and kept it going when the old man's strength began to wane, brought them gin and tonic. Neither she nor her husband ever touched alcohol, but while Goûmi lived, the house would contain the essentials of British hospitality.

"There's not much to tell, really. I was a young conscript, just turned eighteen, on a battlefield near Ypres in the Kaiser war. I'd been on the lines less than a week when we were ordered to charge along a wide front to try to take a weakly-defended German trench. It wasn't a bad assault, as those went. It was well-planned. Most of the line actually managed to get across and we took a hundred yards that day."

He shook his head. "But not my unit. We got pinned between what must have been the only two German machine gun nests that our big guns missed. Everyone else was dead before I knew what happened, so I just sat in a shell crater and cried. Not a scratch on me but I didn't even have the sense to lie flat and play dead. Just sat there waiting for someone to put me out of my misery, sobbing like a little girl lost in the woods.

"And then I heard a rumble like I imagine a dragon would sound. I thought the Germans were coming for me. A beast ten feet tall stopped in front of me. That's when the German machine guns truly opened up. You never heard such a racket. I couldn't move.

"But a man shouted from a metal basket at the top of the beast and I realized the thing was some kind of armored walker shaped like an elephant dragging an armored carriage. The elephant shielded me from the German guns, and another man opened the door of the carriage and shouted to me that I should jump inside, but I was too frightened to move.

"The next thing I knew, a Sergeant Major in beefeater red—the man who'd been up in the basket, in fact—was standing next to me explaining how I was a disgrace to the uniform, and that if I was afraid of a little German lead it was only because I didn't know what he would do to me if I didn't get a move on.

"I got, and that was how I met Watters."

Goûmi shook his head in wonder. "I heard nothing of him. London denies he ever existed."

"I'm surprised to hear that, because many a soldier owes his life to that man. And he insisted that the Behemoth only existed because of you. He made each of us memorize your address and swear that, if we were ever posted in India, we would find you and thank you personally. I suppose I'm not the first."

"You are the first."

"Oh." The man seemed shocked. "Then you don't know."

"Know what?"

"Watters was killed in Verdun. Shot while controlling his machine from its howdah by a German sniper as he rescued ten men from the Jawan Regiment stranded in 'no man's land.' I'm sorry."

"I imagined something along the lines. It was how he would have wanted it to end. And it's fitting that he should have died rescuing Indian troops. Were you there?"

"No. I was in Belgium. But Watters' Irregulars, our loose club of men who loved him, had the best grapevine in the entire war. We knew everything he did, gathered each scrap of information. I have a book with clippings and letters. Some of us wanted to go to the press with our material, make Watters a national hero. But he wouldn't have wanted that. He never craved glory. Unfortunately only a few of us survived the war, which is why I kept the scrapbook."

"It is wonderful that such a book exists."

"It's yours. I'll send it by the next post when I return to Bombay."

Goûmi wanted nothing more than to hold such a book in his hands. He was tempted to accept the offer, to pass what little remained of his years remembering an old friend. Nevertheless, he shook his head. "No. Keep it. It would be wasted on me. My life has run its course, and I have no more wars left to fight. Better that men who have time ahead of them can remember him. But tell me, what happened to the Elephant?"

"The French kept it after the war. I think they stored it in the Paris Zoo, for want of a better place. I haven't heard of it since I returned to England."

"And you?"

He smiled. "I never left the army even after they tried to demobilize all of us. And now it looks like all those years of free meals and staying in top physical form at the government's expense are going to be put to good use by His Majesty. There's another war coming."

"I have heard as much. And what will your role be?"

The man unconsciously touched the collar of his uniform. "The most glorious role of all: I'm a Sergeant Major."

Goûmi smiled. "You would have made him very happy."

Want of Air

Janice Rider

KAREN RAISED HER EYES from a presentation she was putting together in her home office and peered down into the backyard. Outside, her son, Jordan, shoveled snow into a long, cigar-shaped mound. The ten-year-old, bundled so that only his eyes were exposed to the biting wind, worked hard. His creation stretched almost the entire width of the yard and, at one end of it, a protuberance much like the horn of a unicorn jutted out. Curious, Karen thought. Jordan took time to tamp the snow firmly into place. Smiling, his mother recalled Jordan's excitement when he'd been allowed to go outside in spite of the frigid weather. Edward would have delighted in his son's sprawling imagination, his fascination with the natural world. Karen sighed, the whispers of a former life washing over her.

A short while later, Karen heard the back door open and then shut with a bang. She winced. So much for new hinges! Boots dropped to the kitchen floor, feet stomped up the stairs to the second story of their house, and Jordan bounced into the office. Cheeks lit up from the cold and dark eyes bright, he stopped. Clumps of snow fell from his powder blue snowsuit onto the carpet. Having noted their descent, Jordan stooped, catching them up in his mittened hands prior to popping them into his mouth, somehow managing to avoid consuming part of his aquamarine scarf in the process. "Yum!" he exclaimed. "Mom, did you see what I built?"

As Karen looked into her son's face, she felt a welling of vulnerability. Dear God, how she loved this child! Nodding, she responded, "I've been watching you. You're a human bulldozer! That's one amazing heap of snow!"

"Know what it's supposed to be?" her son asked.

Frowning, Karen paused before replying, "I can't say I know for sure, but I think it might be a whale, perhaps?" In a sudden flash of inspiration, based on Jordan's fondness for ocean creatures, Karen guessed again, "A narwhal! I think it's a narwhal!"

Laughing happily, Jordan exclaimed, "You think like Captain Farragut, but you're on the right track!"

"Captain Farragut? Who's he?"

"Wouldn't you like to know?" her son teased.

"Okay, Smarty-pants. Give me a clue."

Jordan exclaimed, "It's incredibly destructive! Positively lethal!" With those hyperbolic words discharged, he vanished back downstairs.

"Be careful!" she shouted after him and soon saw him once again playing amongst the snow dunes.

Leaving her workspace, Karen headed for the kitchen. A stew had been simmering in the slow cooker all day, and it smelled amazing. She breathed in deeply. Oh, yes! The recipe was one she had pulled from an old cookbook her parents had given her when she first moved out on her own. All the recipes in the book were easy to put together, a blessing for single moms. On bitter days, when she felt the enormity of the task of lone parenting, a hearty stew made her feel connected to her parents and the husband she had lost. Edward had been most appreciative of her stews, and he himself had been a fabulous cook.

When Karen went to the back door to call Jordan in for supper, she stepped into a pond of icy water. Her feet protested as her socks absorbed the insult. She bellowed to Jordan, who whooped and charged into the house, a yeti high on glacial chill. As the door banged closed yet again, Karen scowled and pointed. She noted that the yeti took in her sodden socks, stifled a laugh, and affected concern. "I'll clean it up, Mom."

"You'd better," she grumbled.

Soon, Jordan's winter attire hung from four of their kitchen chairs, and the towel he'd used to mop up the floor was spread over two of the chair seats. While they ate, Karen listened while Jordan described his meal. "Mom," he said, pointing at vegetables in the stew, "this seaweed is delicious!" Scooping up some lentils on a spoon, he continued, "These fish should have been cooked more though. They keep trying to swim away!" Karen laughed along with her son. Outside, snow had begun to fall again, large alabaster flakes spiraling down from a darkening sky. Karen could not recall a time when there had been this much snow. The world was being buried, buried alive. She felt gratified to be inside amidst warmth and light while the world was reconfigured, any deformities and disfigurations vanishing. When they had eaten, Jordan cleaned up while Karen went back to work. Normally, the two of them tidied the kitchen together, but Karen was pressed for time to finish off her PowerPoint lecture for *Ocean Environs*. Her presentation could make the difference between the choice to protect an offshore marine area or to leave it without the protection necessary to support the biodiversity there.

Checking on her son later, she found him in his bedroom, on his bed, chin propped in his hands, deep in a book. The walls of Jordan's room peeked shyly out from behind numerous posters that had accumulated over time. Some depicted illustrations or photographs of ocean creatures—octopuses, sponges, corals, sea stars, and whales. Others depicted ships—frigates, galleys, longboats, schooners, and galleons. The most recent addition to his walls was a submarine. Shelves above Jordan's desk held stuffed toys—a squid, a shark, a dolphin, a walrus, and a harbor seal—and model ships. Books about ocean creatures were there, too, including one about stingrays, written by his father, who had been an oceanographer. Whenever Karen spotted that book, she felt a sadness so profound it was like being engulfed by all the tears in the sea. She swallowed and inhaled, pulling air into her chest in order to avoid feeling overwhelmed.

Edward had died of lung cancer, which Karen considered ironic as he had never touched a cigarette in his life. Of course the reason for his cancer was probably a result of exposure to second-hand smoke in his family home while growing up. A vital, active man with a lively mane of hair, Edward had become emaciated, reminding Karen of the driftwood that washes up with the tide—pale and attenuated. Together, the family visited the sea for as long as it was possible for Edward to do so. He reveled in Jordan's energy and all the treasures he found to show his dad—limpets, shells, snails, crabs, and clams. Her husband would sit on the beach taking in great gulps of wind-blown air redolent with salt and seaweed. "I'll miss breathing when I'm gone," he'd once commented as Jordan danced naked on the beach. "Breathing and hearing the breathing of those I love." Karen had hugged Edward then, nuzzling up under his chin, as grief flooded her eyes and ran down her cheeks. He had rocked her back and forth in his arms until Jordan had come running in for a "group hug."

Karen pulled her attention back to her young son, so engrossed in his book he didn't look up. "Good book?"

"Hi, Mom," Jordan responded, without turning to face her, "the crew are in trouble."

"The crew?"

"The crew of the *Nautilus*!"

"*Twenty Thousand Leagues Under the Seas?*"

"You've read it?" She heard the surprise in her son's voice, but he still didn't turn around.

"I have." Then it dawned on her. "Aha! We have a submarine, the *Nautilus*, not a narwhal in our backyard."

The boy gave her a thumbs up as he finally turned in her direction. "The *Nautilus* has a ramming prow to puncture ships and send them to the bottom of the sea! Captain Farragut thought it was a dangerous narwhal!"

Sitting down on the edge of Jordan's bed, Karen placed a hand on the calf of one of his legs. "That book is a great adventure!"

"Did Dad ever read it?"

"Oh, yes, he read it for the first time when he was about your age, and it was always a favorite of his. He introduced me to it. In fact, it was the first gift he ever gave me. Not flowers, just *Twenty Thousand Leagues Under the Seas*. An unusual gift."

Jordan wove his brow into ridges and became pensive. "Think I'd like to be the captain of a submarine, Mom. Imagine all the things I'd see! Maybe I'd come across the world's largest squid!"

Fear lapped at her heart as Karen envisioned a squid beckoning to her son with a lengthy tentacle. Although part of her wanted to cry out and forbid him to leave her for waves and water, she bit her tongue and simply said, "Hate to break the news, but it's bedtime!"

"Ah, Mom, not yet!" Annoyance and a hint of something else resonated in her son's tone of voice.

Holding out a hand, Karen waited for Jordan to hand over the book. He did not relinquish it. "You're going to keep it!" Jordan accused her.

"Just until tomorrow, Jordan," she sighed. "We've been through this before. If I leave the book in your room, you're not going to sleep, you're going to read."

"I'll pay you five dollars if you let me keep it. Captain Farragut offered money for the first one to see the monster. So, what do you say?"

Karen shook her head. "No. You've got school tomorrow. I'll be back in a bit to kiss you goodnight." Jordan scowled, smacking the book down on the bed and turning away from her. He had always resisted going to bed, and his resistance was growing.

After taking the book, Karen put it on her night table beside a mystery she was reading, marveling at the fact that, one hundred and fifty years after its publication, Verne's classic still had the power to weave a spell over readers. The cover of the book depicted an enormous scarlet squid with its arms wrapped tightly around a submarine. Small figures were frozen in horror at porthole windows.

Looking in on Jordan a short time later, Karen found him standing on his bed looking out his window at the white vista beneath him. He wore warm flannel pajamas with sailors on them. "Time to turn out the lights!"

"Couldn't you give my book back - just for a few minutes?"

"Sorry."

"I'm worried about the crew."

"You'll find out what happens to them tomorrow. Come on, I want you under the covers, not on top of them."

Jordan hesitated, then crawled under his blankets, his face strained. Karen felt herself soften. "Everything alright?" She knew he hated to admit to any childish fears.

"I'm feeling kind of funny."

"Funny?"

"Dizzy. And I have a pain in my head. Am I purple?"

"Purple?" Karen looked at him, pursing her lips thoughtfully. "Not any more purple than usual," she kidded.

"Are my lips blue?"

"Why would they be blue?"

"I'm not breathing right."

Karen felt a tidal swell of concern in her belly. She was asthmatic and sometimes suffered from episodes of wheezing and shortness of breath. Her beloved husband's struggle to breathe as fluid filled the space in the chest cavity around his lungs came to mind. At the time, she recalled thinking that he was going to drown on land. Watching her son, Karen noted that his breathing was fast and somewhat shallow. Nonetheless, the color in his face was good. "Honey, does your chest feel tight?" she inquired.

Jordan nodded. "Mmmhmm. I feel suffocated. Maybe you should open my window."

"Open your window? It's freezing out there! It's still snowing, and the wind's coming up!"

"What if there's not enough oxygen in the house?"

"Our house is special. Whenever the furnace runs, which it does a lot on nippy winter nights, fresh air is pulled into our home."

Her son appeared unconvinced.

"Listen, if you start to feel worse, let me know."

Leaning forward, Karen laid a gentle hand on Jordan's cheek and kissed him on the forehead. He responded by wrapping his arms around her neck in a fierce embrace and returning the salute on one of her cheeks. His kiss was mildly wet. She felt a thrill of tenderness run through her. Jordan snuggled into his blankets as Karen drew his quilt up over his shoulders.

"Goodnight, Jordan. Sleep well."

"I'll try," he replied, his eyes sober. Leaving Jordan's room, Karen decided to treat herself to an early night. "Why not?" she thought. Winter evenings were long. Without the companionship of books, they would also have been unbearably lonely.

As she climbed into bed, clad in winter pajamas, *Twenty Thousand Leagues Under the Seas* caught her eye as it lay on her night table. Her plan had been to continue with her latest murder mystery; now, however, Jules Verne's classic was speaking with a persuasive vehemence while the mystery novel lay mute beside it. The cool blue of the water on the cover gave her the shivers. She picked the classic up, sliding under the warmth of her blankets and down quilt as she did so. It was a most inhospitable night. Karen recalled other similar nights wrapped in Edward's long arms, his breath in the waves of her hair, his presence solid and real and stabilizing. Her husband had had a remarkable capacity for immersing himself in the mystery of other living things. "Diving deep" he had called it. His research introduced her to the immense diversity of life in the ocean. She had been startled, at first, by the intensity of his interest in creatures like sharks and rays; but, later, she embraced his passion herself. He would have been delighted to see his son reading Jules Verne's novel.

She planted her pillow behind her back, tucked her quilt up under her arms, and, curious, opened the book to the place where Jordan's bookmark lay. The first words her eyes came across were, "Half stretched upon a divan in the library, I was suffocating. My face was purple, my lips blue, my faculties suspended." Karen's eyes widened, and she laughed. This novel had inspired Jordan's vivid imagination. No wonder he was concerned about a lack of oxygen in the house. She went back to the beginning of the chapter. *Want of Air* was the title. She laughed again. The chapter's first words read, "Thus, around the *Nautilus*, above and below, was an impenetrable wall of ice." Karen continued reading, as enthralled as Jordan had been. It turned out that the crew of the *Nautilus* had only enough oxygen to last forty-eight hours. Captain Nemo and his men were in a real bind. It had been ages since Karen had read this book. How fantastic it was to reconnect with old friends! Not that she'd ever liked Nemo very much.

The longer she read, the more Karen felt as if she'd been entombed in ice. Strange. Reading in bed tended to make Karen feel cozy and pleasantly drowsy. Not now. She listened for the furnace. It was running. No problem there. In fact, it seemed to run non-stop. Moaning, she slid out from under the covers. As her bare feet contacted the rug, they encountered a frigid draft. Goosebumps erupted on her skin. Karen made her way down the hall to her son's bedroom. She felt cruel winter fingers reach for her toes from beneath his door. Upon entering, she plunged into a frosty lair. Karen gasped as the soles of her feet made contact with the brisk, polar bite of snow! Jordan's window was wide open, and swirling snowflakes settled on bedding, desk, shelves, and carpet. The snow seemed eager in its desire to devour and consume. A huge mound of woolen blankets, which had been stored on the shelving in Jordan's closet, monopolized Jordan's bed. Beneath the mound was a cave-like opening near her son's pillow. Large eyes and a small nose were at the opening.

"Hi, Mom," Jordan said tremulously.

"You are going to catch your death of cold, and I'm liable to catch my death, too! I'm going to close your window!" she rampaged.

"I need the oxygen," her son insisted. "Don't close it! Please!"

Karen recalled the crew of the *Nautilus* and felt a frisson of guilt. "Oh, I see. Well, there's extra oxygen in my room because… it's bigger than yours. You can snuggle in with me for a bit." She slammed Jordan's window shut against Winter's bleak breath and took her son's hand. The two hurried back to her bedroom.

Once there, Karen pointed to the book laying on her pillow. "I began reading it," she admitted. "Much better than my murder mystery. I think we should finish the chapter *Want of Air* together. What do you think?"

"Now?" Jordan asked.

"Yes. Right away."

Jordan grinned and bounced in on the opposite side of the bed. Nestling close, they took turns reading to one another until the *Nautilus* broke through the sea ice, and a panel in the submarine was opened to allow life-saving air to rush in amongst the crew.

"How do you feel, now?" Karen asked.

"I'm not suffocating anymore," Jordan assured her.

"Time for us to sleep, then. You can stay here tonight."

A minute later, Jordan was sound asleep. Gazing at him, Karen considered life's fragility, its ebb and flow. It was at one and the same time tenuous and tenacious. A quote from *Leagues* came to mind, one Edward had been fond of, "I ask no more than to live a hundred years longer, that I may have more time to dwell the longer on your memory." Yes, she still had the memory of Edward, and sometimes that memory was so powerful, she could not only see him, but smell him, taste him, and even feel him. Karen closed her eyes and visited Edward, telling him all about their son. As she set the book down, Karen's eyes flitted over a passage in the next chapter—"All our past suffering was forgotten. The memory of our icy imprisonment was fast fading from our memories. We only thought of the future."

Nellie and Jules Go Boating

David A. Natale

I

Nellie yawned and pulled her shawl close against the cold train compartment. The stuffy carriage smelled of mildew, strong tobacco, and stale cheese. Through a swirl in the fogged window a French winter countryside blurred past.

Next to her on the bench Tracey Greaves, the London Correspondent for the *New York World*, snored like a bulldog. His derby hat was tilted over his eyes. Nellie adjusted her feet on the one foot warmer in the center of the carriage. She stepped on someone's toes then smiled meekly across to the Frenchman who glared at her through his pipe smoke.

When Nellie had alighted at Southampton, Greaves was there with a message.

"Monsieur and Madame Jules Verne have sent a special letter asking for you to see them."

"How I should like to see them!" she answered. "But can I do it without missing my connections?"

"If you're willing to go without sleep and rest for two nights," he said, "I think it could be done."

"Then I'll do it," she said.

"Follow me," Greaves said as he winked at Nellie and clutched her elbow.

Nellie pulled her arm away and said, "I have no need for a chaperone, Mr. Greaves."

Greaves flushed and said, "But I have the tickets. The train leaves any minute."

Nellie considered her options. "I said I'd make this journey on my own," she thought. "I don't need this bounder! But an interview with Jules Verne is too good a scoop to miss. Besides, the visit would count as just a side jaunt. And Greaves does know the way."

She took another look at the pouting Englishman. Then she said to him, "Very well, Mr. Greaves. Lead on!"

"Please, call me Tracey," he said as he reached for her small valise.

"Thank you, Mr. Greaves. I can carry my own bag."

And they were on their way to Amiens.

The train switched tracks with a jolt. Greaves' hat tumbled into her lap. He continued to snore as Nellie, careful not to wake him, set it back on his balding head.

"How can he sleep?" Nellie marveled to herself. "I'm going around the world!" Until a couple weeks ago, this assignment had been a mere pipe-dream.

Ideas are fuel for a newspaper writer. And in her first year at the *World*, Nellie's boiler was stoked. She posed as a factory girl to show their plight. She busted a baby-selling ring with her undercover reports. She put the screws to the King of the Albany lobbyists and caught his extortions red-handed.

And then there were the ten days at Blackwell's Island.

"I didn't sleep then either," Nellie remembered.

She had forced herself to stay awake for two days and passed as insane in order to gain access to New York's notorious asylum. Her stay at Blackwell's was a sojourn in a realm of abuse and misery—and her feature exposed the horrors for women inmates.

It also made her career.

Nellie Bly was now one of the most well-known reporters, man or woman, in the country.

But she still needed ideas. And ever since the madhouse they came to her more slowly. Nellie got headaches. Safe at home in her flat, she still had trouble sleeping. She would stay up late and re-read her favorite adventure books. One night it was Jules Verne's, *Around the World in Eighty Days*, published sixteen years earlier.

"I wish I were at the ends of the earth," she sighed as she closed the cover on Phileas Fogg's journey. It was already Monday. Her wall-clock chimed three. In a few hours she must tell the editor her next brilliant lede. The lamp at her bedside flickered. Pillows and blankets became mountains and ocean swells. "I need a vacation," Nellie whimpered. "*I* should take a trip around the world."

Then she bolted upright.

"That's it!" she shouted. "If I could do it as fast as Phileas Fogg, I would go."

Nellie clapped her hands with glee. Then she linked her fingers and made a shadow face on the wallpaper like her mother had taught her. The mouth moved and she said in a low register, "A woman traveling alone, ridiculous!"

"It's not ridiculous at all," she answered in her own voice.

The shadow jabbered, "I'm Phileas Fogg, and you can never go as fast as I."

"That's what you think. I shall beat your time around the world!"

On her way to work Nellie stopped at the White Star shipping office and gathered all the sailing schedules she could lay her hands on. The meeting with her editor wasn't until noon. So, she pored over itineraries all morning at her desk.

"London to Suez. Suez to Columbo," she thought.

Then the 'Fogg' in her head asked, "Why not Bombay?"

"Colombo in Ceylon is faster," Nellie retorted. "Then I can jump to Penang, Singapore, and Hong Kong."

"I crossed India from Bombay to Calcutta," Fogg said. "And then I went directly to Hong Kong."

"Jules Verne put that in his novel so you could rescue the maiden and ride an elephant."

"Maidens need rescuing in all good stories," proclaimed Phileas.

"Your story is fiction; my story is real," said Nellie. "And I won't need rescuing."

"We'll see about that," said Fogg.

A new voice cut in, New York and nasal. "Bly, what have you got?" It was her editor, John Cockerill.

Nellie took a breath and said, "I want to go around the world in less than eighty days. I think I can beat Phileas Fogg's fictional record. May I try it?"

Cockerill smoked his stogy like a locomotive. Sweat shined on his round fleshy face.

"That's a brilliant idea," he said. "Original, sensational, tremendous!"

"Thank you."

"We've thought of it before."

"I see," said Nellie.

"Our intention was to send a man."

"That's not so very original, sir."

"Don't get me wrong, Miss Bly; I'm all for you going. But it's impossible."

"Why?" she said.

Cockerill blinked at her in shock; then addressed her as he would a child, "In the first place, young lady, you're a woman."

Nellie rolled her eyes.

"You would need a protector!" he barked.

Nellie glared at her boss and said, "I survived travel in Mexico, I survived work in sweatshops, and I survived the madhouse at Blackwell's all without protectors. I can handle myself."

"All right," Cockerill said, "even if you could travel alone, you'd need so much baggage you couldn't make rapid changes. A woman traveling around the world can modestly expect to make the trip with eleven steamer trunks."

"I'll have no trunks," Nellie said, "only one bag."

"But what about the formal dinners, the balls?"

"If one is traveling simply for the sake of traveling," Nellie said, "and not for the purpose of impressing one's fellow passengers the problem of baggage is simple."

"Besides, you speak nothing but English," he said with a puff. "There's no use talking about it. No one but a man can do this."

"Very well, Mr. Cockerill" she said, "start the man, and I'll start the same day for some other newspaper, and I'll beat him!"

The editor bit into his cigar with a growl and mopped his brow with a yellowed hankie.

"Hold on," he said and lumbered off towards the publisher's office.

Nellie put her elbows on the desk and rubbed her throbbing temples.

"I wonder if the *Times* is hiring?" she thought.

Then Nellie heard her name called in a hushed Hungarian lilt, "Miss Bly, are you alright?"

Nellie looked up. Stooped over her like a dark stork, pince-nez balanced on his beak, was the publisher, owner of the *New York World*, Joseph Pulitzer.

Nellie jumped to her feet. "I'm fine Mr. Pulitzer," she said.

"I am glad to hear that," Pulitzer said. "We'll need you fit if you're going around the world. Can you start the day after tomorrow?"

Nellie's heart thumped hard for a few beats. Then she said, "I can start this minute! But what made you pick me?"

Pulitzer smiled and ran a hand through his shock of black hair. "When I bought this paper six years ago, it had a circulation of fifteen thousand and was losing forty thousand dollars a year. Now we have a circulation of six hundred thousand which makes us the largest newspaper in the country."

"So, what's the problem, sir?" asked Nellie.

"Sales are down this year! I want you to go because you're one of my best reporters. And you're certainly my best-known reporter."

"I try," she said.

"The *Augusta Victoria* leaves for England the day after tomorrow," Pulitzer said. "According to our calculations, you ought to make it around the world in seventy-eight days."

Nellie jumped up and said, "I can do it in seventy-five!"

"That's the spirit!" he said. "You're going to break the record for going around the world and the *New York World* is going to break the record for selling newspapers. So, get packing!"

Now eleven days later, Nellie and Greaves sped through France to visit her inspiration, Monsieur Jules Verne.

Nellie's head ached. She rubbed her eyes, stung by fatigue and pipe-smoke. Silhouettes of hedgerows floated past the train window. She yawned again. With a wail of the whistle the train pulled into a tunnel.

The carriage dimmed. Nellie nodded once, then twice, and her eyes fluttered closed.

She was in a large circular hall several stories tall. A colossal staircase wound up into the gloom like a swirling maelstrom. Each landing was ringed with columns.

A nurse at the base of the stairs beckoned to Nellie. The woman wore a white cap and a striped dress covered with a white apron. Around her waist was a chain of keys.

Nellie felt compelled to follow her up and around until, at the top, they came to an iron door under a great green dome. The nurse unlocked it and pointed to the room beyond. Nellie tried to flee, but the nurse pushed her in and slammed the door behind her. Nellie clutched the knob in vain as the bolts clanged home. She was locked in.

Nellie looked around. A single overhead gas lamp struggled to light the misty haze. In the center of the chamber sprawled a full tub the size of a rowboat. Water in it cast a queasy glow on the wall. The clammy air chilled her. In one dark corner Nellie perceived a figure of a man. He leaned on a cane and faced away from her.

"Hello?" Nellie said to the silent sentinel. Without turning, he pointed to the tub with his stick. Then she heard a sloshing. Someone or something was in the water. Against all instinct she stepped closer, touched the rim of the tub and peered into the liquid murk. Bubbles erupted on the surface. Then with a fishy reek, a purple tentacle shot forth and enclosed her arm like a frozen vice. Nellie screamed.

The train whistle shrieked.

Greaves squeezed Nellie's wrist. "I say, Miss Bly," he said.

Nellie startled awake and pulled her arm away with a jerk. "What is it?" she said.

"We're arriving at Amiens."

II

Jules sat, elbow on his desk, chin in one hand, pen in the other. He tugged at his gray beard with dull despair. The sole latticed window spread diamonds of morning winter light on the worn Persian carpet. A puffy, white, Angora cat batted one of the crumpled papers that had tumbled from a full basket under the desk. Then the feline swiped Jules' tasseled slipper.

"*Arrête*, Passepartout!" Jules growled as he kicked the puss. Passepartout spat and ran out the door.

"*Merde*!" Jules cursed as pain shot through his leg. He tossed down the pen in frustration. He took his cane hooked on the chair and with careful concentration slowly stood. Winter was worse for his leg. But at least it took his mind off his stomach which seemed to pulsate and contract with a mind of its own. "It produces more excrement every day than I can write in a week," he grumbled.

As Jules limped towards the door of his writing room, he thought of the letter that had recently arrived from Paris. '*The* Académie Française *regrets to inform that you have not been selected for this year's membership*.' "Again!" he added out loud. He could picture his rival, that bastard, Émile Zola, limp moustache aquiver, laughing at him.

"When will they realize," thought Jules, "that science and fiction are not incompatible?"

He shouted for his wife, "Honorine! Where is my laudanum?"

She answered from downstairs, "Can't you wait, Jules?"

"No! My gut and my leg compete to see who will pin me first."

"But the girl, Jules," Honorine pleaded as she entered the room. She held a cylindrical blue bottle in one hand and a spoon in the other.

"What girl?"

"The American journalist. We're to meet her this afternoon."

"*Zut alors*! I forgot." He grabbed for the bottle and ignored the spoon.

"It was your idea to invite her," said Honorine as she moved the medicine out of reach.

"Well, what else was I to do?" Jules said. "I cannot ignore a challenge."

"No one is challenging you, Jules."

"Imagine!" he continued. "A girl who thinks she can best the great Phileas Fogg."

"*Mon chéri*," said Honorine, "the great Phileas Fogg made his trip seventeen years ago. Times have changed and Fogg is fictional."

"But the science is true!" Jules yelled.

"As for fiction," Honorine said softly, "how is it going?"

Jules sighed and whacked a wad of paper with his cane. "It's still Topsy-Turvy. Now, give me my medicine and let me be."

Honorine poured out a spoonful of brown syrup. "Open," she commanded and held it up to his lips. Jules swallowed the tincture.

"*Encore*," he said.

"You must be sharp to meet your challenger."

"Just one?" Jules pleaded, gazing at the medicine bottle.

"And tidy this room," she scolded. "The girl will think you're a madman if she sees this mess."

Jules said nothing and rubbed his aching leg.

"I'm sorry *mon chéri*." She filled half the spoon. "Here you go," she said.

"*Merci, mon chou*," sighed Jules as the narcotic liquid warmed his insides. "Now I must get back to work."

"Don't sleep too long," Honorine said as she exited. "We leave for the station in two hours."

Jules shut the door none too gently. He shuffled back to his desk and hissed like a balloon on his slow descent to the chair. He picked up the pen, then set it down. He yawned. His chin found its old perch in the cup of his hand. His head nodded. His eyes fluttered closed.

— JV —

Seagulls cried and swirled beneath early morning clouds. Eleven-year-old Jules dodged a baker who carried a sheaf of baguettes. He shifted his little seabag and skipped along a cobbled alley to the quay. His young heart raced when he saw tall masts peek above the rooftops.

Along the pier, mongers bartered with fishermen. Jules looked at the water and could tell the tide was poised to ebb.

"Just in time" he said to himself as he ran up the gangway of the shabby brig. He hopped onto the scuffed deck and stopped as half a dozen grizzled faces turned.

"Fresh meat," said one.

"Shut it, you!" said the captain. "It's our new cabin boy. You just made it. Prepare to cast off!"

Jules got settled in below. He thought of his cousin, Caroline. She was older, auburn haired, and lovely.

"I'll go to the Caribbean," he had sworn to her. "And bring you a necklace of coral."

Now, by God, he would!

He heard voices in the companionway. Then the door slammed open.

"Here he is," said the captain with an odd, deferential air to the shaded figure behind him. The captain stepped aside. In stepped Jules' father. He looked down at Jules from an impossible height, his worried eyes ablaze.

The cathedral bell tolled in counterpoint to the thwacks of his father's cane.

He grunted out words as he swung the stick, "I am your father and my word is law."

"Yes sir," Jules whimpered.

"The law is our life and our trade, Jules. And you, my first born, must promise to join the firm. Promise me!"

"I promise I will join the firm." wailed Jules.

"You must also promise me that from now on, you will voyage only in your imagination."

"But *mon père*," wailed Jules.

"Say it, boy!"

"I promise I will voyage only in my imagination!"

His father's eyes softened and filled with tears. He lowered his cane.

"One day you will thank me," he said.

Then the scene morphed into a quavery rendition of Verne's study. Jules' aged frame was frozen at his desk. Through the undulating panes of the window, he perceived the floating faces of his beloved characters, Fogg and Passepartout. Jules could only observe as the faces argued.

"Passepartout!" said Fogg.

"*Oui, Monsieur*?" Passepartout said.

"We start for Dover and Calais in ten minutes!"

"Monsieur Fogg is going to leave home?" cried Passepartout.

"Yes," Fogg bellowed. "We are going around the world in eighty days, there's not a moment to lose!"

"Perhaps it's true what they say about mad dogs and Englishmen," Passepartout hissed.

JV

Jules awoke in his chair to the needle-prick of cat's claws on his chest. Passepartout's whiskers tickled his nose. Before him, Honorine calmed a large, black, shaggy dog.

"Down, Nemo!" she commanded. "I'm sorry *mon chéri*," she said to Jules.

"How am I to get anything done with this menagerie?" Jules grumbled.

"No time now," said Honorine. "The carriage is ready. It's time to meet the girl."

"*Merde*," Jules mumbled under his breath.

III

As the train pulled into the station Nellie did her best to smooth her auburn hair and dab her face with a kerchief. Greaves took her by the wrist and pointed to the platform.

"There they are," he said.

A diminutive couple slid into view like cut-outs in a magic lantern. The train stopped.

Greaves tried to help Nellie down. Nellie twisted loose, hopped to the platform, and took Jules' outstretched hand.

"*Bonjour, mademoiselle*, I am glad to greet you," said Jules with a heavy accent. "Allow me to introduce my wife, Honorine."

"I am so pleased to meet you both." Nellie said

The carriage ride through the Amiens evening gave Nellie a glimpse of shops, and parks full of nursemaids with baby buggies. They soon arrived at the neat, stone Verne home, Number 2, Charles Dubois Street. Nellie stepped through the gate and was jumped by a huge black dog who whimpered with delight.

"Nemo, *laissez-la tranquille*!" shouted Jules to no avail. Honorine clapped her gloved hands and the dog drooped his tail and slunk off.

They crossed through a tiled outdoor vestibule and passed a little greenhouse full of tropical plants. Honorine led the way followed by Nellie and Greaves. Jules brought up the rear with rhythmic taps of his stick.

They entered the parlor. Honorine lit a pile of dry wood in the hearth and they settled in comfortable chairs around the fireplace. The flames crackled and Nellie looked around. The room was large and paneled with dark hardwood. On the floor was a velvet carpet. Hangings and paintings covered the walls but the images remained obscure in the dim light. As the fire flared, Nellie caught the bronze flash of a statue next to Jules' chair. It was the figure of a harem dancer, scantily clad.

"Scheherazade," Jules said as he caressed the statue with his cane. He spoke something in French. Honorine clucked her tongue and left the room. Greaves nodded to Jules and translated.

"Monsieur Verne wonders," said Greaves, "if you've ever seen his play, 'The Thousand and Second Night?'"

"I'm afraid I haven't," Nellie said.

Honorine returned with a tray of tarts. "Mademoiselle Bly *est une fille gentille*," she scolded.

Greaves grinned and said, "She says you are a good girl."

Nellie ignored Greaves' leer and turned to Jules.

"Monsieur Verne" she asked, "have you ever been to America?"

"Yes, one time," he answered. "*J'ai vu* Niagara Falls."

Greaves popped his bald head into the light and said, "He says he saw Niagara...."

"Yes, I got it," Nellie said. "And how did you come up with the idea for your novel *Around the World in 80 Days*?"

Jules picked at the tart tray and spoke, "I found it in a newspaper. One morning I took up a copy of *Le Siècle*, and there were the calculations. *Mais, ils ont oublié la différence entre les méridiens*."

"They forgot to account for the difference between the meridians," offered Greaves.

"And I thought, *Quel twist*!" Jules continued with glee. Crumbs tumbled off his beard.

"What a twist!" said Greaves.

Jules became serious and leaned closer to Nellie. "Please tell me your route, *Mademoiselle*," he said.

Nellie took a breath and recited, "New York to London, to Suez, to Columbo, to Hong Kong to Yokohama to San Francisco, and back to New York."

Jules' silver brows furrowed and he said, "Why do you not go to Bombay and Calcutta like Phileas Fogg?"

Honorine gave a quiet warning, "Jules!"

Then Jules said, "*C'est incroyable que cette petite fillette voyage toute seule autour du monde.*"

Tracey translated, "He says it is not to be believed that this little lass is going all alone around the world."

Greaves continued to interpret as Honorine said, "Yes, but she is built for it, "Trim, energetic, strong. Jules, I believe she will make your heroes look foolish."

"*Elle ressemble à une jeune fille*!" Jules said with a thump of his cane.

Greaves slapped his chair and aped, "She looks like a young girl!"

"She will beat your record, Jules," warned Honorine.

Nellie watched the volley like a spectator at a tennis match.

"*Quoi*?!" said Jules.

"I will wager with you if you like," said Honorine.

Jules glowered at Honorine, who smiled in return. The room was silent for an uncomfortable moment. Then to the relief of all, puffy Passepartout sauntered into the room. The cat rubbed past Nellie's legs and hopped up into her lap. Then, deflated, Jules smiled sadly at Nellie and said, "You indeed have the character to succeed my dear."

"Thank you, Monsieur Verne," Nellie said as she petted the cat, "Perhaps you would show us where you work?"

"*Avec plaisir, Mademoiselle*," he said. "Right this way."

They trooped out of the parlor and around a corner. Before them, a tall winding staircase spun into darkness.

"After you," said Jules. "My mountain of Sisyphus."

Honorine led the way up and lit gas jets along a corridor. She opened a door and ushered them into the writing room. Nellie had expected a cluttered palace of creativity, ink awash, and pens akimbo. Instead, she saw a bare, modest cupboard and a wooden desk by a window. On the desk sat a manuscript in pristine repose.

Nellie went to the writing, "May I see?" she asked.

Jules looked to Honorine who gave an imperceptible nod.

"But of course," Jules said. "Just a *petit* something I work on."

"Why, it's so clean and complete," Nellie exclaimed. "No additions, no changes, just a few blot-outs. Is this a draft?"

Jules gave a Gallic shrug and Honorine smiled beatifically.

"I am truly impressed sir," Nellie said. "By the time I finish even the smallest article, my papers are all smeared and my desk is destroyed."

Jules only nodded. Greaves took out his watch, then cleared his throat.

"I'm afraid it's getting on," he said. "Won't do to miss the train to Calais."

Honorine and Greaves started down. But as Nellie moved to go, Jules said to her,

"*Un moment, mademoiselle.* I wish to show you something."

Jules ushered Nellie into the hall. With a sweep of his cane, he pointed to a large map of the world on the wall. Nellie saw that it was crisscrossed with lines in blue pencil. She recognized the path.

"It's Phileas Fogg's route!" she said.

"*Exactement*!" said Jules. Then, with a thump, he lunged the tip of his stick into the heart of India. Nellie jumped and looked around. They were alone. Verne leaned his face so close to Nellie she felt the tickle of his beard. His eyes burned black and he said in almost a whisper, "I have always wanted to visit India."

"But Columbo. . . ." Nellie began as she backed away.

"I know," Jules said. "It is faster through Ceylon. I have studied your itinerary."

"You have?" Nellie said.

"That is not where you will find your trouble." He added. "To cross the Pacific this time of year is, *comment dit-on*. . . chancy.

"I see." Nellie said.

"If you make it home in seventy-nine days," said Jules, "I shall applaud with both of my hands."

Jules moved closer to Nellie. She poised to retreat, but saw that his eyes had cooled and he looked sad. She relaxed. Jules offered her his hand and she took it.

"*Mademoiselle*," he said. "I must admit that I am jealous of you."

"But why?" asked Nellie with real concern.

"I envy your action, your youth, your strength," he spoke. "You inspire me. For my entire life, my dearest wish has been to travel the globe. But a promise I once made many years ago kept me from it. And now that I am finally free to do as I please, ill health, injuries, and, alas, age require that I continue to voyage only in my imagination."

"*Monsieur* Verne, it is you who inspires me." Nellie protested. Without your imagination, I should never have even thought to begin this trip."

Jules smiled and they descended arm in arm.

Jules said. "I have claimed before that anything one man can imagine, other men can make real. I believe I shall now amend that to include women."

They reentered the parlor, laughing.

JV

It was nearly midnight by the time the train pulled in to Calais. On the platform, Nellie pulled her checkered shawl tight to block the winter wind. She was so tired that she did not bother to protest when Greaves took her wrist and led her to the Brindisi mail train.

"Doesn't leave for an hour yet, Miss Bly," he said. "But you can board and get settled."

There was one passenger coach, a Pullman Palace sleeper with full accommodations. Nellie freed herself from Greaves' grip and boarded. Alone at last, she sat down with a sigh. She raised the shade and startled back from Greaves' face pressed against her window like a full moon.

"Safe travels Miss Bly," he shouted, "And look me up when you're in London."

"Thank you, Mister Greaves," Nellie called back.

"Please," he said with a final wink, "call me Tracey."

Nellie shut the shades on him with a snap. Then she slid into the bunk. Her eyes were closed before the train pulled out.

In Amiens, Jules sat in his parlor chair. Passepartout purred in his lap and Nemo snored by the fire. Honorine proffered a spoonful of medicine and left the room. His head dipped, his beard slid down his chest and he entered the world of Morpheus.

JV

Jules and Nellie were in a rowboat. It ghosted along of its own accord on a glassy midnight sea. Nellie watched from the bow and Jules held the tiller astern. On the horizon a beacon spun its feeble light through swaths of fog.

"Where are we?" Nellie asked.

Jules said, "I don't know."

The fog thickened until it seemed as if they floated through space. Then the boat lurched. Phosphorescent bubbles peppered the hull.

"What was that?" said Jules.

"I don't know," Nellie said. She looked over the side. Something swam under the boat.

Then a tentacle shot up and wrapped her wrist with an icy grip. The boat tipped. Nellie tried to break free. But she was held tight. She felt desperately about the bilge and clutched an anchor. Nellie hefted it aloft and swung the fluke into the appendage. It released her.

At that moment several more lengths of purple tentacles burst from the deep.

One wrapped trunk-like around Jules' middle. He felt his stomach squeeze. Again, Nellie rifled around the hull and grabbed something long and smooth, a harpoon. She stabbed at the limb that encircled Jules until it let go. Another arm clamped to Nellie's head. Jules hacked it with an ax and freed her.

To the starboard, a mountainous mound of flesh emerged from the froth. Higher and higher it rose until it resembled a small island. It was a gigantic, bulbous head!

"*Mon Dieu*," cried Jules. "It is my father!"

"It's my editor!" Nellie yelled. No, it's Greaves!"

"A monster!" they screamed in unison.

Together they attacked. Nellie threw her harpoon and Jules flung his axe. The axe stuck fast into the purple pate and the harpoon hit the monster in an eye. The giant blinked and roared with rage and pain. Tentacles shot up all around and crashed down on the water causing waves to swamp their craft. Then slowly, the head sank gurgling back into the deep.

Nellie and Jules supported each other in the foundering boat. They were soaked to the waist.

"We won," Nellie said.

"The demon is defeated," Jules said. "It has gone to rest."

Suddenly the night was pierced by a whistle. Off the port-side came the chug of an engine. Then a steam launch burst through the mist.

"There's not a moment to lose!" yelled a man on the launch.

"*Oui Monsieur*!" answered another.

"It's Fogg," said Jules.

"And Passepartout!" cried Nellie.

"We are here to rescue you!" said Fogg.

Nellie looked around at the calm sea.

"You're too late, Fogg," she said. "We did it ourselves. I told you I didn't need rescuing."

"I see," Fogg replied. Well then, how about a ride? That tub of yours seems to be foundering."

"I will join you, Fogg," Jules said.

"Not me," said Nellie. "I'd rather row my own boat."

"I applaud you, *Mademoiselle*," said Jules as he climbed aboard the launch. "Passepartout," he ordered, "help her bail! Fogg, start the engine!"

"Yes master!" they said in unison.

The night had cleared to reveal a black sky swathed with stars.

"I'm headed that way," Nellie said, pointing to the far distant shore. "How about you?"

Jules looked heavenward and said, "We shall see."

The Brindisi train blew its whistle and lurched into motion. Nellie sat up. She shook her head and blew out a breath. "Phew, that was quite a dream," she sighed. She lay back in the bunk and looked out the window to the clear winter night. She felt calm, confident, and free. She was sure now that she could complete her journey without help. And that she would beat Fogg's time.

"No matter what!" she said to herself. Then Nellie rolled over and slept, sound and deep, the whole night through.

Jules jolted awake in his chair. "Honorine!" he called.

"*Oui, mon chéri*," she said as she entered. "Would you like some more medicine?"

"*Non, mon chou*," he said. "Bring me a bolster, some paper, pen, and ink."

His eyes sparkled. "I have a journey to begin!"

Then Jules turned to the window and looked up at the winter stars.

"*Merci*, father," he said.

The Highest Loyalty

Mike Adamson

***Who* could possibly** be writing a letter to Captain Nemo?

One of the intractable qualities of an existence divorced from the surface world was the surrendering of all communication beyond the iron hull of the *Nautilus*. Nemo regarded any breach of that anonymity as unwelcome. Yet, to the captain's frowning gaze, the envelope in his hands heralded a strange call to unknown possibilities. He stared at it, then out at the blue waters beyond the salon viewing panels, and his heart raced. Did he really want to entertain the concerns of outsiders? Yet, as a man who had reinvented himself, was he not of rich enough spirit to at least consider an entreaty?

Few places in the world furnished a finer variety of seafood to Captain Nemo than Green Cay, in the Bahamas. Diving teams from the *Nautilus* collected fish, crab and lobster, and a thousand strange delicacies from its sunlit shoals, while the submarine lay in the blue gloom of the Tongue of the Ocean, an intrusion of the deep sea within the Bahama Bank.

Green Cay also served as one of his exchange points for contacts with his surface agents around the world. Though well-paid, none of these agents could identify Nemo or even knew of the *Nautilus.* From them he collected newspapers and volumes of up-to-date learning, books and technical journals, to swell the *Nautilus*' library, and bolster Nemo's specific knowledge. An unparalleled knowledge of the oceans did not blind him to the danger of growing out of touch with scientific advances. On this day in April, 1867, Nemo's divers arrived at the secret contact point, recovered a watertight crate, and delivered it to the *Nautilus*, placing it in the library for the captain to open.

Awaiting full darkness before getting under way, so as to make the daily recharge of the air banks on the surface, Nemo opened the container at his leisure, and none was present to see his expression as something unprecedented greeted his gaze.

Atop the tightly packed collection of papers he found the envelope, addressed in a flourishing hand, *To Our Mysterious Friend.* Thus he had taken it up with a frown and a glance at the chronometer, to sink into a comfortable seat by the open viewing ports, and, when his private soul was at last ready to entertain the thoughts of an outsider, tear open the envelope.

To Our Mysterious Friend,

> *Some years have gone by since we were last in touch, to arrange your most valued service in facilitating the escape of slaves from the Confederacy to safety elsewhere. In accordance with your wishes, none have ever asked how you accomplished this miracle, nor spoken of your involvement.*
>
> *However, a situation has arisen of sufficient desperation to warrant an appeal to wartime channels, and I pray our old schedule of contact times remains active. White Fox and cubs*

are surrounded, den being watched, the situation is believed lethal. I appeal to your good and just nature one last time, to snatch a small group from certain death at the hands of those for whom the Civil War shall, in fact, never be over.

Your servant, in direst need,
The White Fox

In previous correspondence the sender never included a physical address, a security measure guarding against the conceivable interception of messages. This time, the letter showed an address in Swansboro, North Carolina, and Nemo sighed as he stared at it, his mind working quickly. The dynamic of deep loyalties remained the only certainty left in the world for one who had forsaken the whole human race—save his sympathies for the oppressed and exploited—and he knew at once this desperate adventure called him to duty. During the period since the letter's date, eight days earlier, anything could have rendered a rescue an exercise in futility: but he must try. Perusing the handwriting with the eye of a scholar, he held no doubt the letter owed its authorship to a woman. Previous messages, during the war, had been in a carefully disguised script, and this revelation gave him further cause for deep thought. He pocketed the letter and went forward to the navigation table in the salon, where he found the Mate reviewing the shoals and islands. "Course, sir?" the Mate asked, in the secret tongue of Nemo's own creation.

"North, for the ocean. From Nassau, steer north-east for Abaco, thence a direct bearing for Cape Hatteras. Revolutions for twenty knots."

The Mate laid calipers over the chart's scales and checked distances. "We'll be diving with full tanks by nine, be off Nassau by midnight, then, abreast the capes of Abaco by dawn."

"Very good. Half an hour to full dark, then get us under way."

Nemo had watched the American Civil War unfold with the greatest interest, as well as a conflicted heart. Slavery was perhaps the most hateful of all human institutions, and he had been presented with the dilemma of whether he should act, for to oppose the Confederacy was to assist the Union, and it was, after all, *all* humankind with whom he was at war. He remembered too well his own chains while a prisoner following the failed Indian Mutiny of 1857. He knew well the brutalization of nation states hell-bent on power and how they used up men, women and children, including Nemo's own family, to achieve their aims.

Slavery was a stain upon the world, an offense to every decent human being, and he had no difficulty in providing material support to the Abolitionist movement. The *Nautilus* became operational as the American Civil War raged, and Nemo insinuated himself as a silent partner with those courageous souls who operated hidden routes into the Union, along which thousands of slaves flowed to freedom. And it was his privilege to provide a further route, as on a number of occasions he had taken escapees aboard, blindfolded, in the dead of night, transporting them to a convenient landing point on the Union coast. Secrecy was preserved by use of the blind, internal compartment, sedatives in their food, and other measures, and the captain took neither credit nor acclaim for having assisted.

Upon these things, he meditated as the *Nautilus* sped north during the night, and all the next day and night. When they approached the Carolina capes, shoreward of the warm river of the Gulf Stream, he knew what he must do. It all began with a letter, which he penned in his quarters, with a strange sense of both destiny and closure.

— JV —

One of the few crewmen who could speak English posted Nemo's letter. Set ashore in the dark hours by the *Nautilus*' small boat, he took residence in a cheap sailor's inn near the waterfront on the east side of the White Oak River estuary. He gave the inn as a return address, and there awaited a reply, studying a map of Swansboro, or drinking at a local tavern, with tales of serving on a whaler.

A letter arrived the next day, and the seaman took a walk by the dark waters of Bogue Inlet, along the marshy reaches of Myrtle Island, and, on a lonely stretch of reeds and rippled sand, he met the returned skiff, with a crew of four men and Captain Nemo. Shading the letter from the morning sun, the captain read quickly, dark eyes darting along the hurried hand-writing.

Our Mysterious Friend,

I am overjoyed to receive your letter. Please come quickly. I have barely dared leave my home in weeks, and spend each night in terror of assault. The police I suspect of indifference in this matter, and have not approached. I have observed strangers watching my house, apparently in shifts, and believe they will kill me should I show my face for more than a moment. They may decide to force an entry, and though I shall give good account of myself, I cannot help but feel I shall be done for.

Praying for your prompt arrival,
The White Fox.

Turning his face from civilization had been a vow he took seriously, yet what measure of man would he be to place such a choice before the wellbeing of an associate? He was not a man who had 'friends,' but the White Fox shared at least some of his ideals, and now this brave soul who had shepherded the helpless from a land of cruelty faced such wrath herself. This stirred memories—memories of his dearly beloved wife, his children, lost long ago in the cycle of horror that had propelled his creation of the *Nautilus*. For her sake, her humanity, he could not turn away. He must tread one last time the cursed land.

The crewman who had carried the message pointed out their destination on the cheap town map he had purchased: a modest house on Walnut Street, opposite the Ward Cemetery, a few streets back from the river frontage on the other side of the inlet. Nemo nodded as he assimilated their route, and his men saw his determination in his face. He would save The White Fox or die in the attempt.

Nemo and his crew bore weapons Nemo had sworn he would never touch again. Each man checked his 1864 Metropolitan Navy Percussion, a licensed copy of the Colt Navy six-chamber handgun. Nemo had considered arming his party with the electric weapons of his own invention, but decided against it. A single weapon, or even one charged pellet, left ashore could reveal his technology to the undeserving. The Colt pistols would suffice. They were excellent weapons, but took time to load with black powder and shot; each man had been issued a pair. Between them, they had sixty rounds—but not one to spare.

The skiff was equipped with a stepped mast and sail, but the wind lay against them and the hands rowed smartly, Nemo at the tiller. They had a two-mile journey from Myrtle Island west around the peninsula, inland of the gaggle of shoals and marshy islets behind the barrier beaches, and oil lamps in the town streets were a string of fireflies off to starboard. They felt the chop increase as they came abreast the Main Channel which led down to the sea, then it smoothed out as they turned inland with the curve of the river, up toward old Swansboro town.

The peninsula on which the town had stood since early colonial times was barely half a mile across, so nowhere was far from anywhere. They found a berth at the hundred-year-old Town Dock among ramshackle river traffic and the odd small coaster, a forest of masts that moved gently against the glow of the town. The *Nautilus*' metal boat seemed strange among painted timber hulls, and Nemo hoped it would not arouse unwanted interest.

A sleepy dock inspector accepted Nemo's soft words about having rowed over from the newer parts of town. They headed up into Swansboro by Front Street and Church Street, and in ten minutes were on the corner of Walnut. The cemetery dominated the north side in a mass of dark oaks, all ominous shadows, and Nemo identified where the town's watchers would most likely be. The house in question was fifth from the corner, and no light burned at its door. A picket fence gleamed below a newly rising moon, and the house seemed deserted, shutters closed and garden unkempt.

"Keep watch," Nemo hissed. His men fanned out behind the fence in the shadow of bushes, to watch the cemetery with guns drawn. The Captain made his way to the porch of the timber-siding house and knocked. He waited a few moments, knocked again, and sensed movement on the other side of the door. "White Fox," he said softly, "your 'mysterious friend' has come."

Bolts slid, a lock turned, and the door opened to a pitch-dark hall. "Come in," a feminine voice whispered, and when Nemo slipped inside, pistol in hand and senses prickling for danger, he heard the bolts slide back again. A silhouette moved against the glimmer of an oil lamp turned to its lowest, and a hand gestured for him to follow. He made his way after the vague outline into another room with shuttered windows, then the lamp was set down and the wick turned up.

She was an attractive, dark-haired woman, in early middle age, or younger, he thought, given the cares and terrors life had held. "White Fox?" he asked in a whisper, and she nodded. He smiled with the ghost of a shrug. "All these years, I always imagined you were black."

Now she smiled too. "More whites than you might believe were appalled, sickened, by slavery, all across the South.... Since General Forrest founded his so-called 'social club' to oppose the interests of Emancipation, and to punish Abolitionists in particular, this land is no more safe than during the war."

"The law was of no use?"

"My dear sir, the law in this state pays only lip service to the Federal statutes. Sheriffs, judges, governors, all across the old Confederacy, are slow to uphold them. And even slower to obstruct the interests of those many see as continuing to fight the South's battle, no matter the end of open hostilities." The catch in her voice, the white-knuckled clench of her hands before her, bespoke her tension, yet her smile suggested she now dared hope. "You saved hundreds of lives during the War. Now I ask only one thing—that you perform the same service for myself and my children."

"The 'cubs' you mentioned?"

She spread her hands. "I may have been part of the secret network that shepherded souls from hell to freedom, but I am also a mother and widow... I shall not tell you our names, and ask none of you in return, for only in secrecy do we find what safety exists."

"Very wise," Nemo replied, already tense, eager to be away. "You're ready to travel?"

"We have a small bag packed, little enough to salvage from a whole life. Sir, I place our lives in your hands."

"I've a boat at the Town Dock. Four men outside, armed."

"I don't think those who watch me will risk an open conflict, they're usually murderers who lynch at will. Usually, but not always...." She nodded and swirled on a cloak over her skirt and jacket, calling her children with a whisper. Many years had gone by since Nemo had laid eyes on children, and he felt a clutching at his soul as they entered the room. They were a boy and girl, the boy perhaps six years of age, dark haired, silent, and afraid, the girl perhaps two years his elder, a frown also unbecoming so tender an age. They were dressed warmly, as if each night they had expected to make some desperate journey. She paused, looked once around her home, and laid a hand to a wall, as if saying goodbye.

Nemo gave her the moment, then inclined his sea cap to the hall. "Madam?"

She turned down the lamp and shepherded her children to the door, and as she drew the bolts by touch alone, Nemo reached into his jacket and drew a pistol.

Soft moonglow lit the street. Leaving the family in the cover of the dark porch, Nemo went first to his men by the fence, one shadow among many. "All clear, sir," a seaman murmured in their private language. "There are men in the graveyard, two, possibly three, looking unsure of themselves."

"They probably weren't sure if the house was even still occupied," Nemo murmured. "No matter. We take the first turn to the left, two streets south, left again and straight on to the docks. Maybe they'll not start something in town. . . ." He turned back to the house, whistled quietly, and the White Fox and her children hurried down the steps. "We'll form a guard around you," Nemo whispered in English, and one of the seamen took the valise she carried.

They stepped out onto the street, and at any moment Nemo expected a flurry of shots. He carried his pistol openly and scanned the darkness of lawns and stones across the way, ready to fire at any muzzle flash. In moments they made the corner of Broad Street and hurried south for the waterfront.

Every dozen breaths Nemo looked back, and they were at the corner of Elm when he saw a figure appear, shuffling, hands in pockets. "They have a man keeping touch," he hissed to the others. "Don't pause for a second."

Fifty yards on, they turned onto Water Street and the lights of the docks glittered ahead, torches and oil lamps shimmering on the river. Three hundred yards to their boat. . . . Nemo glanced back and saw not one but three men tagging along, and a fourth joined as he watched. Two hundred yards, no one else was about, just a faint sound of music from a tavern near the docks. Would their pursuers depend on the indifference of the law, to make it a fight here on the foreshore?

A hundred yards, they were near the wood jetties now, among fences, the strong smell of the estuary. Fifty yards, and Nemo looked back at the men, who seemed in no particular hurry. . . .

The docks were deserted but for a few anglers at the end of the jetty, and under their barely curious notice the seamen guided their charges down a wooden ladder, into the skiff. They cast off and pulled for the channel in moments and Nemo sat with the tiller in his left hand, pistol out of sight in his right. The shadowy figures appeared on the jetty and seemed to be reporting to someone, meeting with two, three more....

"Smartly, men, into mid-channel, then we'll hoist the sail."

The moon was well up now over the marshes and islets, providing light to work by, and they exchanged oars for sail with the skill of seasoned sailors. The wind was good for a fairly straight course south and east between the larger islands in the river. Having studied a harbor piloting chart before leaving the submarine, Nemo felt confident steering them. Fortunately, the skiff drew very little water, giving him reason to doubt they would run aground on the mudbanks, even now at low tide. The Main Channel was a mile away and as they felt the roughening water, twenty minutes from the dock, Nemo brought them about into the passage. The boat pitched on the incoming rollers, and the sail jibed over on the course change. They were cruising now, heading for the sea between reedy islets, the passage a comfortable five hundred yards wide or more throughout. Moonlight on the waves a mile ahead promised freedom, and every moment brought them closer.

Halfway to the mouth of the White Oak River they saw a sail astern, a sloop of some sort, without doubt pursuing them, scudding between the banks in the hands of someone who knew the river well. "Steady, men," Nemo said in their unique language. "Stay the course, we can do this." With gritted teeth he took them as close to the shallows as he dared, his keen eyes darting back and forth between the islands and the beacon lights that burned here and there.

Ten anxious minutes later they were abreast of Emerald Point and felt proper waves under them, the skiff starting to pitch in earnest. The bed fell away safely and Nemo sent them directly out to sea, the freshening breeze filling the sail and heeling the craft. As ocean nights went, it was mild, but the children would be cold soon enough. With a glance back, Nemo knew they had several minutes before the sloop cleared the point, and he ordered the sail trimmed against the wind for best speed.

"Right, men, get the signal up," he whispered, and one of the sailors opened a compartment under the bow, to bring out lanterns and open each in turn to switch on electric globes. Then the three were strung to a halyard and run up, so the skiff presented three white masthead lights, a signal known only to the crew of the *Nautilus*.

The flat *bang* of a weapon astern reminded them of their pursuers, and several rifles joined in with what sounded like old muskets. Every ball went wide, but Nemo shook his head, knowing the Moon gave the shooters a clear target, the skiff outlined against the light on the sea. He whispered to the White Fox, "They have the speed on us, so it's only a matter of time."

"Then....?" the woman asked hoarsely, clearly very afraid now.

"Have no doubt, that signal will be seen," Nemo replied, seeming unconcerned, but deep down he knew they were on a razor's edge. The sloop had a better hull, five times their sail area, and twice their speed no matter how well-handled the skiff may be, and he took them a little north of east to move out of the moon-glare. Come what may, they had a hunter behind them—but also a barrier ahead. The great river of the Gulf Stream poured by the Carolinas between ten and twenty miles offshore, depending on season and year, and in these latitudes began its great turn north and east to cross the Atlantic. Should they find themselves in it, they could be swept a long way from land, and the skiff was not a very seaworthy craft for a prolonged voyage. She was rising and falling to the swells now and cold dollops came over the gunwales.

The lanterns burned against the April stars and Nemo's eyes swept the dark. Out there somewhere, he knew, the *Nautilus* was prowling, her lookouts searching the sea with field glasses, and when they picked up the triple spark she would come. There was no more to the plan than that, but they must come *soon*.

The sloop closed the distance with distressing speed, the moon-touched arch of her mainsail growing by the minute against the receding ribbon of lights ashore. The children were crying now, afraid, cold, and tired, and their mother, on the stern bench at Nemo's side, could only hold them close, praying in a whisper, both for her family's lives and for those of the brave men who had come to their assistance. When the sloop opened fire again, a hundred yards back, they heard lead balls whine over them like angry wasps, punching holes in the sail. The children yelped pitifully.

"Steady," Nemo growled in the dark. "Hold your fire. If it comes to it, make every shot count." The men on the sloop were reloading, a minute or more respite before the weapons rang out again. Most shots were still well off target, but another passed through the sail and one chimed harshly against the hull. "Stay low!" was Nemo's command, thrusting the woman and her children into the damp, uncomfortable well of the boat and crouching as best he could, the tiller still firm in his grip. Not wanting to reveal his desperation to the others, he kept his scans of the horizon brief and infrequent. *Where is she?* he thought, over and over.

Another volley was better on target, several ricocheting, others singing low over their heads, and Nemo raised his head to find the sloop a few boat-lengths behind. "Get ready," he ordered. "Let them close up, if they mean to, then we rise and fire as one, using one pistol only. Sweep their deck and with luck we'll take enough to discourage the rest."

Now they could hear the shouts of the chasing sloop's crew, jeers and encouragements, the curses, and promises of a violent end flung into the night. The woman whispered to Nemo alone, "Good sir, promise me you will do us the kindness? Do not let them take us alive. . . ."

Before he could answer, the sloop's next assault broke out in a ragged volley, and in the darkness Nemo half-collapsed forward amid the pain of a hot, wet line streaking across his left shoulder. His arm went numb, forcing him to hold the tiller between his forearm and torso. Nemo panted with gritted his teeth as the cold and the boat's motion compounded his struggle. The woman seemed to know, he felt her touch, and in the moonlight his eyes entreated her to silence.

"Ready," he growled and glanced back. The sloop a length behind, he saw men on her deck, wrestling with weapons. *Close enough.* "Now!" Nemo's men rose from their crouches, and .45-calibre pistols hammered in flashes of flame and powder smoke. A crackle of thirty rounds blasted across the sloop's deck and men went down, some flinging themselves into cover, two with cries of shock and pain, and the sloop's tiller went over at once to veer them off, two, three, four lengths.

"Second pistols," Nemo ordered, the strain in his voice now clear. "If they come on again, no mercy, for they'll show none!"

The skiff raced on, cutting creamy wakes across the Atlantic, the spring phosphorescence marking their passage, and when the sloop turned for them again Nemo's mouth was dry. Was this where the grand dreams ended, in a pistol duel with anti-abolitionists off the Carolina coast? How strange, he thought, to be defeated not under the seas, but above them.

Abruptly, a sulfurous glow, a yellowish-green radiance built ominously in the waters beneath them, and they heard uncomprehending yells from the sloop. But as the craft surged obdurately on to intersect with the skiff, the light abruptly faded, then in a roar of waters, a crashing of foam, a long, dark shape rose from the waves. The sloop collided with a screech of timber on metal, rebounded and went over on her beam ends, righted at the last moment and wallowed, tons of water in her belly. Her crew now had more to worry about than General Forest's agenda, and she hove away, limping, her sail flapping against the mast.

A light showed in the dark against the long, low outline of the submarine, and Nemo, with a sigh of relief, ordered down the sail. Then he collapsed against the side of the boat and panted in the distress of his wound.

– JV –

Upon reaching the safety of the vessel, their clothes were taken and dried, and mother and children were afforded warmth and comfort in a windowless compartment. When their clothes were returned, Nemo joined them, his wound already tended, and a meal was provided, the blandest elements of his oceanic larder. Not for them to know, the food was laced with a strong sedative, and the last the family would recall was of the woman speaking earnestly with the strange sea captain before the exertions of the day overtook them, and they fell into a deep, sound sleep.

– JV –

Sunrise was an hour away when the skiff returned from the Delaware coast. Nemo waited on the *Nautilus*' surface platform, left arm in a sling, and took the Mate's report that The White Fox and her children had been set ashore, with skillfully forged coach tickets, by the foreshore of the town of Lewes, on the west coast of Delaware Bay. The shore party had made sure to point the family, still groggy from the sedatives in the night, in the right direction, and ensured they boarded the coach without difficulty. This was old Union territory, from which they could make their way in safety.

Thus was Nemo's security preserved; the White Fox had seen little by night, and Nemo was confident she had understood nothing at all. He knew she was glad merely to be alive, and he trusted her with whatever scraps of insight she may have gleaned.

The Mate oversaw the stowing of the skiff and awaited orders. The captain breathed the sea air, staring off at the glimmers of the mainland, and was glad he had been able to help those who had helped others. Such was only ever right, and the loyalty he prized above all. Now they were over, he could reflect on those desperate hours, and found he was not torn between the creeds of isolation and magnanimity—he must meditate upon this, but saw at this point no conflict between the extremes. He was done with the human race, but not with *humanity*.

"Secure for sea," he ordered, with a glance at the coming day. "We'll be diving directly. Let's see what the ocean will yield this day."

Hatches closed, tanks vented, and the submarine slid gracefully beneath the waters, turning away from the concerns and conflicts of humankind, to seek nature's peace in the arms of the deep.

Embrace of the Planets

Brenda Carre

Eleanora stared through the crowd milling in the street, just to make sure her eyes weren't deceiving her. They weren't!

The window on the antique shop door still looked dark, but the red '*Closed*' sign within had been turned to read, '*Open by Inter-Planetary Agreement*'.

Eager now to see inside, Eleanora pushed herself up from her bistro table. A challenge with two forearm crutches and a twisted spine, but she did it. She'd been wanting to get into Trove the entire month she'd been here. She'd heard the owner, Mr. Nemo, was an eccentric. He only sold stuff to people he liked and opened at very weird times. Clearly a quirky soul like her.

She chuckled at his sign's allusion to Port Millicent's Equinox celebration—an unusual one with the moon's golden balloon riding at perigee on this warm British Columbia evening.

Both pubs and the Tai-Chi Bistro had tables out in the street. The whole town was jiggy with pizza and beer, with Millennials and Gen-Xers her own age chilling out after work. The air smelled of hot-dogs, fish-and-chips, and cappuccino. A bunch of seniors and under tens gyrated unashamedly to the sixties band on the corner. Teens huddled, giggled, and texted in doorways.

She was almost at Trove's big blue door when her phone went off.

"*Ah-oo-gah*!"

Two pre-teen girls in shorts and checked shirts giggled at her ringtone.

"Dive! Dive, Lady!" called the pink-shirted one. Eleanora gave her a thumbs up. A quick look at her phone told her this was her agent.

She hated it when people entered a store talking on the phone. Nor did she like to discuss business with Max on a crowded street corner.

She turned on her earpiece and stuck the phone in her pocket.

"Look, I'm busy, Max; can I call you back? I told you before, I don't do interviews for papers like that! No! I don't care how much money they're offering. It's nothing but sensationalism. If I wanted that kind of money, I could write for erotic lit!"

"Well!" The suntanned mom who'd come up to the two pre-teens sent her a shocked expression.

Eleanora winced and dropped her voice to a mutter. "I don't want to talk about my accident, okay? No! I don't need a shrink to help me deal with it, Max, I need to learn to walk through crowds without falling on my hiney."

She hung up on him in the middle of his reply and put her phone on 'buzz'.

Even ten years later, the horror of the terrible crash was still fresh in her mind and now this idiot wanted to sell the whole deal to some sleazy magazine. He wanted her to tell him what it had been like to lose her mom and her brother on that same wintry school trip to New York. He wasn't the one using crutches. He wasn't the one who woke up three days later in ICU remembering way too much: the screams of her drowning classmates, the wrenching pain of broken bones, the taste of ice and dirt and blood, the black, freezing water rising in the back of the school bus. Worst was the terror when she knew she couldn't hold her breath any longer.

She'd died. She'd gone over. The EMTs had brought her back. Only her. She refused to talk about the multitudes of worlds she'd seen on the other side. Not to the papers, not to the movies, not to the doctors who'd helped her walk again.

Breathing hard, Eleanora grabbed Trove's heavy bronze door latch. "Please be open, please be open…."

The handle turned and gave an inviting, well-oiled clunk. An exquisite presentment tingled through Eleanora's spine. A bell above the lintel dinged as she opened the door and stepped deep into darkness.

The heavy door shut behind her with a thud—closing out the sounds of Port Millicent. The lights came on. Her heart leaped with terror as the vivid flash made her eyes wince closed. The delicious smell of furniture polish, fruitwood, and potpourri teased them back open.

Here was a world of wonders such as she'd glimpsed on the other side of death. A huge human skeleton stood just to her immediate left. Her five-foot-eight height came to mid-chest on the giant.

Oh, my giddy Maiden Aunt!

She stayed where she was to let her eyes adjust to the brightness and catch her bearings. Sabers and cutlasses dazzled from their wall mounts; mirrors glistened. Furniture beckoned, carefully placed on the big room's smooth floorboards. Elizabethan benches, Georgian chairs, Gustavian clocks ticking like hearts contented. Imperial Chinese chests, Japanese tables. Tables and benches so organic they looked like they'd grown right out of the ground.

Light bathed Eleanora from an ornate tin plate ceiling, from which hung at least twelve crystal chandeliers. A second chamber in back seemed just as large with green velvet curtains defining the arch that divided the rooms. A faint whirr of machinery came to her ears. There was something big and spherical back there she intended to investigate later.

These big rooms seemed too large for the small space Trove took up on the street of Port Millicent. A bit of 'fool-the-eye' *trompe-l'oeil*, she reckoned. Even so, there were inexplicable things in here. Like that Victorian diver's outfit complete with its helmet hoses and brass gauges, light dancing from brass fittings. It hung as though floating mid-room above the shop desk.

Eleanora grinned at this artistry. No wonder Mr. Nemo didn't part with his stuff very often.

A low row of medieval iron shelves filled with books fronted a shop desk as huge as a horse cart. A thick tome lay on it perhaps too heavy, or too valuable to locate too far from Mr. Nemo's immediate reach. Beside this tome was a wooden crank-operated cash register and shadowed just beyond these what appeared to be a bowed, combed-over head of sparse white hair.

"Hello?" she called.

No reply. A frisson of worry filled her. Was this another construct like the diver and the skeleton, or the actual Mr. Nemo? He was old, she knew. Was he dead? Nonsense! He could be hard of hearing, or asleep.

Leaving the door-guarding skeleton behind her, Eleanora leaned into her crutches and made her way past a neo-gothic-style table covered with rolls of star charts. A framed map depicting the route taken in *Journey to the Center of the Earth* was propped against the table's near leg. Since her accident, she'd lived in the works of Jules Verne and the certainty that like her, Verne had glimpsed the truth of the universe.

Eleanora took note of oak glass-door cabinets lining the wooden walls, everything accessed by a sliding step ladder mounted on a sturdy brass railing. Within lay the kind of artifacts and paraphernalia that spoke of a world-travelling explorer—albeit one from the 1800s. A collection of sauropod skulls with disquieting teeth glimmered white in the light. Perched above them was a beautifully preserved Dodo. Atop another cabinet, a trio of brass barometers and a one-tenth scale model of Ferdinand Lagleize's Ballon-Poisson airship that did indeed look more like a fish than a dirigible.

"H-hello? Mr. Nemo?" she ventured.

Mr. Nemo's head with its obvious pink bald spot stayed bent. The head of a man of at least seventy, maybe more. A head that bobbed a little. Her keen ears heard a rustle that could be the turn of a page. She grinned now. She herself had been lost in a book more than once.

She approached like a devotional pilgrim, taking care with her crutches. The tannins of parchment and the vanilla of centuries enveloped her.

The tome she'd first noticed appeared to be hand-bound in tooled calfskin and titled *Embrace of the Planets*. The page edges were marbled.

"Hello?" she breathed softly, peering to see what was capturing the old man's attention.

Oh! By all that was rich and lovely, he was reading the 1873 first edition of *Le Tour du Monde en 80 Jours*!

"Around the World in Eighty Days," murmured Eleanora, overcome. Mr. Nemo shut his book and gave her a nearsighted squint.

With his head down, she'd not gotten the full effect of a man as unique as his store. An emaciation of advanced palsy had claimed his body. Two deep pain lines defined his narrow mouth and gave him a permanent Eeyore-type frown. His head had been squashed into a long thin baguette shape. Mr. Nemo's teeny, black eyes reminded her of raisins, close-set on either side of his prominent nose.

He frowned at her scrutiny. She guiltily straightened.

Oh, how rude of me to stare, especially knowing how it feels to be stared at.

A loud hiss to her immediate right made her flinch, expecting a reptile of some kind. Instead, a beautifully scrolled little *bergère* chair had appeared where no chair had been a minute before.

"How...." she began.

"Be careful. She bites," said Mr. Nemo. "She isn't certain she likes you. Make no sudden moves until you know. Sentient chairs bond to one person only."

Eleanora blinked at the chair. It sent her a cat-like growl and backed away with a clicking noise and skittered out of sight.

"S-sentient?" she breathed, dizzied now by the implications.

"Ah-oo-gah!" Her phone klaxoned.

"Oh, I am *so* sorry." Confused, she pulled out her phone. "Stupid thing! I put it on 'buzz'. I don't know *how* it rang."

"Mobiles don't usually work in here at all, be they on 'buzz' or not," Mr. Nemo murmured, looking bemused. "Now yours has. Go ahead, I don't mind, it must be important."

She nodded and turned on her earpiece. This was the executive editor of one of the small presses she worked for.

"Hi, Robert? Sorry, I can't talk to you long; I'm out of country. Okay, I know your guy's book on Verne is due before Christmas. You do know I can edit anywhere in the world, right? Yeah, why am I not surprised he's balking at my suggestions. Listen, just tell him I found this amazing shop and I'm looking at an actual Jules Verne first edition right now."

Eleanora smacked her forehead. "No, I am not lying. Ok, forget about my suggestions. I'll line edit and deal with his additions this week, I promise. Yeesh!" She ended the call and turned her phone off.

She caught Mr. Nemo's sympathetic look and the amused tightening of his narrow lips. "Can I do anything to help you gain a little extra time?" he asked.

Now what a strange thing to say. Way more than the usual, 'Can I help you?'

Nonetheless she played along. "I doubt you can alter time, Mr. Nemo, but I'd be pleased if you could show me every blessed thing you have in here that's connected with Mr. Verne. I think I came to the right place for inspiration, don't you?"

Mr. Nemo regarded her with a sudden sparkle of interest. "Why not start here then, shall we?" He nodded at *Embrace of the Planets*. "As far as I know this is the only copy of Verne's private theories of the universe, in his own hand, bound into one volume."

"*Jules Verne* wrote this?" Eleanora breathed, wanting desperately to touch what looked like the softest calfskin.

"He did," said Mr. Nemo. "*Embrace of the Planets* is a brilliant compendium of Verne's theories of the universe, bound in 1886 by his longtime publisher, Pierre-Jules Hetzel. There were fears among a secret scientific body that humanity would advance too fast, would discover too much, even discover their existence should Verne bring *Embrace* to the public at large. In desperation they hired a young man among their number to shoot Verne and steal the book. He got the book, but only wounded his target."

"The crazy nephew? Gaston?" Eleanora interrupted him.

Mr. Nemo went a bit red. "Yes. Gaston. Historical records say he was committed to an asylum—not true. Gaston vanished from the public eye back to the Council of Worlds, bringing with him the only copy of *Embrace* in existence."

"Really? The Council of Worlds?" she replied, amused and distracted by the allure of the book.

"Yes. The Council liked *Embrace* so much, it became a kind of bible to them. They rewarded Gaston by promoting him within the Council. Meanwhile, after the death of Hetzel that same year, Jules Verne's visions turned darker, more wary about the dangers of science and technology. The Council's aim was achieved, the danger of too much knowledge averted. The works of Jules Verne are now lauded for the sense of wonder they provoke."

Mr. Nemo winked at her. "Conspiracy or fact?"

She laughed at his whimsy. "Might I touch this or does it bite too?"

He chuckled back at her. "Go ahead, Miss....?"

"Watson. Eleanora." She stroked the embossed gold writing on the huge cover. "Wow," was all she could manage. She thought again about what she'd seen after she'd died. That too could brand her as crazy. "And how did you—?"

"So, what brings you here?" he said at the same time.

She laughed. "Oh, I've been trying to get into your store for a long time. Is your name *really* Nemo?"

"No." He grinned. "My real name vanished a long time ago. I have a lot of Verne memorabilia in here, so the nickname stuck. You've been asking about me? Why?"

"About the store. It's intriguing both outside and in. I love that quirky sign of yours, and I love the fact that you don't appear to care that your shop is right in the middle of a rather self-complacent Main Street. It's exactly the kind of place I would own," (and never leave, she wanted to add), "if I had the bucks to put together an inventory like this one. Just, Wow!"

He looked around with a wistful pleasure. "Yes, it is rather 'wow' isn't it? Like an old friend who never fails to surprise you? A little wearing after such a long time, though. No chance to really see the world with such a yoke about my neck, but nevertheless. Tell me more about yourself, my dear."

Eleanora looked toward that second room she still wanted to check out. It had to be well past eight o'clock by now. "Oh, but really—"

Mr. Nemo tucked his beloved first edition of *'Le Tour de Monde'* out of sight and shook his pointed head. "I tell you what. I so rarely get a kindred spirit in here. May I make you some tea? I have scones as well and I found some lovely clotted cream at the British Shop a few doors down."

Eleanora thought about the files waiting on her phone. She thought about the fact that she was disabled and alone with a stranger—albeit a very old and equally disabled one. At the fierce look from those deep-set eyes of his, a bizarre image flashed through Eleanora's mind of old Mr. Nemo and her lashing out at each other with crutches and maybe a borrowed saber or two.

She laughed. "Alright, sure. I love clotted cream. Ten thousand calories in every bite, but I don't care."

"Lovely! My kitchen is in the back of my work room. While we take a break, might you lock the front door and turn the sign for me, please?"

"Of course," she agreed.

After doing so, Eleanora couldn't help snooping a bit on her way to the kitchen. She heard Mr. Nemo humming and the whistle of his teakettle. She studied the contents of several lighted display cases. These held everything from stone age tools to what appeared to be Greek and Roman coinage and some Spanish pieces of eight.

Just beyond the tied-back green velvet curtains that marked the division between the display room and the 'work room' was a sturdy fix-it-bench complete with a side vise and labelled drawers with brass cup-pulls. The smell of machine oil, metal polish, and sealing wax teased at her nose. Five deep drawers were half-open, sectioned off to hold a variety of vacuum tubes. A pile of what appeared to be oddments of rusty armor lay heaped upon the bench's pitted top, along with a pair of leather aviator's goggles, a pith helmet, and two long scythe blades.

She edged past three wooden crates on the floor containing switches, resistors, relays, and transistors to stare upward in awe at the spherical structure she'd spotted from the front of the store. Here was a pristine and polished Victorian diving bell and beside it the steam-powered equipment needed to pump air to a diver walking a sea floor fathoms deep. The whirring hum she'd heard earlier didn't come from the bell but from beyond it. Just next to the open kitchen door a wall of blinking lights and active vacuum tubes clicking and clacking. Ingenious. This might be the power source for the intense lighting in the main room. Or was it a computer like the Colossus, that World War II machine? Or cleaners, perhaps, to get rid of an old shop's dust and mold?

"I know you want to see everything my dear, but let's have tea first, shall we?" called Mr. Nemo.

"The tea smells delicious," she said, joining him in the kitchen.

As in the front room, a cut-glass chandelier lit the table. Though tiny and windowless, this meticulous kitchen might have come straight out of the French countryside. Black-and-white checked tiles. A tall armoire. A blue gingham curtain covered the waste area beneath the deep farm sink. A mid-century white wood table held two dainty spindle chairs. Bone-handled knives and silver spoons. The fat white teapot had a goose on it. Two delicate-looking teacups sat ready, alongside a two-tiered plate of scones and *pain au chocolat*.

"The tea flavors are honey, as well as ginger and lemon. Sweet. Tart and sour. Like me. Sit please," he said.

She obeyed with pleasure. It felt good to lay down her crutches.

Mr. Nemo brought out a small, blue-striped Cornishware pot of clotted cream from a tiny wooden icebox. He poured. They sipped tea and cozily nibbled scones-and-cream for a while. Eleanora couldn't remember when she'd felt so at ease. His unusual face had gone from 'strange' to 'filled with character.'

When asked again to tell him about herself, Eleanora did, to reveal what she'd never told another living soul before: How even before the accident she'd felt like some kind of changeling, born out of her own time and place, never fitting in. She told him about the accident, what it had felt like to die and see there was more after death, to be brought back to a body that didn't work right, and the aftermath. How she'd never have kids, about the black moods that demanded a retreat into complete invisibility, her fear of being called mad, and how she could never keep a job that required her to stay only in one place.

"I admire you for keeping up this place so long," she said. "How long have you actually been—er—*open* here in Port Millicent?"

He chuckled at her emphasis on the word 'open'.

"Oh, maybe twenty years? Before that I had a store down in Sedona, also called Trove. And before that I was in England—Totnes—another Trove. . . ."

"You moved all this stuff three times—between different nations, even?"

"More times than that, my dear. I was a lot younger then."

She tried to imagine Mr. Nemo as a young man and couldn't.

"May I show you something?" he said, quietly. "A treasure of mine I haven't needed to pull out in quite some while."

Eleanora grinned. "Please do. I'm ready for anything now that I'm full of tea and scones."

She watched him shamble to the sink, reach under its skirt, and pull out a mahogany box inlaid with mother-of-pearl. It looked like a traveler's kit, early Georgian in style. She expected to see dozens of silver-topped grooming items of the kind a rich gentleman's valet brought along on a carriage. Instead, Mr. Nemo took out a pistol and placed it on the table, closer to him than to her. A dueling piece, well handled, beautifully preserved.

"Oh, my," she breathed.

"This belonged to Gaston Verne. It's the one he used to shoot his uncle," said Mr. Nemo.

"Oh, my," she said again. A sudden worm of unease crawled into her belly.

"Not that accurate, but good enough at close range. I do get people trying to break in at times."

"You'd shoot somebody with that?" she quavered.

He looked at her. He smiled with a certain sly manner. "Wouldn't you? Given what you've seen?"

The question and the avid look in those little black eyes creeped her out. It wasn't what she'd seen, but what she *hadn't* seen. The pistol and something more: a glimpse of the impossible and it terrified her.

"Ummm, you know, I should really go, Mr. Nemo," she said, reaching for her crutches.

Eleanora pushed herself up.

"Oh, please, Eleanora, don't," he cried. "I've frightened you; I see that. I haven't had a chance to tell you anything about the shop—do you know what *ley lines* are?"

"Yes, and I wish such invisible lines of energy existed right now. I could use them, 'cause I don't feel well," she said. There was pain now. In her legs, her back, her head. She had a doozy of a migraine coming on and a four-block walk back to the Strathcona Hotel.

Mr. Nemo gave her a curt nod. He watched her check the time. It was half-past past ten. The festivities would long be finished by now. Main Street would be a tomb.

Eleanora took a deep breath. Tried to slow her pounding heart. She reached into her pocket for a pain-killer and swallowed it dry—the pill should work well enough in the tea she'd drunk earlier.

"Eleanora…."

"No, really, I'll come back, I promise," she lied.

Don't let him see your panic.

Starbursts of pain behind her eyes caused her to stagger past the big diving bell. The strident lighting in the front room brought on the migraine. The unusual skeleton felt like a threatening entity guarding the door. Mr. Nemo was coming after her! She heard the fast scrape of his slippers. Did he still have that pistol with him?

"You turned the sign!" he cried. "Don't go out there, Eleanora!"

She unlocked the door, tugged it open, and froze at the deafening roar. This was *not* port Millicent! The morning air stank of soot and blood. An icy draft shivered her up in her light summer dress. Peasants filled the square, all shouting in French, loud and coarse. Women in mobcaps and long skirts, scarves around their shoulders, *sans-culotte, or lower class,* men in long baggy pants, their bare feet filthy. In the middle of the crowd stood a wooden platform topped with a guillotine.

Before the shriek came out of her mouth, she was yanked back inside. Back into sanctuary. Back within the blue church door. Then she *did* shriek, and Mr. Nemo let her. He was holding his pistol but not to shoot her.

"You're all right. I promise you. Just breathe and let me explain."

He led her to a narrow bishop's pew. She sat, all a whirl, still seeing the rise of that bloody blade, and the roars of glee from the hoard as it fell. Imagination filled in the rest. She'd read Verne's *Flight to France* and *The Count of Chanteleine* and of course Dickens' *A Tale of Two Cities.*

"I was really there in the French Revolution! How is that even possible?"

"The sign on the door read 'Closed'," said Mr. Nemo. "You turned it for me, remember? Closing Trove is a message for the Council of Worlds that I'm available to go where they want me to go, and when. They are not of this world, Eleanora, and many of them have lived for millennia. By their power we can move through time, through space, through galaxies. Though its many outer facades remain anchored in their eras and locations, Trove's interior moves between them."

"That wall of lights! Is that its purpose?" said Eleanora.

"The Wall and the ley lines help move us, yes. This world is constructed with lines laid down by the Council of Worlds. Here the enlightened built their temples to knowledge and power. I was told to open today in Port Millicent to make a new acquisition. One does not just come in or go out of Trove at a whim, Eleanora. Thanks be to the Council of Worlds, I reached you in time. You opened the door without leave; if you did so again, who knows where the other side of my door might be? If you'd stepped out completely tonight, with the sign turned to 'closed', you would have been lost in the French Revolution."

Eleanora wheezed and covered her face. She felt the warmth of his palm on her shoulder.

"You'll get used to this, my dear. I didn't think teleportation existed either, not until the Council of Worlds plucked me out of my time period and put me in charge of Trove. This storehouse is the very essence of the word 'discovery'. The Council of Worlds sends me everywhere in the cosmos, to conserve, study, document, and guard what I find. Lovelies like this. He stroked the silky arm of the sentient chair now pressed to his leg and it shuddered, lifted its arm, and hugged him around the hips!

"The wonder is that Uncle Jules imagined sentient furniture and mentioned them as a future technology in *Embrace of the Planets,* never knowing they already existed on another planet."

Eleanora needed time to digest what she'd just heard, but there was one question that needed an answer immediately. "How do we get back to Port Millicent?"

"We already are. I turn the sign to 'open' when told to, as I did to admit you tonight. I've been given the Trove in Port Millicent. I don't leave

Port Millicent unless I'm sent elsewhere to receive something new. I go out when I choose, as long as I lock Trove's door behind me—I've made some friends."

"Like me?" she snarked.

Mr. Nemo sat down on the sentient chair. It started to purr.

"Oh, especially like you," he replied. "I've been wanting a Verne scholar like you for a very long time. Over a century. As soon as your phone went off, I knew the Council had answered my request. When you spoke of your project, I was close to certain. We had tea and then, in my haste I frightened you! My fault. I'm getting old, Eleanora, and I need an apprentice. There are advantages to living in a shop that can leap through space and time. It will be much easier with an apprentice like you to attend my door and take in artifacts."

A strange excitement mingled with terror flooded Eleanora at the thought of living here, going from world to world in a journey through the impossible.

Oh, my giddy Maiden Aunt!

He'd called Jules Verne his uncle! Mr. Nemo was over a century old! A shop that could teleport!

"I know there's a lot here to assimilate," he continued. "I can give you time to do that." He gestured at *Embrace of the Planets*. "You will have to place your hand on the book at the outset, of course, but your acceptance won't be onerous. You can come and go as you want back into Port Millicent, as long as you obey the rules laid out by the Council of Worlds. You can work from here as if it were your own apartment. You can see the world—see worlds—perhaps those you saw beyond the Veil. There are ways of avoiding incidents like you just faced. The Council of Worlds is concerned with preservation and that includes their conservationists. They don't want one of their Troves floating around unmanned—or unwomaned."

"There are others?" she said.

He nodded.

"Do you ever sell anything?"

He nodded again. "There are rules of barter. You'll learn."

"Why me?" she said now.

"Because you were dead and revived. You've seen beyond the possible and you understand the impossible. You know Uncle Jules in a way that will let you read and understand the mysteries there in his hidden work."

"There's a catch, isn't there?" she said, looking at Gaston's strange elongated face. Not quite human anymore, she decided.

"Yes, there's a catch. Neither I nor the Council of Worlds will let you leave. I'm sorry, Eleanora. He pointed the pistol at her. "At this range, I cannot miss."

"No. Please, don't shoot!" she cringed and squeaked. "I agree! I agree!"

He lowered the pistol and shook his head. "I'm sorry, it's not loaded and even if it were, I could never shoot an apprentice so promising. Any manager or apprentice within Trove must accept the need to shoot someone should they attempt to access Trove's time/space controls. Your world is not yet ready for the truth."

Eleanora shivered. Not with fear now, but with presentment and delight. *Given access to both time and space?*

Oh yes. Now she knew why she'd not spoken about her experiences after her death. Here was discovery of the impossible suddenly made possible. She *did* never want to leave. An icy shiver of bliss rose through her as a doorway opened into a life now transcending her every expectation and limitation.

She wanted to laugh and shout and cry all at the same time. Neither agents nor crutches would define her life here. "So, I have a choice of not belonging anywhere or the chance to *live* in the worlds of Jules Verne with Gaston Verne as my mentor?"

"Yes, but to anyone in Port Millicent or elsewhere, I am Mr. Nemo," he corrected her. The sentient chair purred louder.

"I agree! To Atlantis and back, say I! I guess you're going to have to show me how to use a gun, Gaston."

Then she smacked her palm onto the butter-soft leather of the great tome Jules Verne himself had penned.

Rust and Smoke

Demetri Capetanopoulos

"Rune!" Erik called out for the third time.

This elicited a reluctant stomp across the floorboards above his head followed by a pronounced tramp down the creaky stairs, bringing his son to the kitchen. Ignoring the drama, Erik asked enthusiastically, "Ready to go?"

From under an unkempt mass of curly blonde hair, Rune cast a critical eye on the lunch preparations and shrugged. His father hefted an old steel box onto the counter and began to pack their lunch into it. At this, Rune rolled his eyes. "Why do you still use that old thing?"

"It floats," was Erik's cheerful defense.

The teenager let out an exasperated breath. "Dad, it goes *in* the boat. It's not like we tow it behind."

With that Rune stepped out of the room to grab his jacket, which he began stuffing into a backpack. "Besides, it's like a hundred years old."

"Maybe older," his dad said with a smirk that earned him an icy stare from Rune's sapphire blue eyes.

It was true the ancient box was a bit bulky and sported a worn patina flecked with rust no teenager would ever consider cool. But it had been superbly made with a curious, sealed, double wall that made it buoyant even when loaded down with supplies and lunch. It had served as his father's tackle box, and the frugality of continuing to get use out of it appealed to him. By replacing the long-corroded latch springs and installing a new rubber seal, he had made it airtight once again.

Seeing his son shoulder his pack and head for the door, Erik called after him. He softened his tone in an appeal to break through the teenage derision that had lately become the norm. "Grab that chart on the table. I thought we'd explore someplace new today."

His son paused and let slip a look of interest over his shoulder. Erik hefted the lunch trunk and joined him at the door.

The air outside was clear and crisp with the sharp smell of drying fish on the breeze.

"You can smell the money," Erik announced to no one in particular as he closed the white door of their bright red house. It was the age-old local expression that served to excuse the pungent aroma that violated the otherwise breathtaking beauty of a rugged landscape whose grey rocky slopes tumbled toward the life-giving sea. In another week or two, uncounted thousands of stockfish would be taken down from the racks, or *hjell*, that covered the hills every year from February to May. They would be brought indoors for two more months to complete the natural, unsalted drying process. Then the precious harvest would be surrendered to the graders to be sorted and sold. And in that transaction, the fate of the village for another year would be determined. Rune just wrinkled his nose.

Though they both wore traditional, bird's-eye, wool sweaters against the chill, the late May morning was already hinting at warmer days ahead. By the end of the week, the sun would rise and not set again for two months. Erik felt like time itself had been suspended as the community paused to catch its breath. The frenzied work of cod season had wrapped up and the summer tourist rush had not yet begun. Both activities centered around boats, which kept him busy with repairs in the village marina. Getting there required a ten-minute walk down a rough but green hillside dotted with small, wood, clapboard houses sprightly painted in red, yellow, or white, a bygone hierarchical telltale of one's prosperity.

Rune stayed ahead of him on the path and his father marveled at how tall the boy was already at thirteen. *Just like his grandfather*, he thought. Erik's father had been a Lofoten fisherman like his father before him. Though Erik considered himself primarily a boat builder and mechanic, from the end of January to the beginning of April he was a cod fisherman like every other able-bodied Lofoten man had been for generations. But as he watched Rune slip his ear buds in to listen to whatever was playing on his phone, he wondered if the tradition would continue.

At the dock Erik handed the box with their lunch down to Rune in the boat and then went forward to untie the line, his eyes affectionately following the smooth curve of her gunwale as it swept up to the stempost. She was a classic Nordlands boat, just over seven meters long, with the nearly symmetrical high prow and stern, shallow keel, and clinker construction that could trace its pedigree to Viking ships that had plied these waters a thousand years earlier. Erik had built the boat in his youth, alongside his father, who had taught him the time-honored techniques of joining the overlapping planks that formed her sides. Like most such boats, she was constructed of pine, a lightweight wood that made it a simple task to pull the vessel up on shore. But it lacked durability and Erik had so often repaired the boat that he wondered whether any part of it was still original. At the center of the craft rose a short mast equipped with a single yardarm that could be raised to set the large square sail. More modern boats often sported a lug rig, but Erik preferred remaining true to tradition. As he stepped aboard, line in hand, Rune moved to take a place in the bow. His father nudged him and pointed to the tiller. "I think it's time you took command. What do you say?"

For the first time that day, a smile appeared on Rune's face and his eyes brightened. "Really?" he asked.

"Absolutely. Let's head south along the coast. There's someplace I want to show you."

And with that, he settled himself onto a thwart with the air of a passenger.

They rowed at first, to clear the cluster of boats in the tranquil harbor. The water was so placid and deep that it gave the appearance of spilled ink, with every dip of the oars disturbing an otherwise perfect reflection of the surrounding mountains. But as they cleared the rocky headland, they caught the breeze and Rune hoisted the sail. A little farther offshore, the wind from the northeast was blowing steady enough to occasionally flick spray from the whitecaps, so they made a quick downwind passage along Moskenesøya's inner coast. The island was almost entirely grey bedrock that soared near vertically to a succession of peaks over a thousand meters high, forming a formidable barrier to the fury of Atlantic storms. The lower reaches of these ancient slopes were colored emerald green by tenacious lichens and grasses. Here and there, small colorful houses clung to the hillside or perched on stilts over the jumble where stone met the sea. The grandeur of the landscape made their progress feel slow despite the steadiness of the wind. But in just under an hour, they came abeam of land's end and Erik smiled as Rune skillfully brought the bow to a more westerly heading and adjusted sail.

"So, where are we headed?" his son finally asked.

In English, Erik replied, "I thought we'd go to Hell," deliberately mispronouncing the name. Then switching back to Norwegian, "Well, *Helle*, actually."

Rune's good spirits had apparently freshened with the breeze, for breaking into a wide grin he pointed to port and declared, "Well, if we're bound for hell, perhaps we ought to steer for the eye of the Moskstraumen!"

Already the seas had become choppier and confused as they entered the area where strong tidal currents collided with geography both above the surface and below. The result was one of the strongest whirlpool formations on the planet. Swirling eddies were producing their own ripples, some nearly a meter high, that clashed with the wind-driven waves. Though not truly dangerous, the maelstrom demanded careful attention to the helm, not to mention a strong stomach.

With a quick check to ensure Rune remained focused, Erik said theatrically, "Ah the maelstrom! Swallower of ships and the agent of Captain Nemo's doom! Take care, Captain Rune, that you don't suffer the same fate as the *Nautilus* in these waters!"

The wind snatched the short laugh of annoyance off Rune's lips, "Give me a break, Dad. I doubt that whirlpool could sink this boat, much less a submarine – totally unbelievable end to that story."

Erik felt a pang of regret that he had overplayed the moment. Negotiating the turbulent moods of a teenager was proving to be trickier navigation than even the maelstrom required. But the day remained glorious, and after another ten minutes and a change in course to the northwest, their destination came into view.

Here the primeval rock that formed the coast met the Norwegian Sea in a series of fingerlike projections, only tenuously attached to the mainland. On this side of the mountains, the land was uninhabited and inaccessible by road. Gradually, one of the fjords revealed itself as the inlet to a kilometer-wide bay. Turning to the northeast, they glided silently between stone sentinels that loomed over the entrance to Bugåven Bay. Patches of turquoise betrayed the shallows in the otherwise slate-blue waters of the bay that was encircled by mountains as if caught in the claw of a hand. Once in their lee, the wind died and they returned to the oars, making for a rocky beach opposite the entrance perhaps five hundred meters distant.

Rune jumped from the boat when he heard the soft crunch of its keel touching bottom and scrambled up the shore with a line in hand. Moments later his father joined him, wrapped an arm around his shoulder, and declared, "Congratulations, Captain, welcome to *Helle*!"

Rune's eyes dropped from the jagged peaks that surrounded them to survey the limited expanse of open ground that edged the bay. The terrain was randomly strewn with boulders covered with moss and lichen that was ubiquitous in Moskenesøya. Tall grasses were interspersed among the rocks wherever there was sufficient soil for them to gain a foothold.

"What's so special about this place?" Rune asked.

Wading back from the boat with their lunch box, his father replied, "There used to be a fishing village here."

"Here?" said Rune, his eyes searching the shore with renewed interest.

His father perched the box on a few rocks. "Yes. In fact, your grandfather was born here."

Rune squinted at him, "But there's nothing here. What happened?"

"After the war, the government convinced people to give up living in these little outer coast villages. Your grandfather moved over the mountain in 1950 and this place was abandoned. Even back then there wasn't that much here. Pretty much nothing left now, I'm afraid."

"Pretty much?" Rune asked, gesturing to the empty landscape.

His father smiled. "Oh, if you hunt through the grass and stare at the rocks long enough you can see the remnants of some stone foundations I suppose. It's been a long time since I was last here."

Rune's eyes widened with the lure of adventure and he was soon lost to sight amid the endless jumble of rocks. Erik selected one that made a convenient seat and ran his hand over the cover of their lunch box. His fingers registered the precision of the seams, which so impressed his sense of craft, and the rough patch in the center of the lid where surface rust had nearly obliterated an elegantly engraved letter "N." Their family name was Nilsen and Erik had always wondered where his father or his grandfather could have had such work done. *Certainly not here*, he thought with a smile as he gazed around the bay trying to imagine the world of his ancestors.

January, 1870

Ribbons of green glowing light writhed across the dark sky over the bay. On the rocky shore stood a man, a silhouette, save for the glowing tip of his crudely rolled cigar. With a deep inhale, the pinpoint embers blossomed as if threatening to burst into flame, and then subsided. A large, rough hand withdrew the cigar as he exhaled and then waved the lit end under his nose.

Strange, he thought.

There was a sound of scattering rocks behind him and he knew that would be his brother-in-law, Bjørn. The voice came to him out of the darkness. "Good morning, Lars."

Without bothering to turn he said, "Morning."

Bjørn continued without pause, "Well, are you ready to see if the cod have returned yet? It's certain, we'll be the first ones out on the water this season."

Lars glanced back but the few houses scattered along the shore showed no sign yet of light or life. He nodded, the glow of his cigar marking the up and down motion of his head. Since the government restrictions had been lifted a dozen years ago, fishermen were free to fish wherever and with whatever tackle they desired. But it was usually the case that until a pioneering few reported the return of the cod, there was little about being at sea in January to compel most of them to take to the boats. But Lars had always been in the vanguard, if only because he found comfort in returning to the rhythm of fishing. Now, without the need for a word, the two fishermen moved toward a nearby wooden boat drawn partially up on the beach. Bjørn set the items he had been carrying into the boat and both men leaned their shoulders into the bow. As it began to float, Lars clambered aboard with a practiced habit that defied his age.

Bjørn, though younger, was a little heavier and not quite as tall, and came over the gunwale with a huff. "Okay, well, I have to confess that was easier than moving that iron boat!" he exclaimed.

At this, Lars couldn't help a wry smile. Last season, his brother-in-law had fished with that iron skiff. Few others in the village would have been tempted to buck tradition at all. But although strong and seemingly unsinkable, the metal boat had also proved foolishly heavy to haul out. At the end of the season, Bjørn had persuaded most of the men in the village to help him drag the boat inland and place it, inverted, on top of a stone enclosure he had prepared, forming a handy storage cellar until next season. There had been less enthusiasm about moving it back to the water, and so it was still there, an odd but useful space for Bjørn's growing family to use. At length, Lars simply replied, "*Ja*."

This early in January the sun would be some hours in making its appearance. In the twilight, the men moved about their tasks smoothly, familiar routines returning once again. As Lars steered, Bjørn filled the silence of the landscape that they sailed through.

"I don't even know if I'll put that iron boat in the water this year. Besides, the wife has gotten used to the extra storage space." He paused for a moment and then said, "Where do you suppose those fellows got that thing?"

Lars shrugged and said, "Dunno."

It had been a singularly odd event. On June 22, two years ago, heavy seas and strong winds had delayed the return of several boats back to the village. Nearing midnight, with the sun still well above the horizon, they were a couple of miles south of the inlet to the bay when they caught sight of a strange craft with one man attempting to row clear of the chaotic waters of the maelstrom. As they drew closer, they discovered there were two others in the boat, one of whom had been knocked unconscious. The three were oddly dressed, had no supplies, and understood not a word of Norwegian.

Lars and the other fishermen assisted the men in getting their skiff into the sheltered waters of Helle where Bjørn and his wife had taken them in and attended to their injuries. Their guests had attempted to communicate in several languages, but it proved futile, and despite a week of animated hand gestures, they could learn precious little about the castaways. The tall one had the mark of a seaman and made himself useful in the village, but as the other two recovered their health they chatted incessantly in some foreign tongue and seemed unable to resist picking up and examining everything within reach. Since the telegraph station in Sørvågen closed each April at the end of cod season, Bjørn had ended up sailing the three men all the way up the inner coast to Henningsvaer to catch one of the coastal steamers south toward Bergen. In gratitude, the strangers had made a gift to Bjørn of their impressive, but unusual, iron boat.

Bjørn now squatted in their wooden boat, his legs automatically adjusting for the swell, as he checked the bait barrel. With a wide grin he held up one of the herring. "Once we would have considered ourselves lucky to have enough of these for dinner, now we are so spoiled we use them as bait. Good times indeed, eh Lars?"

For the last several years, never-before-seen quantities of herring had appeared in their waters late in the fall. The vast migrations had ignited a second fishing frenzy to their year and were bringing unheard of wealth and development to the Nordland. Lars gripped the tiller, squinted against the salt spray unseen in the twilight, and nodded, "*Ja*."

They had reached the open sea and Lars saw Bjørn turn his back to the biting wind as he began preparing their hand lines. He watched him methodically check the stone weight affixed to the end of each of the lines. These hundred-foot cotton lines were wound on simple wooden reels to make for easy handling. Then Lars saw Bjørn glancing around the boat, his brow furrowed.

"Where is it?" Bjørn asked, referring to the bucket that normally held the hooks on short leads that would be attached to the lines.

Lars nudged a metal box with his foot and said, "There."

Bjørn cast him a quizzical look and bent to inspect the box. It measured half an alen square at the ends and just about one alen long.[1] There were handles built into each end which he used to place the box at his feet.

"Where did you get this?" he asked.

"Found it." said Lars, fishing a cigar from his pocket.

Running his hand over the lid, Bjørn detected a rough pattern in the otherwise smooth finish. His nose hovered over the box as he tried to make out the elaborate engraving on the lid. "Found it? This looks like a heck of a thing for someone to lose." Lars let him fumble with the intricate latches while he carefully lit his cigar. Never before had he allowed flame of any sort in his boat but these latest cigars he had made had an exotic flavor that he found fascinating, although he was as yet undecided about whether he actually preferred them.

---

1. The alen was a unit of measure used in Norway prior to the adoption of the metric system in 1875. One alen equals 62.7 cm or 24.7 inches, so the box is about one foot square and two feet long.

The lid popped open and Bjørn's face registered surprise. The interior cavity was rather smaller than the outside dimensions suggested. He pressed on the India rubber seal that ran around the rim and grasped the wall of the box to gage its unusual thickness.

"Obviously made with great care." He said, the respect evident in his voice. "Where did you find it?"

At this Lars took a deep draw on his cigar and reluctantly pulled it from his mouth. As he exhaled, he straightened up as if preparing for great effort. "A couple of weeks after you took those strangers to Henningsvaer, I found it floating in the shallows north of the inlet to our bay."

With that, Lars relaxed his shoulders and reinserted the cigar.

Bjørn paused in his exploration of the box and looked up at Lars. "This thing, floating? Do you mean wedged in the rocks? Washed up on shore?"

Lars locked his eyes on Bjørn and with the cigar still clamped in his mouth said firmly, "Floating."

Bjørn turned his attention once again to the box. He tapped the inner and outer walls and said, "hollow."

Then he pressed a finger into the cork that was carefully fitted to the inner compartment of the box. "Do you think it fell off a steamer?"

"Dunno," said Lars. He slacked his line and reached up to strike the sail. "Time to fish."

"Dad!"

The voice brought Erik's thoughts back to the present.

"Dad, you've got to come check this out!"

Rune's voice had an excited tone that Erik hadn't heard in a while. He got up from the rock and turned to see Rune bounding toward him from further inland.

"I found some ruins!"

Rune waited for his father to join him and then led the way among the rocks back into taller grass. "See, it looks like the foundation of an old house that had a metal roof."

That sounded odd to Erik and he stepped through the grass to see what Rune was pointing at. Piles of stones that looked like they might have once been stacked to form a low wall ran in two lines set at a right angle. The ancient, rusted remains of a metal structure had collapsed on top of the rocks and disappeared into the grass and decomposed rock at the far end. It struck him as overly complex for a roof. What panels remained were curved and it was clear that they had been expertly joined with butted seams and countersunk rivets. No one would build a roof this way, Erik thought. In many places the metal had rusted to paper thinness and was riddled with holes large and small. But there were a few places where Erik guessed that the original thickness must have been well over an inch. Suddenly, its form became clear.

"Rune, it's a boat! See, it's inverted, and the aft part of the hull has collapsed inward and rusted away."

From underneath the heap came a hollow banging and Rune's muffled voice, "It's like there was some sort of tank in the bow."

"Maybe a buoyancy chamber." Erik offered. He paced off the steel skeleton and estimated the boat had been perhaps eight meters long and at least two meters in breadth.

Rune reappeared and asked, "How do you think it got here?"

Erik thought for a moment. "Well, I'd say that someone decided it would make a better shelter than a boat so inverted it to form a roof." He gazed back toward the water to imagine the effort it had involved. "How it came to Helle, I have no idea. Or when."

A half hour later they had returned to the shore having exhausted their exploration of the boat, though Rune continued to concoct theories about its origins.

"Maybe it's left over from the war," he hypothesized with some enthusiasm.

"Well, maybe" said Erik, popping the lid on their lunch. "There was a raid here on Moskenesoya in '41."

Rune perked up, "There was? Where?"

His father nodded thoughtfully, "Yes, at Reines."

"What happened?" Rune pressed; his blue eyes wide.

Erik handed a sandwich to his son. "British commandos landed and blew up the wireless transmission tower in Sørvågen."

Rune jumped on the idea, "Well perhaps some surplus equipment found its way to Helle."

To Erik it seemed like the most plausible explanation. The boat would have been a valuable resource to a simple fishing community like Helle during the war, and in the years that followed until the village was abandoned. But as he turned the idea over in his mind, something nagged at him. The boat just didn't look like a landing craft or anything commandos would use. It had the lines of a classic whaleboat, but its construction seemed excessively stout. Even as rusted as the boat was, there was sophistication evident in its metalwork… and yet it felt like something from a much earlier age.

Rune laughed as he lifted the lid to retrieve a drink. "Can you imagine if commandos had tried landing at Helle instead, and ran into the maelstrom? That's one way to keep out unwanted visitors I guess."

And then it clicked. To reel in his son, Erik drew out his words, "I can think of one story that mentions an iron boat appearing in a Lofoten fishing village from out of the maelstrom."

Rune looked up, his eyes wide, "You can?" Then just as quickly, his countenance slumped and his voice took a hard edge, "Aw, come on, Dad, not that again. Be serious. That Verne story was totally unbelievable. Fiction, remember?"

Erik couldn't help poking at his son's pragmatism just a little, "I don't know," he said mysteriously, "lots of old tales often contain a nugget of truth."

Rune gave him a look intended to end further discussion and the two fell silent. Rune wolfed down his lunch and began to fidget while waiting for his dad to finish. Erik was in no hurry. With nothing else at hand, Rune started flipping the latches of the box and then examining the lid. At some point he stopped flipping and tipped the lid to better catch the light. "Hey Dad," he said, peering at the surface, "did you know there's something engraved on the lid?"

Erik washed down his sandwich and crumpled the paper wrapper in his hand. "Yes, the initial 'N.' but it's almost rusted away now."

"No, not on the outside. Something on the inside." replied Rune, still staring at the box.

At this, Erik got to his feet and leaned over his son's shoulder with interest. "Where?"

"Right here," said Rune, running his finger back and forth over the surface. "I can hardly even feel it."

Erik squinted where Rune was pointing but failed to discern anything. "I'm afraid these eyes aren't up to the task." Straightening up, he asked, "What's it say, Rune?"

"I'm not sure. It looks like parts of it are almost completely worn away. I think the first word is '*Mobile*' or '*Mobilis*' and then…." he paused, "the letters 'f', 'i', 'n', 'i'," he paused again, " it's either 'v' or 'u', then another 'i', and then what looks like a 't'. The last part is really hard to make out, but I think that's all there is." Turning to face his dad he added, "Does that make any sense?"

"Sounds like Latin," Erik offered.

Turning once again to peer at the engraving, Rune said, "Latin? What do you think it means?"

"I don't know, why don't you ask your phone?"

His son pulled out his phone. There was no hope for a signal here, but he had a translator app that he used sometimes to read tweets from abroad. His thumbs flew over the screen.

"Nothing matches exactly but it seems something like, 'movement has finished.'"

"Huh." said Erik, puzzled and a bit disappointed. He stepped away to untie the mooring line from where they had secured it, then returned, coiling the rope as he went. Rune hadn't moved. "We'd better pack up and start heading back."

"Dad!" Rune exclaimed, "Don't you remember? In the book. *Mobilis in Mobile* is his motto. Captain Nemo wrote his whole life story, and all he'd learned on his voyages, in multiple languages to be placed in an unsinkable container and tossed into the sea if the *Nautilus* were ever in danger of being lost."

Erik thought for a moment. "I guess I had forgotten that part of the story."

Rune, still spellbound, practically whispered, "Do you think this could be *that container*?"

Erik held his tongue for a minute, contemplating the wisdom of how best to respond. Then, breaking into a wide grin, he tousled Rune's hair and said, "Fiction. Remember?"

There was nothing Lars enjoyed quite so much after a long day at sea than a smoke by a warm fire. Its glow provided the only light in the small, low-ceilinged room; the corners lost to deep shadow. They had returned late, but Lars' wife had a hearty fish stew waiting. The creamy soup studded with what remained of their root vegetables had worked its restorative powers on the two fishermen and they had eaten with determination and in silence. Now with the simple wooden table cleared, Lars reached up to the one shelf in the small room to retrieve the Tiedemann tin containing his tobacco. Next to it was a neat stack of paper from which he drew two sheets off the top. He handed one to Bjørn and placed the tin between them. With great care he folded and creased the paper and then gently tore it to the correct size. As he reached for the tin, he noted Bjørn still turning the paper over in his hands.

"What kind of paper is this?" his brother-in-law inquired.

Lars opened the tin. "Dunno." He replied.

"It doesn't really feel like paper. Where'd you get it?" he asked with a touch of impatience.

Lars jabbed his thumb over his shoulder at the shelf. Bjørn rolled his eyes and opened his mouth to complain but then Lars continued, "It was in that box."

"You mean the metal box you found floating?"

"*Ja*," said Lars as he gently shook tobacco in a line onto the paper.

"This page is covered in writing."

"*Ja*," said Lars as he replaced the tin in the center of the table.

Bjørn leaned closer to the fire and squinted at the paper in his hand. After a minute of careful study, he gave voice to his thoughts, "What language is this?"

"Dunno," said Lars, flicking a few stray pieces of tobacco into line on the paper.

Bjørn appeared to not hear and turned his page over. He scrutinized the back side and declared, "It looks like there's more than one language here."

Lars was focused now on drawing the edge of the paper over the tobacco. "Four." he said, eyes fixed on his roll, "In total."

Bjørn straightened up once again in his chair and looked at Lars.

"All the pages are like this?" he asked, gently waving the sheet in his hand.

"Mostly." Lars replied, satisfied now with his roll, and lifting it to his tongue. "Some pages. . . ." he paused to lick the extended edge of his paper roll, "have lots of fish drawings." He ran a rough finger along the cigar to seal the edge and admired his handiwork. Then he turned his gaze at Bjørn. "I kept those."

Bjørn had a curious look on his face. "Don't you wonder what it might say or why it would be in such an elaborate box?"

Lars leaned toward the fire holding a matchstick. "*Nei*." After a moment, the match flared, and Lars withdrew.

At that, Bjørn gave a quick shake of his head, breaking his momentary trance. He glanced at the paper in his hand, then shrugged and reached for the tin.

Lars held the match to the end of the rolled paper, its writing barely visible. A flame danced on the tip, curling it back until it met the dried leaves inside. Lars drew deeply on the cigar and the embers flared, engulfing the end of the mysterious paper and the treasured tobacco it contained. For one intoxicating minute he closed his eyes as he slowly let out his breath. Then he brought the cigar to his nose. The aroma of tobacco was almost overshadowed by the exotic scent of the unusual paper.

Strange, he thought.

Gabriel at the Jules Verne Traveling Adventure Show

Joel Allegretti

A TAN GREATCOAT WITH a black collar. Brown high-top boots. Pomaded hair parted down the middle. A pencil mustache.

The stranger could have walked out of an illustration in a history book.

His left hand held a sheaf of flyers close to his breast, while the right waved one of them like a handkerchief as he sauntered through Gray Birch, New York, on a warm Saturday morning in June 1947.

"Come one, come all, come this evening to the Jules Verne Traveling Adventure Show," he called out with lung-bursting volume, a French accent adorning his English. Adults eyed him with amusement – they'd seen their share of carnival barkers over the years – and the children, all boys ranging in age from single-digit years to teenagers, followed and encircled him.

"What's your name?" a farm boy in overalls asked.

"You may call me Passepartout." The man spoke rapidly.

"Pass what?" somebody else asked.

"Passepartout," the man repeated. "Passe. Par. Tout."

A few tried to pronounce it and fumbled the guttural sound on the second syllable.

"Where are you from?" asked a boy wearing a tweed newsboy cap.

The stranger looked toward the east, over the roof of the hardware store, the steeple of Redeemer Presbyterian Church, and the treetops.

"I hail from thousands of miles across that watery expanse called the Atlantic Ocean. I am a son of Mother France, the glorious nation that gave us Rabelais, Louis *Quatorze*, Marie Antoinette, and Napoleon. However, I have come to your admirable country from England's capital city, fair London, where I, as manservant, am in the employ of Mr. Phileas Fogg, gentleman, intrepid adventurer, and distinguished member of the Reform Club, who in less than three months saw more of our astonishing world than the vast majority of men will see in their lifetimes."

"I'll say this for him," observed Paul Clark outside the post office. "He's very good." Sam and Artie, the Pearle twins, nodded in agreement. "I read *Around the World in Eighty Days* twice," Paul said.

"I read it once," said Sam.

"Ditto," said Artie. "We read it together."

Twenty-two years old, Paul, Sam, and Artie had served in the Second World War, Paul in the Army, and Sam and Artie in the Marines. While stationed in Paris for six months, Paul picked up a handful of conversational phrases, so he was able to order a glass of rosé and ask if anyone had seen a German soldier. Three years removed from the City of Light and nearly two years after the Allies' victory, he still remembered some of his limited vocabulary.

"I want to find out if that fellow's accent is on the level or if it's just part of his act."

Paul limped a few steps forward – a Purple Heart recipient, he had sustained a bullet wound in his left thigh – and cupped his hands around his mouth.

"Monsieur Passepartout, *comment ça va*?" His accent had more proximity to New England than to Nantes.

The stranger turned to the direction of the voice. He responded with a broad smile and yelled, "*Ça va! Merci beaucoup.*" He shouted something else. Paul threw up his hands to indicate he didn't understand anything beyond the basic pleasantries.

"Does that answer your question?" Artie asked.

"The kids seem to be enjoying him," said Sam. "Your cousin's over there, Paul."

"I see him," Paul said. "Hey, Gabe!" A thin, brown-haired, thirteen-year-old boy in white trousers and a yellow short-sleeve shirt looked Paul's way. Paul gestured for him to come.

"What's that guy giving out?" Paul asked. Gabriel handed him the printed sheet. Sam and Artie read over their friend's shoulders.

"Do you want to go to this thing tonight, Gabe?" Paul asked. "I'll take you if Uncle Lionel and Aunt Ellen are okay with it." They were the boy's parents.

"I want to go," said Gabriel.

"Ask your folks and call me on the phone. If they say yes, I'll drop by the house around six-thirty and drive you out there. It sounds like fun." Paul returned the circular to Gabriel. He laid a hand on his cousin's shoulder and gave it an affectionate squeeze.

"I'll see you tonight," said Gabriel, implying he wasn't concerned about getting his parents' permission. "Bye, Sam. Bye, Artie."

Gabriel folded the handbill in quarters and slipped it in his back pocket. He walked the half mile to his house. He saw his father planting rose bushes by the front steps. Lionel asked his son where he'd been. Gabriel pulled out the flyer and unfolded it. Lionel wiped his brow with his shirtsleeve.

"I heard that was going up. It's on the Brouwers' property. That's three miles outside of town."

"Paul said he'd take me. Can I go?"

"It's fine by me. Ask your mother."

"Thanks, Dad." Gabriel ran up the steps. The screen door banged shut. Lionel heard from inside the house, "Mom! Dad said I can go to the Jules Verne Show with Paul!"

Gabriel closed his bedroom door. He tossed the flyer on his desk and tried to smooth out the creases.

SATURDAY & MONDAY ONLY!!!
THE EXTRAORDINARY & INCOMPARABLE
JULES VERNE TRAVELING ADVENTURE SHOW!!!
See Capt. Nemo & the Crew of the Nautilus Battle a Giant Squid
Explore the North Pole with Capt. Hatteras
Take a Journey to the Center of the Earth with Prof. Lidenbrock
Meet Robur the Conqueror, the Master of the World

– JV –

The Village of Gray Birch, population 941, lay three hundred miles south of the border with Quebec. Founded in 1905 and named for that tree's abundance, it had boasted a higher number of residents before December 7, 1941. One-hundred twenty-six of Gray Birch's young men, who prior to their service in the U.S. armed forces hadn't traveled more than fifteen miles in any direction, gave up their blood and breath in the European theater. The courthouse dedicated an entire wall to their memory, the names of the heroes engraved on individual plaques that would hang as long as there was a Village of Gray Birch.

Among the dead was eighteen-year-old Donny Henderson, Gabriel's brother. Gabriel had just turned nine when the word arrived at the Henderson home. His father didn't cry, because men were supposed to be – expected to be – stoic in the presence of others, even when assaulted by tragic news. His mother cried, because mothers had permission to cry. Gabriel, even at his age, did his best to be strong for her.

On that painful day, Gabriel opened the door to his brother's bedroom. He sat on the bed and ran a hand over the bedspread. He sniffled and swallowed and wiped his eyes. He wished Donny had been closer in age to him, because then his brother would have been too young to go off to war.

Gabriel looked around the room, at the football on the chair by the window, at the pennant above the bed, at the harmonica on the night table. On the desk stood a framed photo of Kathy Haas, Donny's sweetheart. Her brother had fought in the same Army unit as Donny. He came home.

Gabriel saw a book next to Kathy's photo: *A Journey to the Centre of the Earth* by Jules Verne. How could he ignore such a dramatic title? He didn't even look twice at the different spelling of "center."[1] Gabriel took the book back to his room. He read three chapters that evening.

The story's German explorers – Professor Otto Lidenbrock and his nephew, Axel – travel to Iceland, where an extinct volcano contains a passage that takes them to the region promoted in the title. As he read, Gabriel imagined that an entrance to the subterranean realm of giant mushrooms and plesiosaurs lay somewhere in the Adirondack Mountains, unknown to anyone, awaiting discovery. He finished the novel within a week and wanted to read more by the man who had written it.

That Saturday morning, Gabriel walked the hundred yards from his home to the Gray Birch Public Library, which took up the first floor of a two-story house that dated back to 1863. On entering, he saw only one other person, the librarian, who sat at her desk writing. She raised her head when she heard the door close.

"Good morning, Gabriel."

"Good morning, Mrs. Loring. I'm looking for Jules Verne."

"Right over there under *V* in Fiction."

Gabriel cocked his head and scanned the spines. *Around the World in Eighty Days. Five Weeks in a Balloon. From the Earth to the Moon. The Mysterious Island. Twenty Thousand Leagues Under the Sea.* By the titles alone, Gabriel felt he had stumbled upon a world that existed alongside the one he inhabited, a world where if you wanted something to happen, all you had to say was "I want it to happen," and it would. He borrowed and read all five novels, one after another.

What struck Gabriel and Paul as they drove up to the site was the size of the Show. The Brouwers' land comprised four acres. The Show seemed to occupy two of them. It looked nothing like the second-rate carnivals that lumbered from town to town. If anything, it appeared to be closer to a professionally constructed film set that one would expect to see in Hollywood, not on the outskirts of an obscure collection of houses and family-owned businesses called Gray Birch. A string of semi-trailers –

1. At the time the story takes place, the latest English translation of the novel appeared in 1925 from Blackie & Son of Great Britain.

each bearing a logo that consisted of "Jules Verne Traveling Adventure Show" surrounding a portrait of the author – stretched along the perimeter of the property.

"It's like a mini-World's Fair," Paul said. He noticed a hot-air balloon, a submarine the U.S. Navy wouldn't have designed, and vehicles he could think of only as "contraptions."

"They built all that for only two days? And then they're going to take it down, go to their next destination, and build it again? I bet some of those guys fought with us in Normandy."

MOBILIS IN MOBILI

Triumphant in big, thick gold letters, the phrase ran across a white banner that hung over the entrance. Paul read it aloud.

"Why is that up there?" he asked.

"It's the motto of the *Nautilus*," Gabriel said.

"*Mobile in that which is mobile*. It describes us in the war."

"You know what those words mean?" a surprised Gabriel asked.

"I paid attention in Latin class."

A bearded man in old-fashioned garb collected the fifty-cent admission. Gabriel wondered if he was supposed to be the great Frenchman.

Gabriel dug his right hand into his trouser pocket.

"I got it, Gabe," said Paul. He gave the attendant two half-dollar coins.

"*Bon soir*," the bearded man said. "Enjoy yourselves."

"Are you Jules Verne?" Gabriel asked.

The man grinned. "There is only one Monsieur Verne, lad, and I am not he. I am Claudius Bombarnac of Bordeaux, whose name is the title of the novel from whence I came."

"Thanks, Mr. Claud—" Gabriel began, but stopped himself. He wasn't sure he'd heard the man correctly because of his heavy French accent.

"Thank you," said Paul.

Once they passed under the banner, Gabriel asked, "Who did he say he was?"

"I couldn't tell you. I wasn't listening."

"Paul!" a cheerful female voice called. Paul smiled and waved. "Hi, Audrey!"

Audrey Lachlan, who had graduated high school with Paul, ambled up to him while sipping from a paper straw in a bottle of cola. Brian, her brother and Gabriel's best friend, bounded up to the cousins.

"Hey, Gabe."

"Hey, Brian."

"I'm surprised to see you here, Audrey" Paul said. "This doesn't seem like something you'd go for."

"I wanted to stay home and listen to *The Dick Haymes Show* with Cynthia and Mary, but Brian badgered Mom and Dad about this. They told me I had to take him. Dad's picking us up at nine."

Paul looked at his watch. "It's ten after seven now."

"You see anything yet?" Gabe asked Brian.

"Nah, we just got here. Audrey wanted a soda, so we went to the snack bar. The guy there asked me if I wanted to try a squid's tentacle on a roll."

Gabriel's and Paul's faces registered disgust.

"Yuck," Gabriel said.

"You're joking, right?" Paul asked.

Brian sneered. "I'm not, but he was. It was a plain old hot dog with mustard drawn in circles to look like suction cups."

"Hey, Audrey, I have an idea," said Paul. "Why don't you and I go for a walk? Gabe and Brian can have their fun, and we'll all meet here right before your dad comes for you."

"I'd like that," Audrey said.

"Gabe, you and Brian can run off and go around the world in eighty minutes or from here to the moon. You have money?" Gabriel nodded. "Be back here at five to nine," said Paul.

"I don't have a watch."

Brian held up his left forearm. "I do."

"Let's go!" said Gabriel.

The boys' first stop was a room half the size of Gray Birch Junior High School's auditorium. Three of the walls, including the one with the doorless entry, were ten feet high, navy blue, and decorated with paintings of octopuses, seahorses, great white and hammerhead sharks, jellyfish that resembled flower blossoms, marlin, sea turtles, sea anemones, sperm whales, moray eels, starfish, swordfish, dolphins, stingrays, and manta rays.

The fourth wall was a pane of transparent glass, one panel of an enormous tank that contained hundreds of gallons of water.

The ceiling was a slack tarpaulin, also navy, that undulated like the surface of the ocean. The floor was the bare field.

Twenty or thirty wooden chairs faced the glass. Gabriel and Brian sat in the first row, in front of and alongside other boys, some of whom were friends from school; some they hadn't seen before. They guessed the latter lived in Woodbine, eight miles down the road. A few girls and a couple dozen fathers completed the audience. Those who didn't have a seat stood along the walls.

Seven men in diving suits, armed with spearguns, descended into the tank. The audience whooped and applauded as if on cue. A monogrammed *N* stood out on the front of each diver's helmet. Brian hadn't read *Twenty Thousand Leagues Under the Sea*, so Gabriel told him what it signified.

A giant squid made its appearance. Only its sinister tentacles were visible. To the children, they looked genuine, and the adults had to admit the effect represented an impressive feat of engineering.

"FIVE WEEKS" read the words on the balloon's wicker gondola. In actuality, the rides lasted only twenty minutes apiece, two per hour. Passengers ascended a hundred feet and then descended. The balloon remained tethered to the ground.

The gondola had room for five occupants, one of them being the pilot, who dressed like Abraham Lincoln and, with a refined British accent, introduced himself as Dr. Samuel Fergusson. Gabriel figured him to be as old as his father.

Gabriel enthused about going up. Brian, on the other hand, balked.

"Come on," Gabriel said. "How many chances do you get to say you looked down on the planet Earth?"

Their friend, Toby Van Dorn, sided with Gabriel. "Don't be a scaredy-cat, Brian," he said. "We'll be with you. So will my dad. Come on. Do it."

"You'll be okay," Mr. Van Dorn assured Brian.

The boy relented. He stayed in the center of the gondola by Toby's father and Dr. Fergusson, who said, "It can be rather unnerving the first time. It was for me." Gabriel and Toby, however, leaned over the side, pointed, and shouted to the people waiting in line for their turns, "We're the masters of the world!"

Gabriel gazed at the star-littered sky. Though a mere thirty-odd yards in the air, he and his companions were closer to the stars than anyone else from Gray Birch. He felt like Impey Barbicane in *From the Earth to the Moon*.

As soon as Gabriel, Brian, Toby, and Mr. Van Dorn returned to the ground and disembarked, Brian announced that he wanted to go up again.

"I guess your friend finally got a taste for space," Mr. Van Dorn said to Toby.

"The line's too long," Gabriel said. "Besides, we don't have time. There's lots of other stuff to see."

Toby said he'd go with them, but Mr. Van Dorn told his son, "It's getting late."

A disappointed Toby said goodbye to his friends. "I guess I'll see you at church tomorrow."

Brian groused about missing another balloon trip. Gabriel ignored him and suggested they board the *Albatross*, Robur the Conqueror's flying machine. He didn't know if the aircraft would lift off and therefore satisfy Brian, but it intrigued him because he knew Robur's name only from its appearance on the flyer Passepartout had given him. Both their attentions, however, were diverted by a group of boys clamoring for autographs from one of the Show's characters.

"I'm getting Captain Nemo's autograph," Gabriel said. He found a stray flyer and added himself to the cluster. Brian followed.

"Watch me get his attention," Gabriel told his friend. He exclaimed, "Prince Dakkar!"

The white-bearded ruler of the *Nautilus* raised his eyebrows. "Who said that?"

Gabriel raised his hand. "I did."

"You know your Verne. What might your name be?"

"Gabriel Henderson." He handed Captain Nemo the handbill.

"Gabriel? Did you know Gabriel was Monsieur Verne's middle name?"

He didn't. The captain's fountain pen scribbled some words in filigreed script on the blank side of Gabriel's flyer.

"Prince Dakkar?" Brian inquired as he and Gabriel walked away.

"It's his real name. He's Indian royalty." Gabriel read the inscription aloud. "*To Gabriel – Who may regard himself as an honorary member of my crew. Yours respectfully, Dakkar, Rajkumar of Bundelkund*[2]*, alias Captain Nemo.*"

"The what of what?" Brian asked.

"I guess it means 'Prince of Bundelkund.'"

"What's Bundelkund?"

"The part of India he's from. Did you read *The Mysterious Island*?"

"Uh-uh. That guy's probably from Syracuse, and his name is something like Henry." Brian checked his watch. "It's a quarter to nine."

They headed back to meet Paul and Audrey.

"I don't know a lot about Jules Verne, but this is a neat show," Brian said. "I want to come back. I'll ask my mom and dad. I'm sure they'll say no. You want to come back here, right? You think your parents will let you?"

Gabriel didn't answer.

"Gabe? Hey, I'm talking to you, Gabe."

"Huh? What"

"Skip it. You look like you're a hundred miles away. You still with the giant squid?"

"Sorry."

– JV –

Gabriel dreamed of Donny that night. The brothers rode the *Nautilus*, Gabriel in his pajamas and Donny in his Army khaki uniform. Donny played "Red River Valley" on the harmonica. Captain Nemo observed a pod of killer whales circling the submarine and ordered his men to repel the creatures. Donny grabbed a harpoon.

The dream ended there.

At the Sunday morning service, Gabriel let his mind wander during the pastor's sermon on the readings from Romans and the Gospel of John. He pictured the church as the *Nautilus*.

After dinner, Gabriel sequestered himself in his bedroom. He took out a writing tablet and pencil. Recalling his dream ("Why killer whales?"

---

2. The spelling of Bundelkhand in Verne's text, retained in the 1875 English translation by W.H.G. Kingston, which is the version that likely would be in Gabriel's local public library. The spelling also appeared in numerous nineteenth-century British documents.

he asked himself), Gabriel proceeded to fill up five pages with his first attempt at a short story, which he titled, "More Adventures of Captain Nemo." He omitted himself, but included Donny as one of the crew.

He switched to a blue pencil and copied out the story twice, word for word. One copy was for him. One was a spare, maybe to give to Brian, maybe to Paul. The original was for the man who portrayed the titular hero.

Gabriel opened his desk drawer to place the manuscripts there, then had a second thought. He picked up the blue pencil and scribbled, "To Donny," under the title on one copy. He folded the pages in half and brought them to his brother's room, which still looked as it did when they both lived in the house. He slipped the copy between the front cover and the flyleaf of *A Journey to the Centre of the Earth.*

Gabriel knew his father wouldn't let him deliver his story to Captain Nemo on a Sunday—the Sabbath belonged to God and family—so he asked if he could go to the Show on the closing night. His father said yes, but "the admission fee will come out of this week's allowance." He added, "You know the guy's an actor playing a part, don't you?"

"I know, but...."

"But nothing. I'd like to see you show this much enthusiasm for your schoolwork. I haven't forgotten your C in math last term."

"Yes, sir."

Early Monday evening, Lionel gave his son a ride to the Show.

"Good Lord, Gabe. You weren't exaggerating. This is some production."

Gabriel opened the passenger door. "You coming, Dad?"

Lionel shook his head. "Let's not make a night of this. I'll wait in the car. Be back here in thirty minutes."

Gabriel plowed through parents, children, and dating couples, "Excuse me" seeming to punctuate every other breath. He ran into two friends from school, Theo Richter and Jon Abernathy.

"Slow down, Gabe," said Theo. "Me and Jon are going to take the balloon ride. Want to come?"

"I can't. My dad's waiting for me outside. You see Captain Nemo? I have something for him."

"We just saw him," said Jon.

"Where?"

"By a big mechanical elephant hitched to a fancy, little house on wheels." Jon turned to Theo. "What was that whole thing called?"

"The Steam House," Theo replied.

"Thanks, guys! See you!" Gabriel sped off.

He hurried along a lane of fake cobblestones bordered by gas streetlamps. He saw the Steam House up ahead, but not the object of his search. In his mind, Gabriel heard the seconds ticking away. He caught sight of Phileas Fogg and a young Indian woman, arm in arm, strolling toward him. Gabriel practically leaped in front of them.

"Miss Aouda, Mr. Fogg, I'm looking for Captain Nemo."

"My excited fellow," Fogg said, "you will find him where you will find any good captain: on his ship."

"Thanks!" Gabriel spun on his heels and dashed in the opposite direction.

"Prince Dakkar, it's me, Gabriel," he announced when he boarded the *Nautilus*.

"Ah, Young Gabriel has returned. Have you come back for more adventures?"

The last two words astonished the boy.

"I came to give you this." He handed Captain Nemo the rolled-up pages with an excited smile. "I wrote it just for you."

"Allow me to express my thanks." The captain unfurled the manuscript. He read the title aloud. "You and I are like-minded." He perused the first page and gave Gabriel a puzzled look.

"Donny? There is no one named Donny on the *Nautilus*."

"Donny's my brother," Gabriel explained.

"Why did you put him in the story? Is he a seaman?"

"No," Gabriel said. "He fought in the Army. He died defending his country."

"I see," said Captain Nemo. "Patriots like Donny deserve our admiration and gratitude. I shall keep his valor in mind when I read your story."

Gabriel suspected that the man behind the character had lost a son in the war.

— JV —

Waking on Tuesday morning, Gabriel wondered if Captain Nemo, or "Captain Nemo," had read his story. He stretched, yawned, and glanced at the clock on the dresser. 6:55. Today the Show would come down and move on to the next stop, wherever that might be. It would have to take at least a day, if not two days, to dismantle and load into the trailers the walls, platforms, and pedestals; the aerial, aquatic, and terrestrial machines; the streetlamps; and the assorted odds and ends that all had transformed a couple of acres in rural Upstate New York into a representation of a nineteenth-century French writer's marvelous imagination. Gabriel pictured Captain Nemo, Phileas Fogg, Passepartout, Professor Lidenbrock, and Impey Barbicane out of costume, dressed, and talking like everybody he met day in and day out.

Gabriel washed, dressed, and went downstairs. He took his seat at the kitchen table. After grace, he began wolfing down his scrambled eggs and ham. His mother grabbed his wrist. "How am I raising you? In this house we eat like respectable people." Gabriel slowed down, but his left leg bounced. He cleared his plate and drank his milk.

"May I be excused?"

"Not so fast, Champ," his father said. He handed Gabriel a list of chores.

Gabriel read it over and asked, "Can I do my chores later?"

"I don't think so. Later isn't a good time. In fact, later is a very bad time. You know what's a good time? Right now."

Gabriel at that moment didn't dare reveal why he wanted to delay doing jobs around the house and running errands for his mother. However, he had no doubt the man knew.

— JV —

Shortly before eleven, below an overcast sky, Gabriel set out on his bike. He worried the whole trip about getting soaked. Fortunately, rain didn't fall.

As he approached the Brouwers' property, he saw crew members breaking down the Show. They all wore the same black uniform with the logo on the back. He was astonished by the amount of work they had finished by late morning. Then again, he reasoned, they do this so often, they must have it down to a science. Gabriel surveyed the grounds for any of the characters or anyone who might portray a character. He saw neither.

A large four-sided canvas tent stood near Dr. Fergusson's balloon, now deflated. Gabriel rode toward the tent. He got off his bike and laid it on its side. The crew didn't pay him any attention.

He peeked through the flap that served as the entrance. He saw the performers still in period clothes. Phileas Fogg, Professor Lidenbrock, Dr. Fergusson, and Axel played cards at a round table. Passepartout read a newspaper next to a long table that held books, which lay side by side. Off in a corner, Aouda knitted. The rest of the individuals, with the exception of Captain Nemo, conversed and drank from china cups. The captain sat cross-legged on a dark red rug with white fringes. He played a strange musical instrument that Gabriel hadn't seen before, an oblong wooden box with a green bellows attached to the back. One hand pumped the bellows and the other played a keyboard. The sound resembled that of an accordion. Captain Nemo, in a mellow voice, sang in a foreign language.

"Your Highness, how does the harmonium compare to the organ on the *Nautilus*?" asked Phileas Fogg.

"How does a pearl compare to an emerald?" Captain Nemo replied. He stopped playing.

"What was the song you were singing?" Professor Lidenbrock asked. He grimaced as he examined his cards. "Today is not my day for whist."

"It was a love poem in Urdu called a *ghazal*."

Gabriel felt tempted to walk into the tent. His body refused to move.

Phileas Fogg withdrew a pocket watch from his vest. "Well, my good people, I see it is approaching that time. We shall reunite in our next location. Come, Aouda. Come, Passepartout."

"Yes, Monsieur Fogg," said Passepartout, who rose from his chair and placed his newspaper on it.

Aouda laid aside her knitting. She and Fogg joined Passepartout by the book-covered table. "*Adieu*, till the next time," Fogg said, at which point he, his beloved, and his valet turned into columns of smoke, which vanished into one of the books.

Gabriel thought he'd witnessed an illusion, but one by one, two by two, three by three, other characters executed the same transmutation and disappearance until only Captain Nemo remained. The commander of the *Nautilus* got to his feet and walked over to the books. "I know you are here, Gabriel. I saw you." The boy showed his uncomprehending face. "Enter, please." Gabriel hesitated; nevertheless, he obeyed.

"I read your little story about my further exploits," Captain Nemo said. "You honored both me and Monsieur Verne. Yes, we must make time for more adventures. Life would be quite dreary without them. Never forget it." Then he, too, evaporated.

Gabriel approached the display with caution. He saw all the Verne books he knew and loved. He also saw books he didn't know. *The Green Ray. The Castle of the Carpathians. The Archipelago on Fire. Facing the Flag. Michael Strogoff. An Antarctic Mystery.*

Bewildered and frightened, Gabriel reached for *Twenty Thousand Leagues Under the Sea*. The edges of a few sheets of paper stuck out from between the front cover and the flyleaf. He lifted the cover and found his short story, folded in half. He opened the manuscript.

Above the title, he saw "G. pays a commendable tribute to his brother" in Captain Nemo's handwriting.

His eyes welled up. *Twenty Thousand Leagues Under the Sea* fell onto *Topsy Turvy*[3]. Gabriel bolted from the tent, mounted his bike, and headed back to Gray Birch as fast as he could pedal.

Minutes later, two crew members brought in an empty leather trunk, which they dropped in front of the table. They packed the books, tossed in "More Adventures of Captain Nemo," and then locked the trunk and carried it to the lead trailer.

3. The title appeared as *Topsy Turvy* on the spine and as *Topsy-Turvy* on the title page of the first U.S. edition, published in 1890 by J.S. Ogilvie of New York.

Tyranny Under the Sea

Christopher M. Geeson

"And I could imagine founding cities in the sea, agglomerations of underwater dwellings which, like the Nautilus, *would come up to breathe on the surface of the oceans each morning, free cities if ever there were any, independent cities! And yet, who knows if some despot...." Captain Nemo finished his sentence with a violent gesture... as if to chase away some unhappy thought.*

– *Twenty Thousand Leagues Under the Seas*, Part 1, Chapter 18

There came a day in the boiler room, shoveling coal into the furnace, when I'd been pushed around so many times that I hit back.

Sergeant Dulleson was the overseer: a hulking, bitter white man in a grey uniform, who only cheered up when he forced someone to cower beneath him. That day, six slaves cowered beneath the onslaught of his truncheon and every terrible threat and foul name he could think of. The two children—George and Phineas—spent the shift in tears, whilst old Robert looked ready to drop from exhaustion any moment. That wasn't enough for Dulleson. He wanted me to cower too. But I threw down my shovel in protest.

"Pick up your spade, boy," Dulleson yelled at me over the roar of the furnace. The four bored guards sensed trouble and closed in.

"It's not right, you treating us like this," I said, sweat streaming down my face and back. Even my last owner before the war had shown some mercy. But not Dulleson.

He glared at me. "Pick it up."

I looked at the other slaves, saw Ellen's eyes imploring me to obey, Silas' and Maria's uncertainty, the fear on the faces of the others. A life of abuse and injustice makes you feel powerless. All they could see was a futile struggle, with punishment—or death—at the end of it.

Dulleson noticed their reactions. "What you all gawpin' at?" he bellowed and swung his truncheon at them. *Them,* not me. He swung viciously left and right, smashing into Robert's shoulder and then hitting Ellen on her back. As the four guards rounded up my fellow slaves, Dulleson turned on me, drawing back the truncheon to strike.

I held up my hands in surrender, hoping I looked contrite enough. "Yes, boss," I said, stooping to reach for the shovel.

"That's right—I'm the boss," Dulleson said.

Wrenching up my shovel, I swung it in Dulleson's face. His jaw went sideways, and he collapsed in a heap. Everything seemed to freeze for a moment. Even the roar and heat of the furnace faded. Ellen, Silas, and the others stared in amazement.

"Samuel!" Ellen shouted, rushing towards me. "What have you done?"

But there wasn't time to think about what I'd done. One of the guards ran for the door and a second guard came at me. In a moment he brought his truncheon down sharply. It collided with my shovel, sending a jolt up my arms. Before he could attack again, I stabbed the blade of the shovel down onto his feet. He doubled over and I threw him to the deck.

Across the chamber, Robert and Maria wrestled the third guard to the floor and knocked him out. The fourth was already down, Silas standing over him with a blood-smeared shovel. By the open door, George and Phineas shouted: "The other guard's run off!"

"The admiral will kill us for this," Silas said.

"Not if we get away," said Ellen.

I started for the door. "Come on—follow me!"

I hurtled down the fort's dim plate-metal corridors, making for the harbor room. My six companions followed. George and Phineas came first and then Ellen, Silas, Maria, and Robert. Nothing got in our way and soon we arrived in a small chamber dominated by three sealed metal doors in the wall, each leading to launch bays for the Hunley submarines. Every door had a set of levers below it—we slaves had operated them many times before. Hanging on hooks from the back wall were diving suits, breathing tanks, and spherical helmets. A large Confederate flag loomed over everything.

Quickly, I unfastened the heavy bolt on the door to Launch Bay Number One. "Everyone through!" I shouted. "Get inside the Hunley and wait for me." One by one, my fellow slaves rushed through the door to the tunnel-like launch bay beyond. Ellen waited until the others had gone.

"What about the floodgate?" she asked from the doorway. "Someone has to stay to open it."

She was right. On a regular launch, someone would stay in the harbor room to open the floodgate at the end of the launch bay. The only safe time to do that was after a Hunley's crew sealed themselves within their submarine. But no one from the fort would open the floodgate for us today.

"I'll open it," I said, "and follow you."

"No Samuel!" Ellen said. "You'll drown if the floodgate's open before you get inside the Hunley."

"Not if I'm quick."

"Put on a diving suit."

"There isn't time!" I could hear the guards' footsteps as they ran down the nearby corridors, searching for us. "Go!" I told her. "They're coming."

She leaned forward and kissed me and then she vanished through the door into the launch bay.

The guards' footsteps drew nearer to the harbor room.

Yanking down one of the levers, I set the clockwork mechanism moving which would crank open Launch Bay Number One's floodgate, letting the sea pour in. I took one last look at the flag I hated, then dashed through the door and bolted it behind me with a clang. From the catwalk, I heard the submarine's tunnel-like launch bay echo with the rush of incoming seawater as the large floodgate at the far end of the chamber ground open.

Forty feet long, the Hunley resembled a bullet, tapered at both ends, with an empty torpedo spar at the fore and two short conning towers spaced along the top of its metal hull. At that moment, I saw Ellen squeezing herself down through the hatch of the aft conning tower. She was the last one, pulling it closed above her.

Water poured rapidly into the launch bay, already overlapping the thin strip of catwalk. In less than a minute, it would cover the Hunley. I sloshed along the catwalk, ankle deep in the rising flood, and scrambled up the rungs on the side of the Hunley, the water level chasing me. Reaching the top of the forward conning tower, I swung open the hatch, and climbed over the rim. As I squeezed feet-first into the narrow well-like opening, the dark seawater already obscured most of the rungs I'd just climbed on the submarine's outer hull. Too close. With a last effort, I shoved myself down the inner ladder into the vessel, pulling the hatch down and sealing us in.

We'd crewed the Hunleys scores of times, but the confined space always felt oppressive. The gloom was broken by just a few candle lanterns—which Maria passed around—and any light that happened to come through the tiny round portholes. The cramped interior forced us to stay seated; the metal plates touched our heads and shoulders whenever we moved. My six companions huddled together side by side along the length of the single bench, hands gripping the long zigzag of the hand-crank, ready to power us. Ellen sat farthest from me, next to the aft ballast tank.

This time we were piloting the Hunley for ourselves, not for any of our masters. I took my position at the bow, hunched over the controls for the rudder, and the levers which operated the diving planes. Looking out of the tiny porthole nearest me, I saw the floodgate ahead was completely open and our vessel had submerged. "Start cranking!"

My companions began turning the crankshaft to spin the screw—a laborious task, especially as it was usually a job for eight. Now, only four adults and two children strained at the crank, while I manned the helm.

"Release the clamps!"

Ellen pulled the levers which detached the clamps on the outside, and the vessel advanced slowly along the launch bay tunnel. But up ahead, the floodgate started to close again. Our masters were cutting off our escape!

"Faster!" I yelled.

My companions turned the crankshaft with more determination than ever before. For the first time, we had a purpose of our own. As the gate came down, the Hunley sped up. I held my breath.

With little room to spare, we cleared the lowering gate to head out into the depths of the ocean.

"Will they follow us?" George asked.

"They might," I said, "but we've got a head start."

"That was a foolish thing you did," Ellen shouted from the other end of the vessel, "flooding the bay before you got inside the Hunley. You could've drowned."

"I can't argue with that," I said, "but it was the only way—nobody else was gonna do it for us."

Face pressed to the small front viewport, I steered to avoid tangles of weed and rocky outcrops. Shoals of fish fled before us like we were a mighty marine beast. Even the sharks avoided us. As we rose through the depths, there were less obstacles to avoid. I swapped with Phineas to do my share of the cranking, while he took over the steering. We continued underwater for two hours. When we surfaced, Ellen and I rushed to open the conning tower hatches, letting in the sweetest, freshest air we'd tasted in years.

"What can you see, Samuel?" Silas called from below.

"The ocean!" I said, laughing. "Nothing but water for miles around—and no one to tell us what to do."

Squeezing around one another, we took turns at the hatches while the Hunley drifted.

That first night, we closed the hatches and floated on the waves as we slept on the hard bench. We headed East the next morning, but when we surfaced for another break, things suddenly changed. It was George's turn in the forward conning tower, when he yelled down: "Samuel! Come quick! It's a sea monster!"

As skeptical as the others, I made my way to the foot of the ladder. "Let's see." George jumped down so I could clamber up the rungs. I squeezed through the hatch and looked. The thing I saw was like one of our Hunleys—a long cylinder, metal-plated and pointed—but it dwarfed our craft. It must have been more than two hundred feet long. As it approached, it broke through the waves like a whale, sending out huge swells. When it drew alongside us, it stopped. A hatch opened and a man looked out. A man who wasn't white.

— JV —

After taking us aboard, our benefactor introduced himself as Captain Nemo. We enjoyed his hospitality for two days, having left our Hunley floating on the surface. His crew fed us well with bluefin tuna and sea mullet. They gave us strange silky clothes made, Nemo said, from the fibers of shelled sea creatures. The submarine, the *Nautilus*, even had a library which delighted Ellen—she'd been taught to read by her old mistress and had since taught all of us, secretly, at the fort.

On the second day, my fellow escapees and I spent the morning with Nemo in the salon of the *Nautilus*, gazing through the glass panels into the depths of the Western Atlantic. Nemo asked us many questions about our former masters.

"Amazing!" he said when I described New Richmond. "An underwater city which rises to the surface to renew its air supply, just like my *Nautilus*."

"Every few days—but they never let *us* see the surface," I said. "They just refill the ballast tanks, and it sinks slowly back to the seabed, where it's anchored next to the volcano." I told him about the huge extinct volcano stretching from the seabed to the surface, how it had a coal mine hidden within it where slaves toiled in diving suits, while other slaves transported the coal to the fort and shoveled it into the furnace.

"I've been a fool!" Nemo said. "I was convinced no one else on Earth knew of such hidden seams of coal."

"It powers just about everything in New Richmond."

Nemo turned from the viewport, smiled and shook his head. "No, my friends, it is you and your people who power it. Without you, the coal would still be under the sea, unless they had the courage to dig it out of the volcano themselves."

A bitter smile spread over my face. "You're right about that." A sense of mutual understanding passed between us.

"But slaves will power this underwater city no longer," he said. "In this vast ocean, chance has brought us together."

It was a wonder to look out at the depths of the ocean from the wide glass panels and see it illuminated—for what seemed like a mile beyond—by the amazing lamps which the vessel bore. New Richmond had nothing like it. The fort stood below us, anchored next to the slope of the extinct volcano. From the outside, the Confederate city under the sea looked a little like the picture I once saw of Fort Sumter: a three-story pentagon but standing on five squat pillars. Lying in wide coils within the area enclosed by the pillars was the vast chain which ended with an anchor buried in the rock of the seabed. The fort's metal-plated walls were covered with hatches and portholes and on the roof was an ingenious valved vent, emitting bursts of steam which bubbled up through the water.

"An impressive construction it may be," Nemo said, "but it is a tyrant's folly. That chain tethers them less than their philosophy does. Have they learned nothing from four years of civil war? Don't they realize their tyranny is utterly defeated?"

We were still reeling from what Nemo had told us earlier: the war was over. The Confederacy had surrendered six months ago, and all the slaves were free. *We were free!* We could return to America and our families.

"Our masters must've known the war was over," I said. "They've been sending Hunleys out to pick up supplies."

"They knew, alright," Ellen snapped angrily. "They just never told *us*."

"No," said Nemo, "they wanted to keep you in chains, fearing for your lives while you worked for them." He took a deep breath. "You said there are fifty slaves there?"

"Yes."

"And thirty-five Confederates?"

"At the most," I said. "Southern gentlemen, soldiers, overseers."

"And the leader of these *gentlemen* is Admiral Donohoe?"

"Yes, "I said. "He was the one who took the design of the original *Hunley* and built the new ones—in secret."

"*We* were the ones who built the Hunleys," Silas said. "*We* did the work."

"The British Empire filled their coffers on the backs of my people too," Nemo mused. "Must the greatest advances of the human race always come at the expense of its humanity?"

Ellen squeezed my hand. We knew we had an ally, a powerful one.

"This Donohoe might have a handful of Hunleys and an undersea fortress," Nemo said, "But I have the *Nautilus.* And there's something else we have that he doesn't."

We all looked at him, waiting on his words.

"We have justice on our side."

I never wanted to see my tormentors again; but I knew I was going to face them one final time. Not as a slave; as a free man.

The *Nautilus* approached Fort New Richmond, lighting it up. Surely the lookouts inside the fort had spotted us from their viewports.

"Their curiosity and their greed will bring them out," Nemo said. "This admiral of an underwater city will be desperate to see an advanced submarine like the *Nautilus.* I expect he will take a dislike to my appearance but he will be in awe of my vessel."

We waited, watching from the salon window, for an hour. Then two floodgates opened in the fort and a Hunley came out of each of them. They were armed with torpedoes, mounted on the spars projecting from their bows. Ten people in diving suits, with lead boots, trudged across from the fort, armed with nothing more than harpoon spears. I glanced at Nemo and saw a dark smile on his face.

The *Nautilus* had a diving chamber which was opened to let in the ten divers. Once they were aboard, some of Nemo's crew operated the mechanisms which sealed the chamber and pumped out the water.

The seven of us watched with Nemo, through a porthole, as the Confederate divers removed their air tanks and helmets. I saw with a stab of anger that Dulleson was among them.

"Is Admiral Donohoe there?" Nemo asked us.

"The tall one," I said, "with the blond hair and whiskers."

Captain Nemo then suggested we wait in the salon for him. "I will show them enough of my vessel to amaze them and then I will bring them to you."

"I like the sound of that," Ellen said. "Won't they be surprised!"

— JV —

Nemo's crew brought us plates of crabmeat while we waited. It was still strange beyond belief to have people bringing us proper food, like they were our servants. Half an hour later, Nemo opened the salon door, bringing in the ten visitors and some of his own crew. The Confederates no longer bore their harpoons. Dulleson and a few of the others scowled—no doubt they objected to a dark-skinned man like Nemo having a superior vessel to their Hunleys—but Admiral Donohoe stared at everything around him with wonder. The admiral's eyes passed over Ellen and I, but he didn't really see us. It was like we were unworthy of his notice—just someone else's slaves.

"With a handful of vessels like this," the admiral said, "I could destroy the Union!" He grasped Nemo's arm. "We have gold, Nemo—come and see Fort New Richmond while we discuss a trade."

"Later," Nemo said, carefully removing Donohoe's grip. "First, meet my other guests."

Donohoe looked around, confused. "Guests?"

"I believe you already know each other?" Nemo pointed to my six companions and me.

Donohoe finally seemed to register our presence, but it was Dulleson who actually recognized us: "The slaves who stole the Hunley! That big fella's the one who hit me. When I get my hands on that filthy—"

Nemo's arm shot out, a barrier halting Dulleson. "You will not," he said firmly.

"Who do you think you are?" Dulleson yelled. "I don't take orders from the likes of you!" Grabbing Nemo by the throat, Dulleson swung his fist. He wasn't quick enough. Launching into Dulleson, I wrestled him off Nemo and slammed him to the deck.

Donohoe drew a hidden pistol from his jacket, but Nemo jabbed the man's wrist and the pistol dropped to the floor. The *Nautilus* crew encircled the salon, each man armed with a strange kind of pistol.

"What the hell is this?" Donohoe spat. "These slaves are our property!"

"Not anymore," I said.

"Not ever again," added Ellen.

Donohoe glared at us and then at Nemo, but the Captain of the *Nautilus* looked unfazed.

"Well, we got plenty more slaves," Dulleson said, getting to his feet.

"And I have room for *all* of them," Nemo answered.

Admiral Donohoe took a deep breath, straightening his back, attempting to muster some control of the situation. "Alright, Nemo, perhaps we can come to a deal," he said, "although we can't sell you *all* of our slaves. I mean, they're not so easy to replace now, are they?"

Nemo looked at the visitors with open contempt. "I do not buy people, Admiral! I am *taking* them away from you and I am liberating them!"

My heart surged inside me at Nemo's words.

"The hell you are," Donohoe said.

Ignoring him, Nemo continued. "You've built a fantastic place under the sea. I admire that. But you have soiled it with slavery."

"They're our workforce. We depend on—"

"Not any longer," Nemo cut in. "You will bring the rest of your slaves to the *Nautilus*. Then we will leave this part of the Atlantic and never come back. You may continue to live in your fort, doing the work yourselves."

"Sure—and wait for the Union to find us," Dulleson said.

"I have little to do with society," Nemo said, "and certainly not with governments, so you can be assured I will tell no one about you."

"You're not taking all our slaves," said Donohoe.

"Then," Nemo said, "you will witness my *Nautilus* in all its power."

Donohoe took time to compose himself. He must have known, as he glared at Captain Nemo, that his two Hunleys would be no match for the *Nautilus*. He took a deep breath. A cunning look came into his eyes that was at odds with his sudden placating smile. "Very well, Nemo, you shall have the slaves."

Nemo nodded, business-like and they set to discussing the arrangements. But I couldn't shake a feeling of dread.

When the Confederates left the *Nautilus*, I drew close to Nemo. "Don't trust Donohoe. He's planning something."

"Would you like to be there to ruin whatever he's planning?" Nemo asked.

For a while, everything happened just as Nemo and Donohoe had agreed. The Confederates returned to New Richmond, gathering all the remaining slaves and furnishing them with diving suits and air tanks—

Nemo had agreed to return all the diving equipment once the slaves were on board the *Nautilus*. Meanwhile, Confederates from the fort took over as crewmen aboard the Hunleys. Soon both Hunleys were back on patrol, guarding the fort and the slopes of the volcano.

Several of us waited in the water to meet the slaves, ready to foil any treachery Donohoe might attempt. With me were Ellen, Silas, and Maria, alongside ten members of Nemo's crew. The rubber diving suits from Nemo's submarine fitted more comfortably than the ones we'd worn in the fort's coal mine, and the air from this breathing apparatus tasted fresher. Each of us carried one of Nemo's air guns, loaded with special glass bullets, which we were told carried a charge of electricity. None of us slaves—*ex*-slaves—was much practiced with a gun, but we were ready to use them if the admiral's men attacked. The Hunleys presented the biggest threat, looming with their torpedoes, but the *Nautilus*—sitting on the seafloor and five times bigger than a Hunley—could surely deal with them.

It took more than an hour, but eventually the hatches opened in New Richmond and fifty slaves shuffled out, in diving suits with weighted boots. I felt a rush of joy as I saw them leave their prison. Free.

The slaves were more than halfway to the *Nautilus* when everything went wrong. There was no charge by an underwater battalion, no attack by the Hunleys, only a change in the movements of the slaves. At first, they just appeared sluggish, slowing down as if exhausted, but then a few checked the pipes running from their air tanks to their helmets. Some waved their arms at us in panic.

"They can't breathe!" I shouted, but no one could hear my voice beyond the diving helmet. I clasped my hands to my throat, acting out a gesture of suffocation and pointing frantically in the direction of the slaves. It only took a few seconds for everyone to understand that something was wrong.

I sped as fast as I could through the water towards the slaves; Nemo's crewmen and my friends came with me. Some of the slaves were already collapsing to the ocean floor. I grabbed hold of one of them and lumbered along with him, making for the *Nautilus*. Ellen took hold of another and the rest of our group followed, helping as many slaves as they could manage. Nemo must have seen what was happening too; his crew opened the diving chamber so we could get the victims inside. All we could do was leave them there for the crew to help, while we rushed back out to rescue more.

But everything took too long. There were only fourteen of us to rescue the remaining thirty people, all of whom were clawing futilely at their helmets and air reservoirs. As we came back with the next group of victims, divers poured out of the *Nautilus* to assist the rest, but it still wasn't enough.

One of the Hunleys swept towards us, its deadly torpedo spar leading the way like a lance. The *Nautilus* divers lunged out of its path, but it advanced on Nemo's submarine, blocking any chance we had of reaching the safety of the diving chamber. Clutching a rescued slave in my arms, I could only watch, helpless, as the Hunley ploughed into Nemo's craft, the torpedo exploding the moment it made contact. The explosion sent a bubbling torrent towards us, catapulting us all through the water. When the turmoil cleared, my heart leapt. The *Nautilus* was still there, undamaged, but the Hunley had been ripped apart by its own weapon. Mangled bodies floated out of it as it sank. Sergeant Dulleson was one of them.

We were almost back again at the *Nautilus* with the second rescue group when the other Hunley bore down on us. They were using their advantage while they had it, knowing that once everyone was aboard the *Nautilus*, the great submarine would enter the battle itself.

Supporting the slave I'd rescued, I drew the air gun with my other hand. I fired. The shot went wide but it was enough to inspire some of Nemo's diving crew. Dozens of shots erupted from our party and I fired again. Several glass bullets hit the Hunley, bursting and sending electricity arcing across it. One of the shots smashed through the bow porthole, right where the steersman would have been at the controls. That was the beginning of the end. The crew could've released the ballast and saved themselves, but they didn't. I imagined them panicking in the confined space as it slowly flooded, with an unconscious or dead steersman at the controls and no slaves to do the rest of the work for them. The Hunley took on water, tilting bow-down as it sank. Turning our backs on it, we guided the rescued slaves to the *Nautilus*. I was the last one inside, climbing through the diving chamber hatch and sealing it, just as the Hunley hit the seabed and exploded with its own torpedo.

When we all returned to the *Nautilus*, the results of Admiral Donohoe's horrific plan became obvious. Twenty-one of the fifty slaves had died from asphyxiation, gasping for breath when their reservoirs ran out.

"The admiral's men must have emptied the air tanks before they gave them to our people," I said.

"Leaving just enough for them to get into the water and die," Ellen said, her voice full of anger.

But most of us had escaped and survived. That was something. I felt neither satisfaction nor regret that the two Hunleys had been destroyed, taking perhaps sixteen of the Confederates to the bottom of the sea.

When I found Captain Nemo in the salon, he was pacing up and down. He swung around, his face showing the pain he felt. "I couldn't save them all," he said, his voice choked with emotion.

"It's not your fault. We did our best."

"And Admiral Donohoe did his worst. The worst thing a man could do."

"I only hope he drowned aboard one of the Hunleys," I said.

Nemo froze. He clenched his fist to his chest. "No. Admiral Donohoe wasn't on one of his Hunleys. He is a tyrant—and by their nature, tyrants have armies do their killing for them." He stormed past me.

"Captain Nemo?" I called.

"Let's finish this, Samuel."

The *Nautilus* turned in a wide arc, until we were a great distance from New Richmond, but with our long, pointed prow aimed directly at the fort.

I stood with Nemo in the pilothouse that protruded from the upper forward part of the submarine. Everything was lit up before us by the powerful electric lamp on the submarine's hull. The steersman had been sent away; Nemo was at the controls, piloting us towards the fort.

I asked a question which I feared I knew the answer to already. "What are you going to do?"

Nemo didn't look at me. Instead, his gaze was fixed on the underwater fort as we gained speed. "I am the law! I am the judge! I am the avenger!" he bellowed.

The fort began to rise in the water.

"They're pumping out the ballast!" I yelled.

Within the pillars of the rising fort, the anchor chain uncoiled.

"Fools!" Nemo shouted. "Do you think you can escape me?"

We accelerated to a speed far faster than anything the Hunleys had been capable of. The fort rose above us, the chain stretching out beneath as the structure rocketed up to the surface. Nemo operated the submarine's diving planes, angling us upwards as we chased the fort from below.

Steeper.

Closer.

Faster.

Until the deadly pointed prow of the *Nautilus* tore into the lower plates of New Richmond. With a deep groan of ripping metal, the wall of the fort ruptured, crumpling before the onslaught of the *Nautilus*.

I watched, heart hammering in my chest, as Nemo turned his vessel to starboard, lengthening the rip in the wall, before he disengaged the *Nautilus* from the battered fort, which was still tethered to its anchor in the rock below. Nemo swung the *Nautilus* in a tight loop, rounding once again on his prey, but a further attack was not needed. Inundated with water, the metal city plummeted through the depths, crashing onto the slope of the volcano.

— JV —

July 1866

After a month aboard the *Nautilus*, Captain Nemo landed my companions and I ashore, at a secluded bay on the Delaware coast, giving us a box of gold to start a new life with. The seven of us are headed westwards now, free at last. Vowing to stick together, we plan to form our own settlement in Iowa, a vast distance from any ocean. Others will join us, as we write to old friends and family, spreading the word. Maria has decided to take care of George and Phineas. Robert and Silas are already making plans for a farm where we will all work together, without master and overseers. Ellen and I will soon have a child of our own to raise. She sits beside me now, as we camp in our wagon, west of Columbus, Ohio.

I look again at the newspaper I bought while we stayed in Pittsburgh: an article about a sea monster and a list of all the dates and places around the world it's been sighted. Now a frigate, named after President Lincoln, is going to search for this monster. But all the monsters of the deep I know of have been destroyed already.

Trumpets of Freedom

Kelly A. Harmon

VASQUEZ SLIPPED THE SCREWDRIVER into the seam of the faceplate on the clockwork man and pried the dented shield away from the brain cavity. He sighed. Felipe's components were in worse shape than he thought from when the automaton had fallen from the top of the nearby forty-foot lighthouse. Vasquez loosened nuts and bolts, moved aside the metallic roll that contained Felipe's programming, and removed two broken springs and a handful of twisted cogs—some of the smaller ones were missing—and sand. Always, he found sand gumming up the works when he opened the machines.

But had this sand gotten in while the clockwork man had polished glass at the top of the lighthouse—perhaps blown in on the ever-present wind coming off the sea? Or, had it entered after the seal broke around his face when he hit the rocky beach below? Vasquez grabbed a soft towel and cleaned out the cavity. He would never know.

Either way, the mechanics were ruined. Felipe would never blink his eyes or raise his eyebrows again—at least not until Vasquez could remake them. He knew it was absurd to give the machines expressions—or names—but it made living with machines much more interesting. It gave them *personality*.

He checked Felipe's large neck spring—the heavy-duty wind-up that enabled the automaton to walk and lift his arms—and found it had been severed from the cogs managing Felipe's shoulders. *How did that happen?* He wrapped his palm around the spring, lifting it gently to look behind it—and found a bullet. No wonder Felipe had fallen over the railing. He'd been forced over by the momentum of a gunshot.

"Who the hell shoots at a clockwork man?" Vasquez yelled.

A mechanical seagull whistled from her perch on the windowsill above the table. She careened down and deposited two tiny gears by Vasquez's right hand before swooping back up to land on the sill. "Bombs away! Bombs away!"

Vasquez smiled. The birds always brought him interesting bits from outside. These had been knocked loose from Felipe's head, Vasquez knew, seeing his own stamp on the metal. He looked at the bird's markings. "Thanks, Martina," Vasquez said. "Go patrol."

Maybe whoever had shot Felipe hadn't realized he'd shot a mechanical man. Maybe Vasquez's own life was in danger. Vasquez sighed. He thought he was done with that nonsense when the Conquest of the Desert ended two years ago in 1884.

Martina acknowledged Vasquez's command with a whistle, then pushed through the canvas flaps covering the small window high above his work table. Vasquez had built the window just for the birds. "Ines! Olivia! Patrol!" The two mechanical gulls still on the sill raised themselves on copper legs, whistled acknowledgment, and plunged through the canvas.

Vasquez reached for the loose wire near the gears Martina had deposited and unrolled a two-foot length, thinking on how to best repair Felipe. He'd have to cut the damaged portion from Felipe's mainspring before re-connecting it, which would shorten the length of time Felipe could work. It was fitting, Vasquez supposed, since Felipe was his oldest machine. He'd lack energy, as most old-timers do. That made Vasquez smile, until he thought about the dented faceplate. It looked like Felipe had picked up some scars as well. *But don't we all, as we go through life?*

Vasquez clipped the damaged portion off the top of the spring and bored a hole into the end that remained. Martina pushed through the oiled canvas flaps on the window. "Intruder," she sang. "Intruder."

Vasquez looked up from Felipe's broken parts and gave the glass-eyed bird his attention.

"Friend or foe?"

"Suit and tie! Suit and tie!"

Vasquez pulled off his magnifying lenses and stood, catching his balance on the table's edge as his prosthetic leg dragged. *Sand in the knee joint. Again.*

Maldita sea, he cursed. He hadn't expected the representative from the Lighthouse Board until tomorrow. The leg must wait. "Let's see what he wants."

The bird whistled and flew outside again. Vasquez limped to the door and met the man at the top of the porch steps. He didn't recognize the agent, who dressed more slovenly than any Board man he'd met. His jacket barely contained his paunch.

"I wasn't expecting anyone today," Vasquez said. He leaned against the porch rail, preventing the agent from climbing the stairs—and more importantly—resting his injured leg. Martina came to light beside his elbow on the railing, her red eyes gleaming in the hot, Argentinian sun.

"I'm getting an early start," the man said, eyeing the clockwork seagull warily.

Vasquez figured that was as close to an admission of "surprise inspection" as he was going to get.

"Well, as you can see, things are fine."

The agent tilted his head back and shielded his eyes, staring at the three clockwork men polishing glass at the top of the tower. "There are some complaints about the mechanicals, but I admit I thought the problem was your leg." He opened his briefcase. "I have a letter here from a Señor Kongre who says you lost your leg in the war and can no longer walk."

"*¡Hijueputa!*" Vasquez should have known better than to believe his personal war with Kongre ended with Argentina's. His wife was dead, thanks to Kongre, though he'd failed to prove it. And that's why he was here at the end of the world. Because if he hadn't left, he would have strangled Kongre with his bare hands. Then it would have been *him* in jail paying the price for Stilla's death instead of Kongre.

Vasquez cleared his throat. "As you can see, Kongre exaggerated, Señor....?" Vasquez stood up straight. He itched to rub his stump where it joined the prosthetic—but he wasn't going to give the Board a reason to dismiss him.

"Forgive me." The man tipped his hat. "Señor Ignatio Cruz." He pulled a graying, crumpled cloth from his pocket and blotted his forehead. "Could we get out of the sun?"

Vasquez was reluctant to entertain the man—there was much to do, along with the added burden of discovering who was taking pot-shots at his clockwork men—though he now had an idea, thanks to Cruz. "Since you see my leg is fine, shouldn't you file your report?"

"Yes, well, there's the matter of the clockwork men and the unfinished repairs. Let's get out of the sun and discuss it." Vasquez opened his mouth to deny him, but Cruz forestalled him. "If I go back without answers, the Board will replace you immediately."

Vasquez sighed. He needed this job. There were precious few to be found after the war, especially for a man with substantial injuries who relied on clockwork men to help him. He motioned Cruz to the porch and two weathered chairs. Vasquez sat in the far chair, stretching out his left leg, hoping for relief.

Cruz sat and mopped his brow with the dirty rag again. He paged through a thin sheaf of papers. "Regarding the automatons, several men in the neighborhood feel they have put them out of work."

Vasquez sighed. "Those men have lost nothing by my machines. The Board has given me no means to pay for help, so I couldn't have hired them even if I wanted to."

There was no use arguing he'd rather the machines do the work anyway: clockwork men labored efficiently. And no man wanted to stand in the blazing sun for hours at the top of the lighthouse cleaning glass, no matter how much he needed a paycheck. Clockwork men didn't complain, worked sun-up to sun-down, and didn't take breaks for cigarillos, siestas or lunch.

"But you hired men to help you with the lens—"

"And paid them from my own pocket." *Because it would have been impossible for me to do the job on my own—and the Board should have known that.* "When will the Board be reimbursing me?"

Cruz's brow furrowed. "I couldn't say." He made some notes on a blank pad, licking his pencil every few words to keep the letters dark. Vasquez waited in silence until Cruz finished.

"Let's discuss the repair timeline," Cruz said. "Do you want to take me through what's done? You've only a few more weeks to finish, or we'll have to find someone who can complete the work in a timely manner—with or without clockwork men."

Vasquez stiffened. "Señor Cruz, I've rectified the most important problem this lighthouse had before you hired me—it's now in operation. Everything else is superficial."

"Not according to the Argentine Republic."

"Lifting that lens to the top of the lighthouse was a time-consuming, backbreaking job, requiring the help of several able-bodied men—" *which is why the locals were complaining about being out of work now,* he thought: *there's no more work where that came from.* "And there's the matter of the items *not on that list* that needed fixing in order to accomplish that monumental task—repairing structural flooring to support the two-ton Fresnel lens, the eradication of vermin in the oil shed, the rat-infested curtains needed to cover the lens in daylight, the—"

"Señor Vasquez—"

"Did no one *keep* this lighthouse before I got here, Señor Cruz?"

Cruz stiffened. "There was the small matter of some pirates that needed quelling before you arrived."

"Pirates?" *Had* pirates *taken pot shots at Felipe? Jesucristo!* Did he have to worry about marauders, too? "No one warned me of pirates when I took this job, Señor Cruz."

Cruz packed his briefcase. "I believe I have enough information. I think my superiors will agree that you may stay until the end of July—"

"August," Vasquez countered.

"July." Cruz snapped the case shut.

"That's only one additional week."

"With your clockwork men, you shouldn't need the extra time. Good day." Cruz hurried off.

"Well, dammit."

Martina chirped in agreement.

JV

Seated at the table, Vasquez rolled up his left pants leg to mid-thigh and loosened the leather bands on the copper bucket that surrounded his stump. He felt an immediate sense of relief in the limb, then a flurry of pins and needles when blood rushed into the expanding flesh—since *tight* was the only way he could keep the prosthetic attached.

He laid the leg on the worktable. The artificial limb was jointed at the knee and ankle so it could bend and move like a real leg and foot. The casing on the lower half of the leg contained a heavy-duty spring attached to a flat metal plate. He wanted to experiment with a heavier spring to see if he could jump— but first, he had to iron out the problem with the sand, complete all the lighthouse repairs, and stop Kongre—or pirates!—from shooting his clockwork men. Or him.

Vasquez removed the casing covering the knee joint. It looked fine—just like he knew it would, but sand was insidious. It got into everything. He turned the large key in the middle of the joint, testing the tightness of the spring. It was firm, which meant sand gummed up the works. He'd have to take it apart to clean it properly. Maybe he could blow the sand out. He reached for a bellows.

"Intruder! Intruder!"

Now what? Vasquez looked up from the table and spied Ines. "Friend or foe?"

"Uniform! Uniform!"

Surprised, Vasquez lurched upright on his one good leg and looked out the front window. "Kongre." He wore the tattered remnants of his officer's uniform, and plodded toward the lighthouse with an exhausted gait. Where was his horse? Had he walked all this distance from his home in town?

How had the man fallen so low?

Hastily, Vasquez re-attached his leg. He grabbed his shotgun, and strode through the door to the porch, keeping Kongre standing in the sun. Vasquez carried the gun in the crook of his arm, the barrel pointed down. It wouldn't take a moment to lift and aim at Kongre if he became a threat. "What do you want, Kongre?"

Kongre turned the brim of his dirty hat backwards and tilted his head to meet Vasquez's eyes. "Is that any way to treat an army buddy?" He opened his arms wide, smiling at Vasquez.

"You killed my wife, Kongre. That makes us mortal enemies."

"That was never proven," Kongre said.

"You've never denied it."

Kongre frowned. Shoving his hands into his pockets. "Not here to rehash old business. You took my job." He took a step closer to Vasquez.

Vasquez tightened his grip on the gun. *Kongre wouldn't talk about his wife, but he was still angry over a job?* "It wasn't your job, Kongre. The *Coronel* asked for volunteers, and he picked me."

"I was the better man!"

"The *Coronel* didn't think so."

"We lost the house!"

"If you lost your ancestral home over two hundred pesos a month, you must not have managed it well. As I recall, you used to brag about your money. Thought it could buy my wife."

Kongre's face turned red, and he jumped up on the first step of the porch, looking as though he'd like to take a swing at Vasquez.

Vasquez lifted his rifle and planted it in Kongre's chest. "I have no quarrel with you, Kongre. But, one more step and you'll lose your life."

Kongre stepped back onto the hard-packed sand at the foot of the porch. "How do you always come up smelling roses?"

"Lots of people lost things during the war, Kongre. Your house isn't my fault."

"How are you even standing?" Kongre pointed at Vasquez's leg. "I saw them cut off your leg—high enough up you should be wearing a crutch 'stead of a peg. Probably got a settlement—set for life."

Vasquez nodded. "I did get a small settlement from the army. But set for life? No."

"Well, you couldn't've grown a new leg."

Vasquez rapped on his ankle with the end of the gun. "Copper."

"You're still smelling roses, then."

Vasquez sighed. "What do you want from me, Kongre?"

"Justice."

"Justice?" Vasquez ran a hand through his hair. "My wife is dead and you're asking *me* for justice?" How the hell was he going to give Kongre justice? There wasn't enough justice in the world to go around. "My settlement's gone, Kongre. It didn't pay for the knee joint, let alone the copper leg. Even if I wanted to give you the money you missed out on, I couldn't."

Kongre sank down on the front stoop, looking out at the ocean. His voice was soft. “The money doesn’t matter anymore, Vasquez. Everything’s gone—”

“Kongre, I’m sor—”

“Save it,” Kongre said, standing and walking away. “We’re not done, Vasquez. Not by a long shot.”

Great, Vasquez thought, watching him go. A war with Kongre was just what he needed in addition to the Board’s time limit. Would he lose everything, then, like Kongre?

Vasquez was still standing there, staring out to sea, when dark clouds blew in off the water and lightning flashed. The sun behind him nearly washed out the blink, but the resounding boom confirmed it. “Shoot,” Vasquez swore, and hurried down the porch steps and to the lighthouse door. He’d have to light the lamp earlier, which meant an additional trip up the stairs in the middle of the night to replenish the oil. Even if he didn’t have to tote the oil up himself, he still had to pour it into the lamp and trim the wicks. The mechanical men weren’t sophisticated enough to perform the task.

It was going to be a long, painful night.

After the storm, the next day dawned crisp and cloudless. The beach was littered with snails the size of his fist and other sea bounty churned up during the storm. But after missing so much sleep the night before, Vasquez was too tired to gather any.

Vasquez was grateful as he extinguished the lamps and cranked up the weights that turned the lens. The clockwork men could clean the glass, cloudy from the salt spray blown around in the storm—and he could sleep for an hour or two, even with that distant rumbling—almost a buzz—he heard on the horizon. No clouds, though, so a storm was far enough away that he could rest without worry. The birds would wake him if there were a problem.

Vasquez woke an hour later, the same hum still buzzing on the horizon, maybe a little louder now. Had he heard a trumpet playing the Argentinian national anthem? *Mortals! Hear the sacred cry.... Freedom, freedom, freedom!* Absurd. Shaking his head, he made his way to the porch and looked out over the ocean. Still no clouds.

At his worktable, Vasquez reconnected Felipe's mainspring, replaced his faceplate, and stood him up. He turned the key at the back of Felipe's neck just a few times, and watched the automaton move back and forth in the small room. When the spring wound down and Felipe came to a stop, Vasquez wired a paintbrush into his hand and carried him outside.

Vasquez turned the key again and pointed him in the direction of the lighthouse. Then, he grabbed the whitewash and followed. It took but a few moments to condition the automaton to paint.

Three hours later, Felipe was nearly finished whitewashing the base of the lighthouse. He was slow, and his steps somewhat jerky as he paced from bucket to wall, but he was working. *And isn't that all a man could wish for in this world—a purpose?*

The low hum still came from the direction of the sea. Vasquez was no longer convinced a storm was brewing. The sound was too constant, too homogenous, to come from nature. He looked to Felipe, who plugged along gamely. *Could Felipe's mechanics be echoing across the water?* That didn't make any sense to him either.

Vasquez looked out over the sea and couldn't believe his eyes. The humming emanated from a ship—but a ship unlike any he'd ever seen before, with—he counted them—*fifteen* masts down each side, and seven taller ones, located centrally as a spine. Instead of sails, each mast bore a spinning propeller on top, keeping the ship aloft. Horizontal shafts, one on the bow, one in the rear, also fitted with propellers, either pushed or pulled the ship along.

Vasquez lifted his glass and saw the name painted on its hull. As the sky clipper *Albatross* streamed closer, he saw the colors she flew: a field of stars on a black background, and in the center a large, golden sun. Vasquez had no idea which country the *Albatross* hailed from; he'd never seen anything like that flag before.

"Martina! Come!" A trilling whistle sounded from the roof of the house, and Martina flew down to perch on the porch rail. Vasquez scribbled a quick note, wired it onto Martina's leg, then wound her up to full strength. He pointed to the airship. "Deliver this message to the ship."

The bird trilled again and flew off. Vasquez watched through his glass until she was only a black speck in his sight.

"Intruder! Intruder!"

Vasquez looked at the markings on the bird now flying toward him. "Friend or foe, Ines?"

"Uni—"

Ines exploded into a cloud of parts, and then Vasquez heard the sound of a gunshot. A piece of metal struck him under his right eye. He dropped to the porch and crawled into the house, pushing the door closed behind him and locking it. He wiped the blood from his face, and reached for his gun.

Kongre.

Had he meant to destroy Ines, or had his shot gone wild? Maybe Kongre only meant to destroy the clockwork mechanicals so Vasquez would be forced to leave if he couldn't complete the lighthouse repairs.

A bullet struck the wood siding of the house. Then another. Vasquez sighed. Since Felipe was in full view of the beach, and Kongre hadn't shot at the automaton, then it was a safe bet Kongre was after *him*.

"Olivia!" Vasquez called to his gull. "Bombs away! Uniform!"

Olivia whistled her acknowledgment and flew out the window over the work table.

Vasquez crawled to the front window and reached to close the left shutter. A bullet smacked into the hinged wood, slamming it shut. "Dammit, Kongre! Shooting me isn't going to get you anything!" Kongre's reply was another bullet, this one striking the framed photo Vasquez's dead wife, Stilla. It fell off the table. Oil from his shattered bird Ines dripped onto the photo, like blood. Vasquez looked away. It was as though Kongre had killed his wife twice.

Vasquez scanned the beach. There were only a few places Kongre could hide—behind a small patch of scrub pine to the far left of the house, a large rock a dozen yards from that, or a cluttered dune on the right, rife with tall, willowy marram grass and oodles of rats—one job he hadn't yet tackled since the rats were far enough away from the house to cause trouble. Kongre had to be in the dune. It offered a more direct shot of the porch and it was closest.

Olivia whistled and flew over the dune, confirming Vasquez's assumptions. She held one of the heavy sea snails in her feet. Vasquez was amazed she could carry it. "Bombs away! Bombs away!" she called, and dropped the snail.

Vasquez inched the barrel of his gun out the window, and squeezed off a round. Sand erupted from the dune. "I don't want to war with you, Kongre, but I will defend myself."

Crack! Another bullet hit the window frame. "Too late, Vasquez! I want what's mine."

Vasquez shrank back, pulling the gun into the house with him. "Bombs away, Olivia! Bombs away!" Olivia whistled and swooped over the beach. She snagged another fist-sized snail and flew over Kongre again.

"Bombs away! Bombs away!" She dropped the missile.

Vasquez heard a muttered oath from the dune and smiled. The second snail must have connected. "Keep it up, Olivia! Bombs away!"

Vasquez heard her whistle, then heard a second, softer whistle from the window ledge over the table.

"Martina!" Her eyes were dim. "Come!" Vasquez held up his arm and the bird leapt from the sill. Halfway across the room, her eyes went dark and she clattered to the floor.

"Dammit." Vasquez crawled to the bird and picked her up. She'd bent a leg in the fall, but her wings looked fine. Quickly, Vasquez opened the case on her back to wind her up, and found a piece of paper inside—a note from the airship? He tucked it away for later, then wound Martina and set her down. Her eyes lit up, and Vasquez found himself smiling. Martina always was his favorite. "Bombs away, Martina! Uniform!"

Martina whistled, then flew to the window and out. Vasquez watched as both birds dropped missiles on Kongre's location. One bird had been a nuisance, but two seemed to be causing him some aggravation. Vasquez couldn't see Kongre, but he watched the sea grass twitch and sway as Kongre rolled back and forth to avoid the snails. That was going to irritate the—

"Ow!" There was a sudden scream from the dune. "Call off your mechanical rats, Vasquez!" More thrashing. Sand flew in the air, and the grass jerked and disappeared as Kongre rolled harder. Kongre screamed again.

"The rats aren't mechanical!" Vasquez studied the dune. Hundreds of black rats poured out of the base of the dune and swarmed over the top, disappearing into the grass.

Olivia and Martina dropped more snails.

"Call off the birds! They're feeding the rats—which are chewing on me!"

Vasquez doubted the birds—or the snails—had anything to do with the rats, but he wouldn't look a gift horse in the mouth. He squeezed off another shot in Kongre's direction for good measure. "I'll call them off if you leave, Kongre, and promise not to come back."

"Agreed!" Kongre rolled out of the dune grass and ran down the beach.

Vasquez called the birds in and pulled the shutters closed on the window, in case Kongre decided to double-back.

Finally, he could get to the note. He read the message, giving a *whoop!* just as Olivia and Martina came through the canvas. Martina flew into the room, dropping something into his lap, which rolled onto the floor. "Bombs away! Bombs away." She whistled and swooped back to the sill.

Vasquez smiled and reached for the sea sponge Martina had dropped. Inspiration hit him. He knew exactly what to do with it. For good measure, he ordered the gulls to retrieve several more.

Vasquez finished packing after breakfast, everything except for his small hand tools, still strewn about the wooden table, and several of the sea sponges the birds had retrieved. Felipe and the other clockwork men were lined up by the door, silent and still, awaiting their next orders. While he waited, Vasquez finished carving a flat, round section from one of the sponges and placed it over the inner workings of the knee joint on his leg, testing the fit. It had taken an hour to clean all the sand and other crusty sea bits out of the sponge, but he'd been left with a soft membrane to protect the knee and keep sand out of the joint. Even if sand got onto the case, it wouldn't be likely to work its way through all the sponge's nooks and crannies and make it into the gears.

"Thank you, Martina. Thanks, Olivia." The birds dipped their heads in turn to his remarks, then re-settled on the sill. He'd programmed that response, but it never failed to amuse him. And he *was* thankful. He hadn't programmed them to find the sponges—and it was a perfect solution to the sand problem. He tucked the sponge around the key, then closed the cap on the knee. "Intruder! Intruder!" Olivia sang from the perch. Vasquez reached for his handgun. "Friend or foe?"

"Suit and tie! Suit and tie!"

Vasquez nodded. He'd been expecting Cruz any day now. A moment later, he heard footsteps—quick and heavy—on the planks of the porch, then a knock on the door. He was too tired to be polite. "It's open!" Vasquez called out, leveling the gun at the door.

A tall, slender man came through the door: Senior Ortiz from the Lighthouse Board. He'd hired Vasquez. Ortiz doffed his hat with a shaking hand. "Señor Vasquez."

Vasquez set the gun down. "Señor Ortiz! I was afraid I'd be meeting Cruz again."

"Señor Cruz no longer works for the Lighthouse Board."

"I'm sorry to hear that."

"You shouldn't be." Ortiz reached inside his coat and pulled out a thick envelope which he handed to Vasquez. "Did Cruz tell you he was brother-in-law to Kongre?"

Vasquez shook his head. "Why would he?"

Ortiz grinned ruefully. "He wouldn't." He nodded at the envelope. "That contains wages and reimbursement for when you hired the townsmen to fix the lens."

"You know what happened?" Ortiz nodded. "Even Kongre's shooting spree?"

Ortiz tried to keep a straight face, and failed. He said, "Kongre lodged a complaint."

"You're joking."

Ortiz shook his head. "It didn't take long to sort out what happened once Kongre mentioned Cruz. Then, they couldn't blame each other fast enough." Ortiz paused. "Cruz and Kongre concocted the scheme to ruin you. Cruz planned to hire Kongre as keeper once they'd run you off."

"Or killed me."

Ortiz nodded, his face grim.

Vasquez thumbed the edges of the worn bills inside the envelope Ortiz had given him. "Seems there's been a bit of an overpayment here. Even if you'd planned to reimburse me for Felipe—"

"Felipe?"

"One of the clockwork men." Vasquez offered Ortiz a look of disgust. "Kongre shot him in the face."

Ortiz looked thoughtful. "I hadn't heard about Felipe. We were hoping you'd stay and complete the repairs—no matter how long it takes. Consider it a signing bonus. Though we've one request: get rid of your mechanicals. It's no way to run a lighthouse."

"This lighthouse has always been run mechanically." Vasquez thought of the weighted chains that he wound to the top of the lighthouse every morning once he extinguished the lamp. He let them drop in the evening—and as they made their slow, twelve-hour descent to the bottom of the weightway, they caused the lens to turn on its axis once every forty seconds.

"Yes—" Ortiz agreed, "but the lamp doesn't have *a face*."

"*That's* the problem?" Vasquez could hardly believe it. Where he found comfort, others felt menace.

Ortiz nodded.

"You realize that a face is the least of your worries when it comes to mechanics?" Vasquez said. "Automatons will soon put us all out of work—this kind of work, anyway—probably other kinds, too."

Ortiz' lips tightened. "Not lighthouses. We'll always need keepers: men to light the lamps in the evening and snuff them in the morning. A face—a human face—as a protector of sailors."

"And when there aren't any more boats?"

"That will never happen," Ortiz said.

Vasquez thought of the airship, and whether or not lighthouses would be relevant in the future. Maybe Ortiz was right: there would always be ships, so there would always be a need for lighthouses. But it didn't follow that the keeper needed to be human. If men like him could learn how to make a lighthouse turn for twelve hours at a time, they could figure out how to turn them indefinitely—and kindle its lamp—and extinguish it again, all without a keeper in residence.

Apparently, men already knew how to make a ship fly—it wouldn't be long before that made keepers obsolete. But airships? What kind of opportunities would that bring? Vasquez smiled. He would soon find out.

Vasquez peeled several bills away from the envelope and handed the bonus back to Ortiz.

"What's this?"

Vasquez packed his hand tools. "Consider this my notice."

"You told Cruz you wanted to stay."

"That was before I'd seen the airship."

"Airship?" Ortiz laughed, a look of incredulity on his face. "That's impossible."

Vasquez just smiled. The constant hum he'd heard two days ago was getting louder. The ship would arrive soon, and he would join this *Monsieur Robur*, the owner of the ship who has conquered the air, and seeks men like himself to unite nations with secrets of machinery, and to free men, using automatons, from their bonds of work.

The hum grew loud enough to shake the small wooden house, then stopped. "Ahoy!" came a voice from above. Something dropped past the window. Startled, Ortiz swung open the door and stepped onto the porch, Vasquez behind him. A large airship hovered above the rocky cliff, the propellers sounding like thousands of honeybees. It was the most marvelous thing Vasquez had seen. A uniformed man climbed down a rope ladder. "Señor Vasquez?" the man asked, "Builder of magnificent clockwork birds?"

Vasquez grinned. "That would be me."

"Splendid." The man returned Vasquez's smile, removed his hat, and tucked it under one arm, then held out his hand to shake. "I am Monsieur Robur. Your bird is an impeccable reference. I'm happy to offer you a job aboard the *Albatross*."

Ortiz stepped forward. "I'm afraid Señor Vasquez has a contract with the Lighthouse Board, Monsieur Robur."

Vasquez cocked an eyebrow. "A contract I'm unable to fulfill."

Ortiz waved his hand. "I told you we are happy to extend that contract—"

"—only if I abandon my clockwork men—"

"Clockwork men?" Robur clapped his hands. *"Magnificent!"*

Vasquez turned to Robur. "Four of them—and another bird. I'll need help loading them."

Robur nodded. He took a whistle from his pocket and blew. Two men in uniform peeked over the gunwales. "Monsieur?" asked the first.

"Send down the lift."

"Aye, Monsieur," the second uniformed man responded. A square platform swept over the edge of the boat at the end of a boom, and lowered swiftly to the ground. Both uniformed men were seated on the platform.

"Just point out your things," Robur said.

"Inside." Vasquez pointed through the open door at Felipe and the other clockwork men, and two large boxes full of parts and tools. The men made quick work of loading them. Vasquez retrieved his bag, and called to the birds.

"Don't go," Ortiz said. "I believe we can find room in the budget for a permanent assistant and a raise."

Vasquez smiled. "Thank you for the opportunity to get on my feet after the war." He stepped onto the platform beside Robur and the uniformed men, and was quickly lifted into the ship. Martina and Olivia swooped upward and landed on the boom arm of the lift.

"Please—stay." Ortiz begged.

"I'm sorry, I can't," Vasquez said. "I have seen my future, and it's not here."

Standing on the deck as the ship sailed away, Vasquez heard a trumpet bleating from the crow's nest above, *Freedom! Freedom! Freedom!*

Raise the *Nautilus*

Eric Choi

South Pacific Ocean
1,700 nautical miles east-northeast of New Zealand
June 1916

The being that emerged from the depths of the sea was humanoid, but it did not look human. The creature's tough beige hide was the texture of elephant skin. The head was a heavy bronze sphere, its face a cyclopean eye crisscrossed by a metallic grate. A pair of thick tubes protruded below the glass eye, snaking back to a heavy cylinder on its back.

Commander Thomas Jennings watched as the diver was hoisted onto the deck of the research ship RRS *Discovery*. Two sailors helped the diver to a seated position on a wooden bench, where they began to disconnect the tubes and unfasten the helmet. A third man in a brown trilby and civilian attire, tall and gaunt with a sharp nose, stared impassively at the scene.

Jennings turned and looked out to sea. A few hundred yards distant the grey bulk of his ship, the cruiser HMS *Euryalus*, drifted serenely on the sparkling waters. The tranquility was a welcome relief from the fierce storms that had delayed the start of the operation for days.

The sailors lifted the helmet off the diver, revealing the ruddy face of a middle-aged man with sweat-soaked dark hair. He closed his eyes, threw his head back, and inhaled deeply.

"Are you all right?" Jennings asked.

The diver, Jonathan Badders, nodded. "Yes, sir. Thank you."

Donald McCabe, a civilian from the Meta Section of the Directorate of Military Intelligence, stepped forward. "What did you see? Is she there?"

Badders nodded again, this time smiling. "She's there. I saw her. The *Nautilus*."

JV

As the executive officer of HMS *Euryalus*, Commander Jennings was glad to be back aboard his ship. Both *Euryalus* and *Discovery* had been launched in the same year, but the latter seemed much older. *Discovery* was a wooden three-masted auxiliary steamship, the last of her kind to be built in the British Empire. The Admiralty had purchased *Discovery* from the Hudson's Bay Company, refitting the cargo ship to serve as a floating base for Operation Mobilis – the Royal Navy's attempt to raise the *Nautilus*.

Jennings, Badders, McCabe, and the divisional officers gathered around a table in the commanding officer's day cabin.

"What's the state of the *Nautilus*?" asked Captain Richard Powell.

"She's at a depth of 41 fathoms, with a slight list to starboard of about seven degrees," reported Badders. "Her stern is buried in about eighteen feet of hard clay, but otherwise she appears to be undamaged."

"When can the salvage operation begin?" asked McCabe.

"Weather permitting, as early as tomorrow," said Lieutenant-Commander Eugene Seagram, an officer from the Royal Navy Engineers who had been seconded from the Admiralty to support Operation Mobilis.

"About bloody time," said McCabe. "The Smith-Harding report was quite specific about the last known location of the *Nautilus*. I can't believe it took almost a month to find her."

Jennings, Powell, and the key divisional officers had been briefed by McCabe on the *Nautilus* file just before their departure from Auckland. Of particular interest to the War Office was a description in the Smith-Harding report, corroborated by earlier accounts from Aronnax, of "a destructive weapon, lightning-like in its effects" that could stun or kill men. His Majesty's Government was still telling the public that the Great War was going well, but military men like Jennings knew the terrible truth. McCabe's impatience was annoying but understandable. Such a weapon, in the hands of the British, could break the stalemate on the Western Front.

"Badders' report on the condition of the *Nautilus* is excellent news," said Seagram. "It means we can proceed with the original salvage plan with little modification." He spread across the table a schematic diagram of the submarine, copied from a trove of documents seized five years ago during a joint raid by the Directorate of Military Intelligence and the British Army on the ancestral palace of the late Prince Dakkar in the Bundelkhand region of India. "The five pontoons from the *Discovery* will be deployed as follows: Three above the stern, and two above the bow. For additional buoyancy, we will run two hoses down to blow the main ballast tank of the *Nautilus*. The biggest challenge will be the unforeseen need to tunnel the clay under the stern to place the harness and lifting chains for the aft pontoons."

"How long will this take?" Powell asked.

"Three weeks," Seagram replied.

Donald McCabe rolled his eyes and shook his head.

"Very well," Powell said. "Get some rest, gentlemen. We have a big day tomorrow."

There was one other aspect of the Smith-Harding report that had made an impression on Commander Jennings – the fanatical hatred of Prince Dakkar, later known as Captain Nemo, for the British Empire. How ironic it would be if Nemo's invention ended up saving it.

JV

Donald McCabe's cynicism was vindicated. It actually took fifty days for Badders and his team of divers to pass the harnesses and lifting chains under the *Nautilus*, attach the pontoons, and connect the hoses to the main ballast tank. Just tunneling the clay under the stern took the entirety of the originally-estimated three weeks.

But at long last, everything was ready. Jennings, McCabe, and Seagram returned to the *Discovery* to supervise the operation.

"Proceed with blowing the stern pontoons," Seagram ordered.

Jennings watched as the pumps roared to life, the needles on gauges began to move, and the hoses snaking into the water stiffened.

"We're starting with the stern first," Seagram explained, "which will hopefully avoid any center-of-gravity issues that might arise if both ends were lifted at the same time."

Euryalus was anchored a few hundred yards away. She was joined by HMRT *Rollicker*, an Admiralty tug that had been dispatched from Auckland six days ago.

"There!" Yeoman Farley called out excitedly, pointing to a colored float that had bobbed to the surface.

"I see it," Seagram said. "That's good. It means the stern has been lifted off the sea floor. Stop the air to the aft pontoons, and start blowing the forward pontoons!"

The men scanned the surface of the water with binoculars, looking for the second colored float. It did not appear.

Seagram glanced at the pressure gauges and frowned. "The bow should be lifting by now." He shook his head. "It's taking too long. Start the tertiary pump. We'll try blowing the main ballast tank on the *Nautilus*."

After ten minutes, the second float finally appeared. Moments later, the surface of the ocean began to froth violently, like water in a saucepan brought to boil.

"Something's wrong," said Jennings.

Suddenly, both of the bow pontoons popped to the surface. The massive cylinders, twelve feet in diameter and thirty feet long, briefly cleared the water before crashing back down in a torrent of spray.

Seconds later, it was the *Nautilus*.

Jennings gasped as the bow of the submarine came up, smashing into one of the pontoons and tossing it aside. She rose like a giant breaching metallic narwhal, the armored steel spur that protruded from her nose glistening in the midday sun. Then, with a great splash, the *Nautilus* slipped back under the waves and quickly disappeared from view.

"What the devil went wrong?" Captain Powell demanded.

"It appears the center-of-gravity of the *Nautilus* is further aft than we expected," Seagram explained. "When we blew her main ballast tank, the momentum caused the bow to rise so fast it slipped out of its harness, separating it from the pontoons and sending everything to the surface. The impact with the pontoon dislodged the hose and opened the ballast tank vents, allowing water back into the main ballast tank and submerging the *Nautilus* again."

"How could you have not known the location of the center-of-gravity?" McCabe asked. "We have the drawings of the *Nautilus*."

"We have the design drawings, not the as-built drawings," Seagram explained. "The mass properties of the final build appear to have differed significantly from the original design."

"What do we do now?" Powell asked. "The damaged pontoon is beyond repair."

Jennings was in a glum mood. The Admiralty was demanding daily wireless reports and bristling at the delays and costs, even threatening to cancel Operation Mobilis. He thought for a moment, then said, "I have an idea."

"Commander?"

Jennings spread a nautical chart onto the table. "The only reason this operation was even feasible is because the depth of the ocean here is unusually shallow. There was an island here until it was destroyed in the volcanic eruption of 1882. We know from the Fessenden oscillator soundings we took during the search phase that there are even shallower areas nearby." He traced a finger on the chart. "For example, just two nautical miles due east of our present location, the depth is only 16 fathoms."

"Yes!" Seagram exclaimed. "I see where the XO is going with this." He produced a notepad and began to sketch. "We can use the four remaining pontoons, not to bring the *Nautilus* to the surface, but to lift her just high enough off the seafloor for the *Rollicker* to tow her to the shallower area, and then we deliberately ground her there. Her ballast tank vents will have to be repaired, but it will be much easier and safer for Badders and his divers to work at the shallower depth. We'll then use the shorter hoses from the *Discovery* that we couldn't use before to blow both the main and secondary ballast tanks, and we can also use the trim tanks to compensate for the center-of-gravity issue. Taken all together, there should be sufficient buoyancy to bring the *Nautilus* back to the surface."

"You think this is feasible?" Jennings asked.

"I'll need to work out the details with my team," Seagram replied, "but yes."

"How long until we're ready for a second attempt?" Powell asked.

"Three weeks," Seagram said.

McCabe shook his head. "Is that your answer to everything?"

The preparations took almost triple the time. Just lifting the *Nautilus* off the seafloor took three weeks, followed by two days for the *Rollicker* to tow and ground her in the shallower water, and finally another five weeks for the divers to repair the ballast tank vents, reattach the pontoons, and connect the additional hoses and lines.

On the day of the second salvage attempt, it appeared as if every man aboard *Euryalus* had gathered along the portside railing to watch. For a moment, Jennings had the amusing and absurd thought that the ship might very well tip over.

Once again, the surface of the ocean started to foam and bubble, and then the great bulk of the *Nautilus*, this time with pairs of massive pontoons attached at deck level to bow and stern, burst through the frothing water. Pressure-relief valves on the pontoons and the submarine opened, sending up spray that shrouded the *Nautilus* in rainbowed clouds of vapor. Slowly, the *Nautilus* righted herself and settled onto the surface, her bobbing motion sending small waves towards *Euryalus* and *Discovery*.

For a moment, nobody could speak. The men of the *Euryalus* just stood there, mesmerized by the sight. And then, a massive cheer erupted through the crowd.

"About bloody time," muttered Donald McCabe.

The real *Nautilus* bore little resemblance to the version depicted in the popular press during Captain Nemo's infamous reign of terror in the late 1860s, with its ridiculous serrated fins, bulbous viewports, and outsized rivets. The real *Nautilus* was two hundred and fifty feet in length from the tip of the armored spur at her bow to the large propeller and fish-like rudder at her stern. A pilothouse protruded about a third of the way along her deck, below which were mounted large hydroplanes for diving control. She was a sleek grey war machine, in some ways a long-lost ancestor of the Royal Navy's new K-class submarines that were only now commencing sea trials.

Jennings turned to Seagram and shook his hand. "Congratulations!"

"Sir!"

Jennings made his way through the crowd to find Jonathan Badders and the divers, shaking each of their hands in turn. "Well done, gentlemen. Yours was the most vital and dangerous job. This accomplishment belongs to you."

"Thank you, Commander," said Badders.

It took a day to run the towing hawser between the *Nautilus* and the tugboat *Rollicker*, and the following day the flotilla commenced its long journey back to Auckland under the escort of *Euryalus*. The most difficult part of Operation Mobilis was over, but there was still one more task to perform.

Only one body had been found aboard the *Nautilus*, and what to do with it became a rather delicate question.

"Sir, you can't be serious!" exclaimed Jennings, sitting across the table from Powell in the captain's day cabin.

"I am quite serious, and my decision is made," said Powell. "Captain Nemo is to be reburied at sea with honors."

"Sir," Jennings pleaded, "that man was an enemy combatant. All those ships he sank. I would not be surprised if there are men right here on the *Euryalus* who knew some of the people he murdered."

"I'm aware of that," Powell said. "Nevertheless, Captain Nemo was a comrade of the seas, and arguably he was even a subject of the British Empire for a time. Like it or not, he is entitled to the honor."

"I don't like it, sir."

"Your objection is noted," Powell said. "However, if it makes you feel better, think of it this way. What better revenge could we exact than to bury him under the flag of his adversary?"

Jennings thought for a moment and decided that he had greatly misjudged his commanding officer's sense of humor.

So it came to be that Jennings, Powell, and the divisional officers of the *Euryalus* found themselves in dress uniform standing at attention before the Union Jack draped coffin of Captain Nemo. Jonathan Badders and five of his fellow divers served as pallbearers, lifting the coffin and slowly marching towards the edge of the deck.

"The sea is the largest cemetery, and its slumberers sleep without a monument," said Captain Powell. "All other graveyards show symbols of distinction between great and small, rich and poor. But in the ocean cemetery, the king, the clown, the prince, the peasant, the hero, and the villain are all alike, undistinguishable."

The pallbearers set the coffin down on a platform at the edge of the deck, and they removed and folded the flag. Badders pulled a lever, the platform tilted downward, and Captain Nemo returned to the sea.

Commander Jennings kept his face neutral and respectful, but in his mind's eye he was smiling. Captain Nemo had been taken from his beloved *Nautilus*, which in turn had been taken from him. His final resting place would be a remote and obscure part of the South Pacific, amongst the sharks, alone and far from the coral cemetery of his crewmates. The Royal Navy had given Captain Nemo exactly what he deserved.

It was a very British thing to do.

At full speed, *Euryalus* could have made it back to New Zealand in about four days. But after a week at sea, the flotilla was still more than three hundred nautical miles out from Auckland. The problem was the antiquated *Discovery*, which could barely manage eight knots under sail and steam. Jennings was still making daily wireless reports to his impatient masters in the Admiralty, and he knew that every additional day at sea was another day that something could go wrong.

On the eighth day, his fears were realized.

"What is it, XO?"

"We have company," Jennings said, handing his binoculars to Powell.

The captain looked out the bridge windows of the *Euryalus* to where Jennings was pointing. "Are we expecting any Allied shipping in this area?" Powell asked.

"No, sir," said Jennings.

"I'm not aware of anything either," said McCabe.

Jennings spoke into a voice pipe. "This is the bridge. Can we get a range on the target bearing zero-four-nine?" After a few moments, he bent his ear to the pipe. "Probably about thirteen nautical miles," he reported, "but it's hard to tell with the mist. Wait a minute." He held up a finger. "Lookout reports the target appears to be turning. The rangefinder will need a moment to reestablish coincidence."

"I don't like this," Powell muttered.

"The mist is clearing, and the target is no longer turning," Jennings reported. "Sir, the rangefinder has a new solution. Eleven nautical miles, and closing rapidly."

Powell turned to McCabe. "If that's a German warship, how soon until we're in range of her guns?"

"For their Pacific fleet, I would expect it to be a light cruiser like ourselves, with similar weaponry," McCabe said. "Main guns would have a range of around 15,000 yards."

After a few minutes, Jennings raised his binoculars again. "Target now at ten nautical miles, still closing fast. I can see a profile and battle ensign." He flipped through the pages of the silhouette book. "Confirmed, she's German sir! Most likely SMS *Scharnhorst*, an armored cruiser."

The klaxon sounded, and Powell spoke into a voice pipe. "All hands, this is the Captain. Action stations, action stations. Inbound hostile vessel. This is not a drill." He turned and called out to a young man. "Yeoman Farley!"

"Yes, sir!" said Farley, pad and pencil ready.

"Get on the wireless. Make to *Rollicker* and *Discovery*. 'German cruiser inbound. *Euryalus* engaging. *Rollicker* and *Discovery* to maintain current speed and heading.'"

"Yes, sir!"

"Make course zero-one-five to bring the target within the firing arc of the fore-turret," Powell ordered. "Prepare to fire when the *Scharnhorst* breaks seven nautical miles."

From the bridge windows, Jennings could see the turning of the fore-turret and the single barrel of the 9.2-inch Mark X gun beginning to rise. The approaching German cruiser was now visible without binoculars.

"Seven nautical miles!" Jennings called out.

At that moment, a flash and a puff of smoke erupted from the *Scharnhorst*. Seconds later, the unmistakable screech of a shell in flight could be heard, followed by a concussive boom and an explosive geyser of foamy white seawater a few hundred yards off the bow of *Euryalus*.

"Return fire!" Powell ordered.

The *Euryalus* trembled as her forward gun discharged. A plume of water erupted short of the *Scharnhorst*.

"Visual splash spotters, recalculate the solution," Jennings ordered. "Gunnery, open fire when ready."

Euryalus fired again, and this time, the shell found its target. On the *Scharnhorst*, an explosion blossomed amidships.

"Hit, sir!" a lieutenant exclaimed.

Jennings bent his ear to a voice pipe, then turned and peered through his binoculars. "The *Scharnhorst* is no longer closing. She appears to have stopped. However, her guns seem to be –"

A shell exploded a few yards off the bow

"—very much intact, sir!"

Yeoman Farley returned with a piece of paper. "Message from the *Rollicker*, Captain!"

Powell read the telegram, his eyes wide. "*Rollicker* reports spotting another ship bearing three-four-nine, identified as SMS *Gneisenau*."

Jennings called into a voice pipe. "I need confirmation and range to the new target, bearing three-four-nine." Moments later, he said, "Second target confirmed, Captain! Range five-and-a-half nautical miles."

Suddenly, a massive explosion rocked the *Euryalus*, throwing the men to the deck. Powell got to his feet and staggered to the engine order telegraph. "Helm, make course three-five-zero, half speed. I want to engage with a broadside."

The helmsman rotated the steering stand, but the *Euryalus* did not turn.

"I have a report from damage control," Jennings said. "We've been hit astern, probably by a torpedo. Rudder and propeller are damaged. Helm will not respond."

"Bring the aft-turret to bear on the *Gneisenau*," Powell ordered. "Fore-turret, keep firing on the *Scharnhorst*." He looked around. "Where's Yeoman Farley?"

"Here, sir!"

"Make to *Rollicker* and *Discovery*. 'If Germans attempt to intercept or board, make no attempt at armed resistance.'"

"Sir?" said Farley, incredulous.

"Young man, we are in a terrible tactical situation," Jennings explained. "*Discovery* and *Rollicker* cannot run, and we cannot protect them against two cruisers. Their only chance is to stay out of the fight – and pray that these particular Germans are inclined to abide by the London Declaration." He jerked his thumb. "Now, go!"

"Wait!" Powell said suddenly. "XO, what's the depth of the ocean here?"

Jennings consulted a nautical chart. "About 880 fathoms."

"Yeoman!" Powell thought for a moment, then said, "Further message to the *Rollicker*. 'Cut pontoons. Scuttle the *Nautilus*.'"

Farley's eyes widened. "Sending this right away, sir!"

McCabe approached. "Captain, I assume you want me off the bridge?"

Powell nodded. "Get below, Mr. McCabe."

The fore- and aft-turrets fired simultaneously. Another explosion blossomed on the *Scharnhorst*, this time at the bow.

Moments later, a blast ripped through the *Euryalus*.

Jennings struggled to his feet. He touched his forehead and felt blood. "Captain? Lieutenant? Is everyone all right?" Mumbled affirmations drifted across the shattered bridge. Staggering to the smashed forward windows, he looked out and beheld a horrific sight. The fore-turret had been hit, reduced to bent and twisted metal from which smoke poured out of serrated holes.

Hearing a shuffle of feet, Jennings turned to see Captain Powell at his side. They looked at each other for a moment, and both knew what needed to be done. They could not run, and it was only a matter of time before the fire ignited the magazine of cordite charges. When that happened, the *Euryalus* would explode in a fireball.

"All hands, this is the Captain. Abandon ship. I repeat, abandon ship. All hands to the lifeboats immediately." Powell turned to Jennings. "Divide the decks between us. Check as many compartments as you can."

"See you at the lifeboat, sir!"

Jennings raced through the smashed and smoke-filled decks and compartments of the *Euryalus*, calling out and directing dazed crewmen, both able-bodied and injured, to external hatches and lifeboats. The men were afraid but not panicked, the evacuation carried out with a stoic British efficiency that Jennings would later recall with tremendous pride.

The last place Jennings checked was the wireless cabin. He had expected it to be already evacuated, but was surprised instead to find an unconscious Yeoman Farley sprawled on the deck. Relieved to find Farley alive and breathing, Jennings hooked his elbows under the armpits of the unconscious man and lifted him in a fireman's carry. His lungs burned from smoke and exertion, but finally he managed to stagger outside.

Captain Powell, Lieutenant-Commander Seagram, and the divisional officers of the *Euryalus* were already in the last lifeboat. With their assistance, Jennings brought Farley aboard and then hopped inside himself. The derrick swung the lifeboat over the side and down to the water.

"Is everyone accounted for?" Jennings asked. The pained, vacant look in Powell's eyes was the only response he got.

They began to row furiously, joining the other lifeboats in trying to get as far away from the *Euryalus* as possible. Suddenly, there was an explosion. The occupants of the lifeboat turned to watch an ominous mushroom cloud rise into the air. But it wasn't the *Euryalus*. It was the *Scharnhorst*.

Jennings knew *Euryalus* would soon share the same fate, but for now he took grim satisfaction in seeing the German ship go down first. For the moment, *Euryalus* was still afloat, as were the apparently undamaged *Discovery* and *Rollicker*.

And the *Nautilus*.

"Sir!" Jennings tapped Powell on the shoulder, and pointed.

The *Nautilus* was still on the surface, still attached to its four pontoons, still hooked up to the *Rollicker*. A short distance away was the second German cruiser, the *Gneisenau*. Jennings watched in stunned disbelief as a boatload of seebataillon, marines of the Imperial German Navy, came alongside the *Rollicker* and boarded. About twenty minutes later, smoke began to billow from the *Rollicker*'s funnel and the tug began to move, with the *Nautilus* in tow and the *Gneisenau* following behind.

Under different circumstances, the men in the lifeboat might have shouted and cursed. But nobody spoke. Cold and in shock, and physically and mentally exhausted by the battle, the harrowing escape, and the imminent loss of their ship, they just sat in helpless silence as the Germans sailed away with their prize.

London, England

December 1916

A note on the menu reminded customers to limit their order to two items for lunch and three for dinner. Commander Thomas Jennings flipped through the pages but decided he wasn't hungry. He put down the menu and sat back, waiting.

Half an hour later, a tall man wearing a brown trilby exited the War Office Building across from the restaurant. Jennings stood, remembering to push his chair under the table, and walked across the street to intercept.

"Mr. Jennings," said Donald McCabe. "What a surprise to see you."

"You're a hard man to reach," Jennings said. "I've been trying to contact you for well over a month."

"What do you want?"

Jennings gestured. "Let's take a stroll through the gardens."

The two men walked down Horse Guards Avenue, then turned to pass through the black wrought iron gates into Whitehall Gardens.

"The ocean is big, but the German Pacific fleet is not," Jennings said. "Yet somehow, we managed to run into two German cruisers less than a day out from Auckland."

"Perhaps the ocean isn't as big as you think."

Jennings stopped and turned. "And why was the order to scuttle the *Nautilus* not carried out? Or was the order never sent? I found Yeoman Farley unconscious in the wireless room."

"As I recall, we were being shelled and torpedoed by German cruisers. Men tend to fall down under such circumstances."

"This is all a game to you DMI people, isn't it?" Jennings hissed, his anger rising. "Let me remind you of the cost. The *Euryalus* destroyed. Ninety-three injured, many seriously. Twenty-eight missing and forty-four dead, including Jonathan Badders. The crew of the *Rollicker* taken prisoner. And the *Nautilus* in the hands of the Germans."

"Forgive the pun, Jennings," McCabe said with condescension, "but as a Navy man, you're out of your depth."

"Then explain it to me."

McCabe lit a cigarette. "Would it interest you to know that German war production is down almost nine percent from this time last year?"

Jennings was puzzled. "What does this have to do with anything?"

"Kaiser Wilhelm fancies himself a man of science," McCabe continued, "but in reality he is quite mad. He is obsessed with the *Nautilus* and her weapons. Well, let him have it. An armored battering ram is hardly impressive in the age of torpedoes. As for this lightning weapon, I suppose what the Germans would call a blitzwaffe…"

McCabe flicked ash onto the grass. "He can have that, too. Directed energy weapons are years if not decades away from widespread practical military deployment. This war will be won with more ships, more artillery, more guns, perhaps more aeroplanes – not with fantastical inventions from the realm of scientifiction. In the meantime, if it pleases the Kaiser to pursue this folly, every pfennig spent on this fantasy is a pfennig that is not being spent on real weapons that will make an actual difference to the outcome of this war."

Jennings was silent for a moment, contemplating McCabe's words. At last, he said, "I think you're wrong."

"I don't care what you think."

"Then maybe you should care that I know something about you," Jennings said.

"And what would that be?" McCabe asked.

"That your mother was born in India."

McCabe stared at Jennings for a moment, then threw the cigarette butt to the ground and crushed it with his shoe. "It goes without saying that everything I've told you is sensitive and privileged information. I should remind you that the penalties for disclosure under the Official Secrets Act are rather severe."

"So are the penalties for treason," Jennings hissed.

A thin smile crossed McCabe's lips. "We each have to fight the war in our own way." He tipped his hat. "Goodbye, Mr. Jennings. God save the King."

Donald McCabe turned and walked away. Commander Thomas Jennings made no attempt to follow. Alone amongst the greenery of Whitehall Gardens, Jennings wondered when the history of the Great War is written whether Operation Mobilis would be remembered as a success or failure. And by whom.

About the Authors

Mike Adamson holds a Doctoral degree from Flinders University of South Australia. After early aspirations in art and writing, Mike returned to study and secured qualifications in both marine biology and archaeology. Mike has been a university educator since 2006, has worked in the replication of convincing ancient fossils, is a passionate photographer, a master-level hobbyist, and a journalist for international magazines. Short fiction sales include to *Metastellar*, *The Strand*, *Little Blue Marble*, *Abyss and Apex*, *Daily Science Fiction*, *Compelling Science Fiction*, and *Nature Futures*. Mike has placed over 160 stories to date, totaling around 750, 000 words in print. You can catch up with his writing career at 'The View From the Keyboard,' http://mike-adamson.blogspot.com.

Joel Allegretti is the author of, most recently, *Platypus* (NYQ Books, 2017), a collection of poems, prose, and performance texts, and *Our Dolphin* (Thrice Publishing, 2016), a novella. His second book of poems, *Father Silicon* (The Poet's Press, 2006), was selected by *The Kansas City Star* as one of 100 Noteworthy Books of 2006.

He is the editor of *Rabbit Ears: TV Poems* (NYQ Books, 2015). *The Boston Globe* called *Rabbit Ears* "cleverly edited" and "a smart exploration of the many, many meanings of TV." *Rain Taxi* said, "With its diversity of content and poetic form, *Rabbit Ears* feels more rich and eclectic than any other poetry anthology on the market."

Gustavo Bondoni is a novelist and short story writer with over three hundred stories published in fifteen countries, in seven languages. He is a member of Codex and an Active Member of SFWA. His latest novel is *Lost Island Rampage* (2021). He has also published three other monster books: *Ice Station: Death* (2019), *Jungle Lab Terror* (2020), and *Test Site Horror* (2020); three science fiction novels: *Incursion* (2017), *Outside* (2017), and *Siege* (2016); and an ebook novella entitled *Branch*. His short fiction is collected in *Pale Reflection* (2020), *Off the Beaten Path* (2019), *Tenth Orbit and Other Faraway Places* (2010), and *Virtuoso and Other Stories* (2011).

In 2019, Gustavo was awarded second place in the Jim Baen Memorial Contest and in 2018 he received a Judges Commendation (and second place) in The James White Award. He was also a 2019 finalist in the Writers of the Future Contest.

His website is at www.gustavobondoni.com

Demetri Capetanopoulos credits *Twenty Thousand Leagues Under the Seas* for inspiring his career as a nuclear submarine officer and deep submersible pilot. In his creative work, Demetri combines precision and technical knowledge with the wonder and possibility of imagination.

A meticulous re-examining of the most famous submarine in literature was the impetus for his first book, *The Design and Construction of the Nautilus*. In an upcoming graphic novel, *Rage Runs Deep*, Demetri weaves the tragic backstory of Captain Nemo through the seminal historical events of the 19th century. Fact and fiction are blended in a more lighthearted way in *Ned the Nuclear Submarine* and *Hadley the Lunar Rover*, two books written and illustrated by Demetri for children and all those who remain young at heart.

To connect with Demetri or learn more about his creative projects, visit PreciseImagination.com.

Brenda Carre lives on Vancouver Island, on land still steeped in indigenous lore where myth can arise from the waves of the Salish Sea on the backs of Orca. She writes for *Pulphouse Fiction Magazine, Fiction River Anthologies, Pulp Literature Magazine, Heart's Kiss Magazine*, and elsewhere. "Embrace of the Planets" originally appeared in the 2014 October/November issue of *The Magazine of Fantasy and Science Fiction*.

Brenda writes with voice and a kiss of grimdark. Her short fiction crosses borders into the realm of weird fiction, time travel, ghostly visitation, and the unknown: A paranormal sleuth and her side-kick genie solve X-file-style crimes in Victorian England. School girls resurrect road kill to deal with bullies and murderers. Antique stores leap through time and space.

Brenda's debut novel *Gret-of-Roon* will be released this year from Pulp Literature Press. A taste of her prose can be found on her website at https://brendacarre.com/

Eric Choi is an award-winning writer, editor, and aerospace engineer based in Toronto, Canada. He was the first recipient of the Isaac Asimov Award (now the Dell Magazines Award) and has twice won the Prix Aurora Award for his short story "Crimson Sky" and for the Chinese-themed anthology *The Dragon and the Stars* (DAW) co-edited with Derwin Mak. With Ben Bova, he co-edited the hard SF anthology *Carbide Tipped Pens* (Tor). His first short story collection *Just Like Being There* (Springer) was released this year. "Raise the *Nautilus*" first appeared in the anthology *20,000 Leagues Remembered* (Pole to Pole) edited by Steven R. Southard and Kelly A. Harmon. In 2009, he was one of the Top 40 finalists (out of 5,351 applicants) in the Canadian Space Agency's astronaut recruitment campaign. Please visit his website www.aerospace-writer.ca or follow him on Twitter @AerospaceWriter.

Christopher M. Geeson has had several pieces of fiction published, with appearances in *Robots and Artificial Intelligence Short Stories* (Flame Tree Press, 2018), *The British Fantasy Society Journal (*Autumn 2011), *Atomic Age Cthulhu*, *Dark Tales*, and *Anthology: A Circa Works Collection*, as well as a poem in the recent *Spawn of War and Deathiness.* With a long interest in the Civil War, his first works in print were three articles for The American Civil War Society UK, about how the conflict has been portrayed in movies. "Tyranny Under the Sea" is Chris' second story to feature the Civil War era – it also gets an alternate history twist in "The Flower," published in Chaosium's *Steampunk Cthulhu* collection. Christopher is a tour guide in the city of York, UK, and also works in schools, libraries, and museums, running creative workshops for children.

Kelly A. Harmon, MFA, is an award-winning journalist and author, and a member of the Horror Writers Association and the Science Fiction & Fantasy Writers of America. A Baltimore native, she writes the *Charm City Darkness* series. Find her short fiction in many magazines and anthologies, including *Occult Detective Quarterly*; *Terra! Tara! Terror!* and *Deep Cuts: Mayhem, Menace and Misery.*

David A. Natale (www.davidanatale.com) is an award-winning author, playwright, and performer. His latest play, "Around the World in Less than 80 Days," which follows reporter Nellie Bly's 1889 global race, was produced this year at the Key City Public Theatre. David's one man show, "The Westerbork Serenade," (www.westerborkserenade.com) tells the true story of Jewish actors in a Nazi transit camp during WWII. It won a Seattle Times Footlight Award in 2007 and toured the Netherlands in 2010. He also seeks a publisher for his supernatural mystery thriller about a pizza driver, *Pizza Stories: Deliveries from Beyond*. David lives in Seattle with his wife, step-son, and dog.

Alison L. Randall grew up in the small Utah town where Butch Cassidy was born. This is, perhaps, the reason she likes to tell stories set in the Old West and why bandits and robbers often play a prominent role. Some of Alison's short stories have been featured in print and online children's magazines. Another was published as a historical fiction picture book, entitled, *The Wheat Doll*. Alison holds an MFA in writing from Vermont College of Fine Arts along with a bachelor's degree in French. Her 16-month stay in France led to her interest in Jules Verne and to an eventual desire to mix his world with her beloved Old West. Find out more about her and get links to some of her short stories at alisonlrandall.com.

Janice Rider has a background in zoology, English literature, education, and conservation. Her love of the outdoors, young people, animals, and plants informs her writing. In the past, she has raised praying mantises and is fascinated by insects. As well, she has owned a giant millipede, bearded dragons, and two large corn snakes. Currently, a border collie mix lives with her family and ensures that, even on days when she doesn't want to get out, she does so for the dog's sake. For the past seventeen years, Janice has been the director of The Chameleon Drama Club for children and youth. She has three published plays for youth with Eldridge Plays and Musicals. *Honeyguide Literary Magazine* published a piece she wrote about snakes. Should people wish to find out more, they can find Janice on LinkedIn.

Michael Schulkins was born, raised, and spent most of his life in California, but has recently escaped with his wonderful wife Helen to the wilds of Arizona. Michael attended several universities and eventually emerged with two degrees in physics, one in music composition, and minors in math, political science, philosophy, and poker. He subsequently spent twenty years teaching physics, and now writes fiction full time. His novels include the comic crime capers *Mother Lode* and *Sting Suite*, the out-of-this-world political satires *Beltway and Up A Tree: A Jobs and Plunkitt Galactic Adventure*, and the alternate history adventure series *Mark Twain on the Moon*. His work can be found at michaelschulkins.com, marktwainonthemoon.com, and at Amazon, Audible, and other book retailers. All of Michael's books should give you a good laugh, but they may also make you stop and think.

Joseph S. Walker lives in Indiana and teaches college literature and composition courses. His short fiction has appeared in *Alfred Hitchcock's Mystery Magazine*, *Ellery Queen's Mystery Magazine*, *Mystery Weekly*, *Tough*, and a number of other magazines and anthologies. He has been nominated for the Edgar Award and the Derringer Award and has won the Bill Crider Prize for Short Fiction. He also won the Al Blanchard Award in 2019 and 2021. Follow him on Twitter @JSWalkerAuthor and visit his website at https://jsw47408.wixsite.com/website.

About the Artist

Amanda Bergloff is a surrealist digital artist whose cover and interior artwork has been published in *Tiny Spoon Literary Magazine*, *New Myths*, *The Horror Zine*, *Turbulence and Coffee*, *Enchanted Conversation*, *Twisted Sister Literary Magazine*, *Backchannels Journal*, and other publications. She lives in Denver, Colorado and is a shameless collector of books, toys, and comics. Artist website: http://abergloff2.wix.com/artistgallery And follow her on Twitter @AmandaBergloff

About the Editors

CDR Steven R. Southard, USNR (Ret.) drew much of his life's inspiration from *Twenty Thousand Leagues Under the Seas.* After graduating from the Naval Academy with a degree in Naval Architecture, he served in the submarine force. Like Verne, Steve turned to writing fiction, creating characters who grapple with new technologies in far-off places. He co-edited the anthology *20,000 Leagues Remembered.* His short stories have appeared in over a dozen anthologies, most recently including *Not Far from Roswell, Re-Terrify*, and *Quoth the Raven.* Fourteen of his stories form the *What Man Hath Wrought* series. He's written science fiction, alternate history, steampunk, fantasy, and horror. He wrote the upcoming sci-fi collection titled *The Seastead Chronicles.* Order your engines to ahead full and submerge into Steve's website at https://stevenrsouthard.com, where he's known as Poseidon's Scribe. Or steam over to his mysterious islands on Facebook and Twitter.

Rev. Matthew Hardesty first heard of Jules Verne while watching *Back to the Future Part III* when he was 10 years old. A few years ago, he thought it would be a good idea to read *Twenty Thousand Leagues Under the Seas* while on a trans-atlantic cruise, and was hooked. He is delighted to be a member of the North American Jules Verne Society and the co-editor of this, his first anthology. When he's not pastoring three parishes in Central KY, he picks away at other projects, like cross-referencing Verne's first draft, *Uncle Robinson* (*Shipwrecked Family*), with its final form, *The Mysterious Island*, and producing footnotes for *In Search of the Castaways.*

Appendix A
Illustration Credits

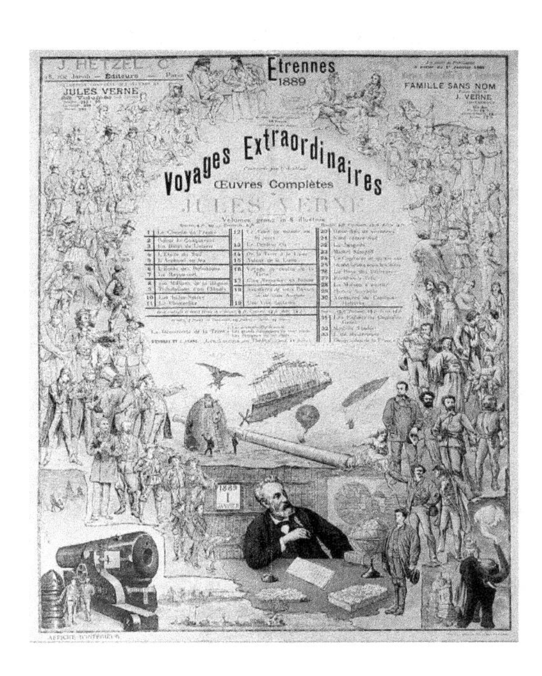

Fronticepiece
Original: Hetzel éditeur
affiche etrennes 1889 /
Hetzel Publishere Poster
New for 1889
Famille sans nom /
Family Without a Name
This poster shows characters
and some vehicles from
Verne's novels that were
published before 1889.

"The Dominion of All the Earth"
Original: 1867 – *Voyage au*
centre de la Terre / A Journey to
the Centre of the Earth
Illustrator: Riou

Le canon de l'île de Malte (p. 42).

"To Hold Back Time"
Original: 1868 – *De la Terre à la Lune / From the Earth to the Moon*
Illustrator: de Montaut

"A Drama in Durango"
Original: 1907 – *L'agence Thompson and Co / The Thompson Travel Agency* (written by Michel Verne)
Illustrator: Léon Benett

Tel était donc le train. [Page [illegible]]

"Old Soldiers"
Original: 1880 – *La maison à vapeur / The Steam House*
Illustrator: Léon Benett

"Want of Air"
Original: 1866 – *Voyages et aventures du Capitaine Hatteras / Voyages and Adventures of Captain Hatteras*
Illustrator: Riou and de Montaut

"Nellie and Jules Go Boating"
Original: 1891 – *Mistress Branican / Mistress Branican*
Illustrator: Léon Benett

"The Highest Loyalty"
Original: 1871 – *Vingt mille lieues sous les mers / Twenty Thousand Leagues Under the Seas*
Illustrator: Alphonse de Neuville and Riou

Palmyrin Rosette.

"Embrace of the Planets"
Original: 1877 – *Hector Servadac* /
Hector Servadac
Illustrator: P. Philippoteaux

Cet objet était une petite bouée. (Page 53.)

"Rust and Smoke"
Original: 1896 – *Face au drapeau* /
Face the Flag
Illustrator: Léon Benett

"Gabriel at the Jules Verne Traveling
Adventure Show"
Original: 1890 – *César Cascabel* /
César Cascabel
Illustrator: George Roux

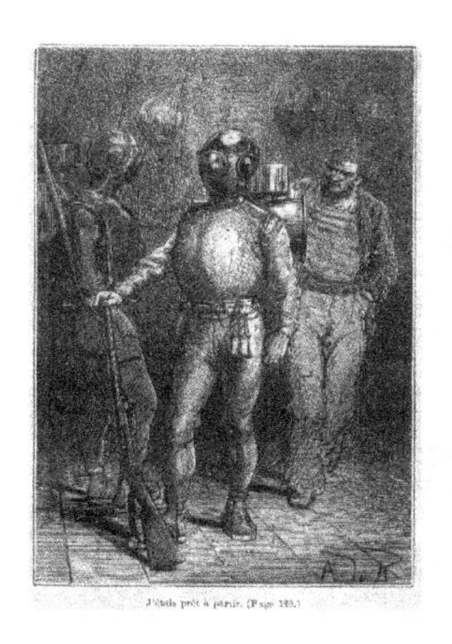

"Tyranny Under the Sea"
Original: 1871 – *Vingt mille lieues sous les mers / Twenty Thousand Leagues Under the Seas*
Illustrator: Alphonse de Neuville and Riou

"Trumpets of Freedom"
Original: 1905 – *Le phare du bout du monde / The Lighthouse at the End of the World*
Illustrator: George Roux

"Raise the Nautilus"
Original: 1896 - *Face au drapeau / Face the Flag*
Illustrator: Léon Benett

Appendix B
A List of Jules Verne's Works

1860 *Journey to England and Scotland* [a.k.a., *Backwards to Britain*] (*Voyage en Angleterre et en Ecosse*)
First published in English in 1992.

1863 *Five Weeks in a Balloon* (*Cinq semaines en ballon*)

1864 *Paris in the Twentieth Century* (*Paris au XXe siècle*)
Not published in any language until 1994 — English in 1996.

1864 *Journey to the Center of the Earth* (*Voyage au centre de la Terre*)

1865 *From the Earth to the Moon* (*De la Terre à la Lune*)

1866 *Journeys and Adventures of Captain Hatteras* (*Voyages et aventures du Capitaine Hatteras*)
2 volumes

1867 *The Children of Captain Grant* (*Les enfants du Capitaine Grant*)
3 volumes

1867 *Illustrated Geography of France and Her Colonies* (*Geographie illustrée de la France et de ses colonies*)
Nonfiction work that has never been translated into English.

1870 *Around the Moon* (*Autour de la Lune*)

1870 *20,000 Leagues Under the Seas* (*Vingt mille lieues sous les mers*)
2 volumes

1871 *A Floating City* (*Une ville flottante*)
Published with "The Blockade Runners" (1865).

1872 *Adventures of Three Russians and Three Englishmen in Southern Africa* (*Aventures de trois Russes et trois Anglais dans l'Afrique Australe*)

1873 *The Fur Country* (*Le pays des fourrures*)
2 volumes

1873 *Around the World in Eighty Days* (*Le tour du monde en quatre-vingts jours*)

1874 *Dr. Ox, and Other Stories* (*Le Docteur Ox, receuil de nouvelles*)
An anthology. Published in French with "Martin Paz" (1852).
* *A Fancy of Doctor Ox* (*Une fantaisie du Docteur Ox*)
1872
* "Master Zacharius" ("Maître Zacharius")
1854
* *A Winter Amid the Ice* (*Un hivernage dans les glaces*)
1855
* "A Voyage in a Balloon" [a.k.a., "A Drama in the Air"] ("Un voyage en ballon") [a.k.a., "Un drame dans les airs"]
"A Voyage in a Balloon" (1851) was later retitled "A Drama in the Air" (1874), for book publication. Included in the Palik Series – Vol 12, *Worlds Known and Unknown.*
* "Fortieth French Ascent of Mount Blanc" ("Quarantième ascension Française du Mont-Blanc")
1872 by Jules' brother, Paul.

1874 *The Mysterious Island* (*L'île mystérieuse*)
3 volumes

1875 *The Chancellor* (*Le Chancellor*)
Published with "Martin Paz" (1852).

1876 *Michael Strogoff* (*Michel Strogoff*)
2 volumes. Published with "A Drama in Mexico" (1851).

1877 *Hector Servadac* (*Hector Servadac*)

1877 *The Black Indies* (*Les Indes noires*)

1878 *A Fifteen Year Old Captain* (*Un capitaine de quinze ans*)

1878 *History of the Famous Travels and Travelers* (*Histoire des grands voyages et des voyageurs*)
3 volumes, Nonfiction work
* *The Discovery of the Earth* (*Decouverte de la Terre*)
1878
* *The Great Navigators of the 18th Century* (*Les grands navigateurs du XVIII siècle*)
1879
* *The Explorers of the 19th Century* (*Les voyageurs du XIX siècle*)
1880

1879 *The 500 Millions of the Begum* (*Les cinq cents millions de la Bégum*)
Published with "The Mutineers of the Bounty" (1879) with Gabriel Marcel.

1879 *The Tribulations of a Chinese in China* (*Les tribulations d'un Chinois en Chine*)

1880 *The Steam House* (*Le maison à vapeur*)
2 volumes

1881 *The Jangada* (*La Jangada*)
Published in French with "From Rotterdam to Copenhagen Aboard the Steam Yacht 'Saint Michel'" (1881) by Jules' brother, Paul. The latter has never been published in English.

1882 *The Green Ray* (*Le rayon vert*)
Published in French with "Ten Hours Hunting" (1881), which is not included in English editions.

1882 *The School for Robinsons* (*L'école des Robinsons*)

1883 *Keraban the Inflexible* (*Kéraban-le-têtu*)
2 volumes

1884 *The Archipelago On Fire* (*L'archipel en feu*)

1884 *The Star of the South* (*L'étoile du Sud*)

1885 *Mathias Sandorf* (*Mathias Sandorf*)
3 volumes

1885 *The Wreck of the Cynthia* (*L'épave du Cynthia*)
Co-written with André Laurie (pseudonym of Paschal Grousset).

1886 *Robur the Conqueror* (*Robur-le-conquérant*)

1886 *A Lottery Ticket* (*Un billet de loterie*)
Published in French with "Frritt-Flacc" (1884), which is not included in English editions.

1887 *The Road to France* (*Le chemin de France*)
Published in French with "Gil Braltar" (1887), which is not included in English editions.

1887 *North Against South* (*Nord contre Sud*)
2 volumes

1888 *Two Year Holiday* (*Deux ans de vacances*)
2 volumes

1889 *Topsy Turvy* (*Sans dessus dessous*)

1889 *Family Without a Name* (*Famille-sans-nom*)
2 volumes

1890 *César Cascabel* (*César Cascabel*)
2 volumes

1891 *Mistress Branican* (*Mistress Branican*)
2 volumes

1892 *The Castle in the Carpathians* (*Le château des Carpathes*)

1892 *Claudius Bombarnac* (*Claudius Bombarnac*)

1893 *Little Fellow* (*P'tit-bonhomme*)
2 volumes. There is no American edition.

1894 *Wonderful Adventures of Master Antifer* (*Mirifiques aventures de Maître Antifer*)
2 volumes

1895 *Propeller Island* (*L'île à hélice*)
2 volumes

1896 *Facing the Flag* (*Face au drapeau*)

1896 *Clovis Dardentor* (*Clovis Dardentor*)
2 volumes. There is no American edition.

1897 *The Sphinx of the Ice* (*Le sphinx des glaces*)
2 volumes

1898 *The Superb Orinoco* (*Le superbe Orénoque*)
2 volumes. Published in English in 2002.

1899 *The Will of an Eccentric* (*Le testament d'un excentrique*)

1900 *Second Fatherland* (*Seconde patrie*)
2 volumes

1901 *The Aerial Village* (*Le village aérien*)

1901 *The Yarns of Jean-Marie Cabidoulin* (*Les histoires de Jean-Marie Cabidoulin*)
Publisher Hachette, changed the title to *Le serpent de mer* (*The Sea Serpent*) upon reprinting the novel in 1937.

1902 *The Kip Brothers* (*Les frères Kip*)
2 volumes. Published in English in 2007.

1903 *Scholarships for Travel* (*Bourses de voyage*)
2 volumes. Published in English in 2013.

1904 *Master of the World* (*Maître du monde*)

1904 *A Drama in Livonia* (*Un drame en Livonie*)

1905 *The Invasion of the Sea* (*L'invasion de la mer*)
First complete English translation in 2001.

Works credited to Verne, but mostly rewritten by his son, Michel

1905 *The Lighthouse At the End of the World* (*Le phare du bout du monde*)

1906 *The Golden Volcano* (*Le volcan d'or*)
2 volumes

1907 *The Agency Thompson and Company* (*L'Agence Thompson and Co*)
2 volumes

1908 *The Hunt for the Meteor* (*La chasse au météore*)

1908 *The Danube Pilot* (*Le pilote du Danube*)

1910 *The Survivors of the Jonathan* (*Les naufragés du Jonathan*)
2 volumes

1910 *The Secret of Wilhelm Storitz* (*Le secret de Wilhelm Storitz*)

1910 *Yesterday and Tomorrow* (*Hier et demain*)
An anthology. Michel removed "Memories of Childhood and Youth" (1890) and *The Count of Chanteleine: An Episode of the Revolution* (1864). He added "The Humbug" (1863/1870), "The Fate of Jean Morénas" (1910), and "The Eternal Adam" (1910). The first English edition in 1965 removed *The Rat Family* (1910) and "The Humbug."

* *The Rat Family* (*La famille Raton*)
1910. The original title, *Adventures of the Rat Family* (1891, *Aventures de la famille Raton*), was shortened by Michel.

* "Mr. Ray Sharp and Miss Me Flat" ("Monsieur Ré-dièze et Mademoiselle Mi-Bémol")
1893

* "The Fate of Jean Morénas" ("La destinée de Jean Morénas")
1910. Michel's altered version of Jules' "Pierre-Jean" (1858). Included in the Palik Series - Vol 5, *Vice, Redemption and the Distant Colony*.

* "The Humbug" ("Le Humbug")
1863/1870. Published in English by the International Centre for Verne Literary Studies in 1991 and in *The Jules Verne Encyclopedia* 1990/1996.

* "In the 29th Century: The Diary of an American Journalist in 2889" ("Au XXIXème siècle: La journée d'un journaliste Américain en 2889")
Appeared first in English by Michel as "In the Year 2889" in 1889, then modified by Jules in French in 1890.

* "The Eternal Adam" ("L'eternel Adam")
1910. Based on Jules' "Edom" (around 1896).

1919 *The Astonishing Adventure of the Barsac Mission* (*L'étonnante aventure de la mission Barsac*)
2 volumes. First serialized in 1914.

Original Manuscripts and Drafts Later Revised by Michel Verne

1897 *In the Magellanes* (*En Magellanie*)
Revised and published as *The Survivors of the Jonathan* in 1910. Original draft published in French in 1987.

1897 *The Secret of Wilhelm Storitz* (*Le secret de Wilhelm Storitz*)
Revised and published under the same title in 1910. Original draft published in French in 1987 and in English in 2011.

1899 *The Golden Volcano* (*Le volcan d'or*)
Revised and published under the same title in 1906. 2 volumes. Original draft published in French in 1989.

1901 *The Hunt For the Meteor* (*La chasse au météore*)
Revised and published under the same title in 1908. Original draft published in French in 1986.

1901 *The Beautiful Yellow Danube* (*Le beau Danube jaune*)
Revised and published as *The Danube Pilot* in 1908. Original draft published in French in 1988. Included in the Palik Series – Vol 8, *Golden Danube.*

1901 *The Lighthouse at the End of the World* (*Le phare du bout du monde*)
Revised and published under the same title in 1905. Original draft published in French in 2005 and in English in 2007.

1903 *Journey of Studies* (*Voyage d'études*)
Completed and published as *The Astonishing Adventure of the Barsac Mission* in 1919. Original draft published in French in 1993. Included as *Fact-Finding Mission* in the Palik Series – Vol 5, *Vice, Redemption and the Distant Colony.*

Plays

1850 *The Broken Straws* (*Les pailles rompues*)

1851 *An Excursion at Sea* (*Une promenade en mer*)
Included in the Palik Series – Vol 11, *Scheherazade's Last Night and Other Plays.*

1851 *Mona Lisa* (*Monna Lisa*)
Never performed. Published in 1974. Included in the Palik Series – Vol 12, *Worlds Known and Unknown.*

1852 *The Castles of California, or the Rolling Stone Gathers No Moss* (*Les châteaux en Californie, ou pierre qui roule n'amasse pas mousse*)
Included in the Palik Series – Vol 10, *The Castles of California.*

1853 *Blind Man's Buff* (*Le colin-maillard*)
With Michel Carré and Aristide Hignard.

1853 *The Adoptive Son* (*Un fils adoptif*)
Included in the Palik Series – Vol 3, *Mr. Chimp, and Other Plays.*

1855 *The Companions of the Marjolaine* (*Les compagnons de la Marjolaine*)
Included as *The Knights of the Daffodil* in the Palik Series – Vol 3, *Mr. Chimp, and Other Plays.*

1860 *Mr. Chimpanzee* (*Monsieur de Chimpanzé*)
With Michel Carré and Aristide Hignard. Included in the Palik Series – Vol 3, *Mr. Chimp, and Other Plays.*

1860 *The Inn in the Ardennes* (*L'auberge des Ardennes*)
With Michel Carré and Aristide Hignard.

1861 *Eleven Days of Siege* (*Onze jours de siège*)
With Charles Wallut and Victorien Sardou. Included in the Palik Series – Vol 3, *Mr. Chimp, and Other Plays.*

1873 *A Nephew From America, or the Two Frontignacs* (*Un neveu d'Amérique ou les deux Frontignac*)
With Charles Wallut and Édouard Cadol. Included in the Palik Series – Vol 10, *The Castles of California.*

1874 *Around the World In 80 Days* (*Le tour du monde en quatre-vingts jours*)
With Adolphe d'Ennery. Included in the Palik Series – Vol 6, *Around the World In 80 Days — The 1874 Play.*

1878 *The Children of Captain Grant* (*Les enfants du Capitaine Grant*)

1880 *Michael Strogoff* (*Michel Strogoff*)
With Adolphe d'Ennery

1882 *Journey Across the Impossible* (*Voyage à travers l'impossible*)
With Adolphe d'Ennery. Published in French in 1981. Published in English in 2003 by the NAJVS through Prometheus Books.

1883 *Kéraban the Inflexible* (*Kéraban-le-têtu*)

1887 *Mathias Sandorf* (*Mathias Sandorf*)
With William Busnach

1989 *Unedited Poems* (*Poésies inédites*)
A collection of previously unpublished poems.

* "The Topmen: Sailor Song" ("Les Gabiers: chanson maritime")
1847. Included in the Palik Series - Vol 11, *Scheherazade's Last Night and Other Plays.*

1991 *Nantes Manuscripts* [Vol 1] (*Manuscrits Nantais* [Vol 1])

* *The Thousand and Second Night* (*La mille et deuxième nuit*)
Included in the Palik Series - Vol 11, *Scheherazade's Last Night and Other Plays.*

* *The Guimard* (*La Guimard*)
Included in the Palik Series - Vol 11, *Scheherazade's Last Night and Other Plays.*

Short Stories, Articles, and Essays

1847 "To the New Bride Caroline"
Poem from Verne to his cousin Caroline Tronson with whom he was in love. She married Émile Dezaunayon on April 27, 1847. Included in the Palik Series - Vol 12, *Worlds Known and Unknown.*

1851 "A Drama in Mexico" ("Un drame au Mexique")
Published with *Michael Strogoff* (1876).

1851 "A Voyage in a Balloon" ("Un voyage en ballon")
Included in the Palik Series - Vol 12, *Worlds Known and Unknown.*

1852 "Martin Paz" ("Martin Paz")
Included in the original French edition of *Dr. Ox, and Other Stories* (1874). Published with *The Chancellor* (1875). Included in the Palik Series - Vol 7, *Bandits & Rebels.*

1854 "Master Zacharius" ("Maître Zacharius")
Included in *Dr. Ox, and Other Stories* (1874).

1855 "A Winter amid the Ice" ("Un hivernage dans les glaces")
Included in *Dr. Ox, and Other Stories* (1874).

1857 "Portraits of Artists: XVIII" ("Portraits d'artistes. XVIII")
Essay

1857 "Salon of 1857" ("Salon de 1857")
Series of seven articles

1863 "About the 'Giant'" ("A propos du 'Geant'")
Article. Predicts the helicopter. Translated into English in 1940. First published in the Palik Series – Vol 12, *Worlds Known and Unknown.*

1864 "The Work of Edgar Allan Poe" ("Edgard [sic] Poe et ses oeuvres")
Article. Published in English as "The Leader of the Cult of the Unusual" in 1978.

1864 "The Count of Chanteleine: An Episode of the Revolution" ("Le Comte de Chanteleine: Un episode de la Revolution")
Published in short story form in 1864 but not in book form in French until 1971. Included in the Palik Series – Vol 4, *The Count of Chanteleine: A Tale of the French Revolution.*

1865 "The Blockade Runners" ("Les forceurs de blocus")
Published with *A Floating City* (1871).

1872 "The Fantasy of Dr. Ox" ("Une fantaisie du Docteur Ox")
Included in *Dr. Ox, and Other Stories* (1874).

1873 "The Meridians and the Calendar" ("Les meridiens et le calendrier")
Article. First published in English in the Palik Series – Vol 6, *Around the World in 80 Days – The 1874 Play.*

1873 "Ascent of the Meteor" ("Ascension du meteore")
Also published as a booklet, "24 Minutes in a Balloon" ("Vingt-quatre minutes en ballon"). Published in 1973 with "Un ville ideale." Included in the Palik Series – Vol 12, *Worlds Known and Unknown.*

1875 "An Ideal City" ("Une ville ideale")
Included in English in the 1965 Fitzroy Edition of *Yesterday and Tomorrow.*

1876 "Note for the Case J. Verne v. Pont Jest" ("Note pour l'affaire J. Verne contre Pont Jest")

1879 "The Mutineers of the Bounty" ("Les révoltés de la Bounty")
With Gabriel Marcel. Published with *The 500 Millions of the Begum* (1879).

1881 "Ten Hours Hunting" ("Dix heures en chasse")
Published in French with *The Green Ray* (1882) and in English in the 1965 Fitzroy edition of *Yesterday and Tomorrow.*

1884 "Frritt-Flacc" ("Frritt-Flacc")
First translated into English in 1892 as "Dr. Trifulgas." Included in the Palik Series – Vol 12, *Worlds Known and Unknown.*

1887 "Gil Braltar" ("Gil Braltar")
Published in French with *The Road to France* (1887). Included in the Palik Series – Vol 12, *Worlds Known and Unknown.*

1890 "Memories of Childhood and Youth" ("Souvenirs d'enfance et de jeunesse")
Article. First appeared in English as "The Story of My Boyhood" in 1891. First published in French in 1974. Included in the Palik Series – Vol 12, *Worlds Known and Unknown.*

1890 "The Diary of an American Journalist in 2890" ("La journée d'un journaliste Américain en 2890")
Appeared first in English by Michel as "In the Year 2889" in 1889, then modified by Jules in French in 1890. In some French journal publications, the year is given as 2890, in order for the story to be set exactly one thousand years after publication.

1891 *Adventures of the Rat Family* (*Aventures de la famille Raton*)
Title shortened by Michel to *The Rat Family* for *Yesterday and Tomorrow* (1910). Published in English in 1993.

1891 "To My English Readers"
Preface to the 2nd edition of *A Plunge Into Space* by Robert Cromie. Reprinted in English in 1976.

1893 "Mr. Ray Sharp and Miss Me Flat" ("Monsieur Ré-dièze et Mademoiselle Mi-Bémol")

1893 "The Future for Women"
Speech to the Girl's School in Amiens. Published in English in 1978.

1893 "An Express of the Future" ("Un express de l'avenir")
First published in English in 1895.

1902 "Future of the Submarine"
Article. First published in English in 1904. Included in the Palik Series – Vol 7, *Bandits & Rebels.*

1903 "Solution of Mind Problems by the Imagination"
Article. Discovered and printed in English in 1928.

1991 *Nantes Manuscripts* [Vol 3] (*Manuscrits Nantais* [Vol 3])

* *A Priest in 1835* (*Un prêtre en 1835*)
1847. Included in the Palik Series – Vol 9, *A Priest in 1835.*

* *Jédédias Jamet*, or *The Tale of an Inheritance* (*Jédédias Jamet ou L'histoire d'une succession*)
Began in 1846 but never finished. Included in the Palik Series – Vol 1, *The Marriage of a Marquis*

* "The Siege of Rome" ("Le siège de Rome")
  1854. Included in the Palik Series – Vol 7, *Bandits & Rebels.*
* "The Marriage of Mr. Anselme des Tilleuls" ("Le mariage de M. Anselme des Tilleuls")
  1855. Included in the Palik Series – Vol 1, *The Marriage of a Marquis.*
* "Pierre-Jean" ("Pierre-Jean")
  1858. Michel revised this as "The Fate of Jean Morénas" (1910). Included in the Palik Series – Vol 5, *Vice, Redemption and the Distant Colony.*
* "San Carlos" ("San Carlos")
  1856. Included in the Palik Series – Vol 7, *Bandits & Rebels.*
* *Uncle Robinson* (*L'Oncle Robinson*)
  1872. Evolved into *The Mysterious Island* (1874). Included in the Palik Series – Vol 2, *Shipwrecked Family: Marooned with Uncle Robinson.*

1993 *San Carlos and Other Unedited Narratives* (*San Carlos et autres recits inédits*)

* "Pierre-Jean" ("Pierre-Jean")
  1858. Michel revised this as "The Fate of Jean Morénas" (1910). Included in the Palik Series – Vol 5, *Vice, Redemption and the Distant Colony.*
* "The Marriage of Mr. Anselme des Tilleuls" ("Le mariage de M. Anselme des Tilleuls")
  1855. Included in the Palik Series – Vol 1, *The Marriage of a Marquis.*
* "The Siege of Rome" ("Le siège de Rome")
  1854. Included in the Palik Series – Vol 7, *Bandits & Rebels.*
* "San Carlos" ("San Carlos")
  1856. Included in the Palik Series – Vol 7, *Bandits & Rebels.*
* *Jédédias Jamet, or The Tale of an Inheritance* (*Jédédias Jamet ou L'histoire d'une succession*)
  Began in 1846 but never finished. Included in the Palik Series – Vol 1, *The Marriage of a Marquis.*
* *Journey of Studies* (*Voyage d'études*)
  1903. Completed and published as *The Astonishing Adventure of the Barsac Mission* in 1919. Included as *Fact-Finding Mission* in the Palik Series – Vol 5, *Vice, Redemption and the Distant Colony.*

Appendix B Sources:

Stephen Michael, Jr., "Jules Verne: A Bibliographic and Collecting Guide," chap. 7 in *The Jules Verne Encyclopedia* (Maryland: The Scarecrow Press, Inc., 1996).

"Jules Verne Bibliography," Wikipedia, last modified May 13, 2021, https://en.wikipedia.org/wiki/Jules_Verne_bibliography.

"Exhaustive Complete List of Jules Verne Titles," by Andrew Nash, accessed May 9, 2022, http://www.julesverne.ca/vernetitles.html.

"Publications," North American Jules Verne Society, Inc., accessed May 9, 2022, http://www.najvs.org/publications.shtml.

"The Palik Series," North American Jules Verne Society, Inc., accessed May 9, 2022, http://www.najvs.org/palikseries.shtml.

"List of Jules Verne's 'Extraordinary Voyages,'" North American Jules Verne Society, Inc., accessed May 9, 2022, http://www.najvs.org/works/index.shtml.

North American Jules Verne Society, Inc.

If you'd like to read more Jules Verne, by the author himself, we invite you to read *The Palik Series* that we published from 2011 – 2018. The series features novellas, short stories, and plays that were translated and appear in English for the first time. You can find out more here:

http://www.najvs.org/palikseries.shtml

In 2002 we published the first English translation of the play "Voyage à travers l'impossible" (Journey through the Impossible). You can find out more here:

http://www.najvs.org/publications.shtml

We also welcome you to join us; you can find membership information on our website:

http://www.najvs.org/

You'll also find us on Facebook, just search for "NAJVS - (North American Jules Verne Society)."

CPSIA information can be obtained
at www.ICGtesting.com
Printed in the USA
LVHW021930120423
744168LV00001B/147